MW01002363

Murder in the Extreme
A Miranda Marquette Mystery
Book 2

J.T. Kunkel

Acknowledgments:

To Donna Pudick at Parkeast Literary Agency. Thank you for continuing to make me a better writer and not allowing me to produce work that is less than you believe I can produce. To me, in many ways the second book was significantly more challenging than the first. I have learned a lot in the process, and I look forward to working together again to get book three in publishable shape.

To Veronica H. (Ronnie) Hart my editor at Taylor and Seale for helping Miranda come to life and having the vision to push me to develop her character. I believe that we have only scratched the surface, and I look forward to many more books in the Miranda Marquette Mystery Series.

To Mary Custureri, CEO of Taylor and Seale Publishing. I am aware how many authors there are out there and how many books are published in a year and I have been honored to be published under the Taylor and Seale name. I hope we have a long association.

To my readers. I have been humbled by your praise of Blood on the Bayou and hope that Murder in the Extreme and the books that follow in the Miranda Marquette series, bring you as much joy as they have brought me, writing them. Thank you for your support. Please visit me at jtkunkel.com for news and information.

Dedication:

I dedicate Murder in the Extreme to my gorgeous wife Susan, the Love of my life. When we met over twenty years ago, we had no idea what our journey together would be like, but we both jumped in with both feet and I have never had a day of regret. I look forward to at least twenty more years and an eternity thereafter. I will Love You Forever.

Murder in the Extreme

J. T. Kunkel

Chapter 1

May 2008

The hair rose on the back of my neck. I could hear only the rush of air at 60 meters per second as I plummeted toward the outskirts of Lauterbrunnen, Switzerland, the base-jumping capital of Europe. After deploying my parachute, the resistance of the opened canopy billowed over me and tore at my arms and shoulders with what felt like a thousand pounds. When fully inflated with air, I floated peacefully downward, awed by majestic snow-covered peaks and lulled into tranquility by bleating sheep on the hillside below.

A scream from above grabbed my attention. Tara, our final jumper, dropped from the sky and plummeted past me. I struggled in vain to change direction, a cold sweat covering my skin despite the cool Alpine temperatures. But I could only watch as she fell. Down, down until there was no sky or wind. Only the cold hard ground.

It felt like hours before I finally landed. I struggled to rip the pack off my back and sprinted to my two other teammates, Annika and Patricia, who had jumped first. They held one another, sobbing with their eyes closed. After a glance, I couldn't look either, at Tara's broken body, the deadly result of a seven-hundred-and-fifty-meter free fall.

Relying on the name on his press pass, I screamed at the cameraman, "Stop filming now, Rocky!" and ran over to join my teammates. The stench of blood mixed with salty tears made me gag with the reality that Tara was dead.

Our three-person survival grip ended when Patricia pulled away. With ashen skin and a blank expression, she sank to the ground. She sat holding her knees, rocking back and forth, moaning quietly. Annika, nearly as pale, stood unmoving, her eyes fixed on Patricia. The police academy training from my former life kicked in. I fished the cell phone from my pocket and dialed 112.

I took a moment before the first responders arrived to breathe deeply, attempting to calm myself. My anxiety had improved considerably since I was acquitted of a murder charge last year, but symptoms of an impending anxiety attack were overtaking me. My ears were ringing, and my vision blurred. I knelt on the ground so I would be close to the ground if I lost consciousness. That had only happened once, but it was frightening and disorienting.

After I shivered in the cold sun for ten agonizing minutes, I started to come out of it. I opened my eyes to see an ancient ambulance chugging into the field where we waited, each in our own thoughts. It was followed by a black and white 1940s Mercedes with the familiar two-tone siren blaring. The first of two officers, who sported an Oktoberfest-worthy beer belly and a brush cut with graying temples, swaggered over to where we stood.

He asked with a heavy German accent, "Which one of you is Miranda Marquette?"

I raised my hand as if in grade school and flipped my long blonde hair out of my face. "I am." I sounded weaker than I had planned.

The other officer spoke up. "Do you want to sit down, Fraulein? You look very pale."

I refused to be a victim. "I'm fine," I spoke louder and clearer, and he looked convinced even if I wasn't.

"*Gut*, then we will take your statements," the first officer barked in broken English. "You," he said, pointing to Annika, "and I will go this way." He turned to me. "You speak with Officer Brecker," and then to Patricia as if he saw her for the first time, "Are you all right, Fraulein?"

Patricia, still ghost white and rocking forward and back, like a headbanger at an AC/DC concert, didn't respond. He motioned to the paramedics to assist her. I stood watching as he and Annika walked through a meadow of daisies, purple salvia, and wild strawberries—a stark contrast to the gory scene behind them.

Officer Brecker and I walked in the other direction, toward the mountains. Twenty minutes prior, I had been in awe of the majestic snow-covered peaks, but as we approached them, I shivered with fear.

We strolled in silence for several minutes when he finally said, "What brought you and your friends to our country?" He read from a black and white college essay notebook.

I spoke, and my voice sounded to me as if reading a press release. "We are the First Extreme All-girl Sports Team or FEAST, four young, successful and independent women seeking fame, fortune, and an adrenaline rush. We participate in several extreme sports, such as BASE Jumping, beach sailing, skydiving, street luge racing, and all types of motorcycle racing, including on- and off-road racing."

I lowered my head when I realized we were no longer a team of four. He touched my wrist and nodded. I flinched and pulled away. At that point, no stranger was welcome in my personal space, especially a cop. My disdain for the police had never vanished since I left the force nearly eight years ago after being ambushed and shot in the face. It remained unclear who had set me up, but several of my co-workers remained under suspicion.

3

Blinking back more tears, I continued. "This was our first BASE jump together. The other three of us had lots of experience, but Tara had only skydived a couple of times, and that was several years ago. I had recently done some ground training with her. She insisted she was ready for this. Now . . ."

I sobbed and buried my face in my hands, wishing I could disappear. I had never been good with people seeing me cry, especially men. I pulled a tissue from my pocket, blew my nose, and was ready to continue the interrogation.

He waited a minute, then looked at me with kind blue eyes and continued in a heavy German accent. "Why do you do this jumping if you know it is dangerous?"

"Extreme sports, for us anyway, are a means of building self-esteem and taking control of our lives. Some believe that simply having financial success is the cure-all for emotional issues. That isn't true. Taking risks is a kind of therapy for us. I've needed therapy since my mid-twenties when I quit my first job on the police force after an unfortunate accident. I don't know how you do it. I couldn't do this every day anymore, living with other people's tragedy."

Ignoring my comment, he reviewed his notebook. "Is there anything else you can tell me about the deceased?"

It took a second to realize he was asking about Tara. "The four of us took a trip to Aruba three months ago to relax and get to know one another. I had recruited them for the team through a nationwide search, and we wanted to make sure we could get along for long periods on the road. So, what better way than traveling together?" I smiled fondly, thinking back on the time we spent together. "It worked out great. We all fit together. No drama. I couldn't believe my luck."

He waited patiently while I thought back for a minute and tried to remember specific details about Tara that might be important. "I know that she got some text messages that she found disturbing while we were in Aruba, but she didn't go into

4

any detail about them when I asked her about it. She is a very private person. Or she was." My stomach churned when I corrected myself to acknowledge that she was dead.

"Did she ever mention being threatened by anyone?" He tried to make the interrogation sound like a casual conversation.

I continued, "I know her ex-husband was very unhappy about their break-up, but she didn't mention that he had been in contact." I provided the officer with his name. "Do you suspect foul play here? Tara's death was just an accident, right?"

"I must ask these questions. It is routine."

I wasn't convinced.

After the officers wrapped things up with Annika and me, they spoke to Rocky. I didn't know him or the other cameraman at the top of the mountain. Two of the girls had come for a few days before the jump, so I felt a little out of the loop. I decided to talk to the others later about whether they had gotten to know either of the cameramen before I arrived. The agency had provided them with instructions to film every possible moment of our adventure from Bernie Weinstein, our publicist. Bernie never missed an opportunity to get our faces in the news.

It seemed like overkill to me when they threatened the cameraman with handcuffs until he gave them his camera as evidence. He stomped around and threw down his hat as if he were a manager arguing a call at a baseball game, but they did not relent.

They received a call on their radio and left with sirens blaring and without interviewing Patricia. She lay on the ground with her feet elevated on a stone in the meadow under a blanket the paramedics had provided, advising her to rest for another half hour. They had treated her for shock as a precaution. But the reality of Tara's death hadn't even begun to sink in.

Annika and I sat on either side of Patricia, each lost in our thoughts. Mine was about the moment just before the jump. The other cameraman had been shooting most of our pre-jumping

5

activities before we plummeted off the cliff, but he and Tara had been in deep conversation before we jumped. It had looked as if he was helping her with her pre-jump checklist, but they could have been talking about anything. With his long stringy hair and mangled beard, I wondered if she was attracted to him. I was going to ask her about it when we landed safely at the bottom. I suddenly realized that he had never come down from the mountain after we jumped. He had disappeared.

Chapter 2

A week later, I arrived at Logan Airport sweaty and jet-lagged from the six-hour flight from LA. Typically Boston was one of my favorite cities to visit, but I hadn't been looking forward to this one. Annika and Patricia's flights had landed within a half-hour of mine, and we reunited after I found my suitcases in the baggage claim area. As usual, mine were the last two off the plane.

As I waited for my bags, I pondered how we had ended up here. Tara, Annika, and Patricia had been hand-selected to join FEAST through a nationwide search less than a year ago. We represented different parts of the country to improve the likelihood that we would attract a broad audience when we launched our reality TV series. Bernie, our publicist, had opened my eyes to the possibilities, and I was pursuing them aggressively.

I had learned to keep one eye on Annika, our Texas girl. Her strikingly tall figure and auburn hair was everything big and brassy. She was as likely to pick up an eligible man while she struck up a conversation at the airport as she was to be on the floor with a two-year-old or a puppy. Everything endearing about her could also be incredibly frustrating if you had a deadline or an agenda. I loved her dearly, but she tested my patience much of the time.

Patricia was the polar opposite of Annika, sleek, with porcelain skin and jet-black hair, people often took her quiet demeanor as snobbishness, but she was shy and reserved at least until you got to know her. She hailed from Denver, and we dubbed her the ice queen but not to her face. She was as likely to be doing the New York Times crossword puzzle as to have her nose buried in a hardcover mystery. Patricia tended to second guess most of her life decisions, which made her a problematic cat to herd.

Tara had been my favorite and our East Coast representative. Her Boston accent and quick wit made her instantly likable by both sexes, but men were particularly fond of her. She had a way of making a person feel like he or she was the only one alive when she gave them her full attention. The team lost a huge asset when she plunged to her death in the Alps. It was still hard to believe she was dead.

Minutes later, I gathered my thoughts, my bags, and my teammates, and we piled into the shabby vinyl back seat of a yellow cab. "First to the Ritz Carlton then to 187 Dorchester," I read from the note I pulled from my jacket pocket.

The cab driver had the leathering skin and the yellowing fingers of a life-long smoker. He coughed, "Dauchesta? Second ride up to Caspa's today. Must be a big shawt's funeral today up theya. Yessa."

Rather than trying to decipher what he had said with his heavy Boston accent, I said, "Guess so," and we all sat quietly the rest of the way as we hung on for dear life.

My feet had never been happier to touch the ground after an exasperating cab ride to the hotel where we hurriedly checked in. Since we were almost late to the funeral, they stored our bags while we jumped back into the waiting cab.

Casper funeral home was in South Boston, an ethnic array of smaller homes and businesses, seemingly a lifetime away from the Ritz Carlton where we were staying, which bordered both the theatre and financial district.

I wasn't sure what I expected, but I was not impressed by the aging storefront with a newly painted sign that seemed almost embarrassed to adorn the place. Even with all the public relations Bernie had been doing for us, I was surprised at all the activity when we exited the cab. Reporters held microphones in

8

our faces as we 'no commented' our way up aging stone steps to the funeral home.

Tara's family barely made eye contact with us as we made our way through the receiving line. Her parents did not invite us back to their home afterward. An outside observer would have thought we killed her. Tara had a substantial Italian family, all speaking loudly in a language we could barely comprehend.

After we paid our respects, I whispered to Annika, "Let's get out of here."

Patricia followed as we slipped out the door and didn't look back.

Catching a cab in South Boston turned out to be impossible, so we managed to negotiate the Red Line back to civilization. It was a gorgeous spring day, so rather than heading back to our rooms, we grabbed an outdoor table with a green umbrella at the Parish Café. It was on Boylston Street, an easy walk from the Ritz Carlton, across Boston Common. We settled in, watching drivers negotiate one of the city's busiest streets.

"A bottle of your best California Cabernet," was all I could think to say when the host came out to ask if we had reservations, pretending I hadn't heard his question. He retreated, mumbling something under his breath as he begrudgingly motioned in our direction to a harried-looking college-aged blonde who I assumed was our waitress.

Patricia, Annika, and I hadn't talked much since Tara died. Every time I thought about it, my stomach tied in knots.

The day before, I'd called Bernie to discuss canceling our scheduled appearance at the Street Luge Nationals in San Francisco in two weeks. Since the accident, as evidenced outside the funeral home, the press had taken an interest in our team. While it wasn't the kind of attention we wanted, he kept reminding me, "There is no bad publicity."

"Really, Bernie?" was the best I could do.

9

Usually, I would have been excited by the sounds and smells of the city, but it was getting to be a hassle yelling over the noise of car horns and loud diesel engines on Boylston. But since we had pretty much stolen an outside table, it didn't seem likely they would transfer us inside.

I wasn't sure if the college girl had rejected us or if the attractive thirty-something waiter had volunteered to take our table, but Annika was delighted. After he brought the wine and poured three glasses, he pulled out a small pad and a pen.

"Can I take your food order, ladies?" He smiled like we were his first table of the day. Perhaps we were.

Annika spoke first. "Just keep the wine coming." She winked at him.

I gave her a look when he departed. "I hope you get this out of your system before we go back to the Ritz. I don't have to remind you how many hotels have made it clear we shouldn't come back upon our departure."

"You exaggerate so much. Okay, there was the fire in the first hotel in Aruba, but that wasn't my fault," Annika protested with the amused edge she always seemed to have.

I smirked. "It would have been the only hotel we stayed in in Aruba had you not almost burned it down. And how about the stolen towels?"

She smiled demurely. "Never mind that now, Manda."

The bags under Patricia's eyes made her look ten years older than the thirty that she was. She spoke for the first time since we left the funeral home nearly an hour ago. "What are we going to do about this luge thing? It's only two weeks away. I say we drop out."

I wasn't really in the right frame of mind, but I replied anyway, "Bernie feels that our possible deal with Bravo for a reality series is toast if we cancel our appearance."

Tears welled up in Patricia's eyes. "Miranda, I'm scared. Maybe this whole extreme sports team wasn't such a great idea.

What if something happens to you, or you, Anni? Before Tara died, I was in the best place I had been for a long time. I don't want to die. I'm also not so sure I want every aspect of my life displayed on national television."

"Let's not worry about the reality series right now. There's a ton of negotiating to be done before that comes together. We'll all have input on our level of involvement, that's if it even gets that far."

Picturing us making our TV series when I was still waking up drenched with sweat and guilt after vivid nightmares of Tara falling from the sky was a stretch, but I wasn't ready to throw in the towel. I couldn't let Annika and Patricia know that I was having second thoughts.

"Sweetheart, we're all supposed to be scared once in a while. Fear is the instinct of self-protection. My therapist taught me that, over time, courage can replace fear. It doesn't come easily, but it's possible."

I saw by the look on Patricia's face; she was hearing 'blah, blah, blah,' so I muttered the truth I had denied to myself for the past two weeks. "I'm scared too."

She frowned. "Don't say that. You're supposed to be the fearless one of the group. If you can't do it, there's no way I can."

I squeezed her hand. "Remember that night in Aruba drinking Tanqueray all night, talking about the future? Wasn't that your idea? Whoever had the wildest idea drank a shot? And you, as I recall, got pretty drunk." She laughed through tear-filled eyes. "That's when the Team was born. I think Tara is looking down right now, cheering us on." I wiped a tear from my cheek.

Annika nodded. "Thanks, Manda. You always know how to bring us back off a ledge."

I rolled my eyes playfully. "You're lucky I love you because no one else gets to call me Manda but you." In a more serious tone, I asked, "So we're on for Frisco?"

11

They both nodded.

I pressed on. "Are you sure? I have no problem telling Bernie it's too soon."

That was a fib . . . but a small one.

"I guess it's better to move forward," Patricia's said. She folded her hands as if she were praying and looked at the crystal blue sky. "I need to believe that's what Tara would have wanted."

I forced a smile. "So, we're going?"

They both nodded. I breathed a sigh of relief and tried to ignore the single bead of sweat rolling down my forehead and the slight ringing in my ears.

Chapter 3

The familiar whinny of my Arabian mare, Misty, made me smile as the electric wrought-iron gate closed behind my car. I admired her sleek features as she ran to meet me on the other side of the paddock. I steered my sky-blue Maserati GranTurismo convertible up to my Malibu ranch house, my safe haven. The mixture of the salt-sea air, hay from the horse-barn, and the bromine from the hot tub were almost enough to make me forget how horrible the last week had been.

Heather, my live-in assistant, smiled and waved from the hot tub on the wrap-around deck above me. She had moved in and kept the company running like a top when I went back home to New Orleans to help my sister with some issues last summer. That hadn't turned out like I planned, but I've found that things rarely do.

Laying her head back on the corner pillow with her eyes closed, it appeared that she didn't have a care in the world. I knew better because I'd been following the e-mail trails she had left while running my Plastic Surgery referral business single-handedly since I left. I recently doubled her salary, and now I paid her a small fortune, but she was worth every penny.

"Come join me in the hot tub! You are a sight for sore eyes." Heather laughed, and my stress melted away. She was so petite that I could barely see her short blonde hair over the side of the hot tub, but I was sure her eyes were as blue as when I left. She had the kind of angelic face that always made people smile.

I adjusted my rear-view mirror to see the disastrous result of another cross-country flight and two hours of LA bumper-to-bumper rush hour traffic. My hair gave a new meaning to 'dirty blonde,' and black circles under my eyes were either from running mascara or lack of sleep. "I'll be right out," I yelled to her as I dragged my exhausted body upstairs to my bedroom.

Five minutes later, I was at the hot tub. Heather had already poured me a glass of Cabernet, and held it out to me. I slipped into the steaming water and settled in across from her. I lay back and closed my eyes, trying to remember my life before Tara's accident.

When I opened them, Heather was staring at me with a concerned look. "I wanted to tell you that we got a notice from the Centers for Medicare and Medicaid Services asking for all sorts of records."

I said as much to myself as to Heather, "They never used to cover any of our services, but with the upsurge in reconstructive surgery after mastectomy, we are suddenly on the Fed's radar. I don't have a good feeling about that." So much for relaxing in the hot tub.

"It said something about a routine audit and some questions about our plastic surgery provider contracts." She shrugged and laid her head back down.

I polished off my first glass in a couple of swallows. "I'm not going to worry about it unless I hear otherwise." I had a sudden desire to do something fun. "Let's go ride the horses."

"Yes!"

"I'll meet you at the barn in five minutes." We ran inside to change.

~*~

Within a week, I was sleeping through the night with fewer nightmares. At nine a.m. on Thursday, two days before the race, I descended the staircase from the upper level. Considering my humble beginnings just south of New Orleans, in Meraux, Louisiana, sandwiched between the Dubouchel Canal and the Mississippi River, I smiled every time I surveyed my domain.

The five-thousand square foot cedar-sided main level was one large room with furniture defining each space: a massive leather sectional framing a stone fireplace on one end and a dining room table for twelve on the other, overlooking the pasture and stables. Ceiling-high shelves, bookended with rolling ladders, housed twelve hundred books. The kitchen boasted stainless steel commercial appliances and solid marble countertops with a bar-height breakfast counter lining the wall with floor to ceiling windows and a dazzling view of the Pacific.

Heather sat at the counter, engrossed in whatever she was reading on her laptop screen, sipping from an oversized Starbucks coffee mug. "Good Morning, sleepyhead. I almost forgot to tell you, you got a Swiss Post overnight letter yesterday."

"Yesterday?" I rushed the rest of the way down the stairs and tore it open in anticipation, read, and threw it on the counter in disgust. "The prosecutor in Thun, who has jurisdiction in the case, denied my request to get Tara's parachute. They claim they need to hold it for evidence while they investigate the circumstances of her unfortunate accident. I doubt they will even investigate. Since tourism represents most of the local economy, the last thing they are going to want is the publicity associated with a trial."

Heather winked. "Well, you know what Bernie says . . ."

We repeated his Mantra in sing-song unison. "There is no bad publicity."

I twisted up my face. "Have you and Bernie been hanging out? Last I knew you barely even knew who he was."

She brushed me off with a swipe of her hand. "No! You quote him so often, I feel like I know him."

I breathed a secret sigh of relief. Heather and Bernie would be a dangerous pair. I had come to learn that she was far more ambitious than she let on. She knew how to play the Valley Girl to a tee, but she was very good at what she did. Or was that my paranoia talking? I recently let her know that I had put her in my will to assume control of the company, since I didn't have dependents or close relatives who had any interest in it. Since then, she had shown a genuine interest in how the business operated, which made me simultaneously proud and uneasy.

I re-focused on the situation at hand. "Did you see that the Swiss authorities issued a press release while we were in Boston, assuring prospective tourists that Tara's death was likely an accident? It was all over the internet. If that was true, what do they need the parachute for?"

Heather had her head buried in her laptop again. She grunted but didn't respond.

I was exhausted because I couldn't get Tara's death out of my head. It seemed almost impossible that it was just two weeks ago today when I had helped Tara pack her parachute. She seemed excited and was all smiles, giving me a thumbs-up as I approached the launching point. As far as I knew, the only person who had gone near her equipment was the cameraman filming us at the top. I knew that Rocky, the other cameraman down on the ground, never went near the parachutes. I didn't want to jump to conclusions, but I wasn't going to sit around and do nothing. The fact that the Swiss hadn't closed the case motivated me even more. I needed to find out the identity of the other cameraman.

I grabbed my phone and punched the numbers on the keypad to call the agency that provided the camera crew for our jump, We Got Film. "Only in L.A," I mused to myself.

The cheerful young woman at the other end of the line was about as helpful as voicemail, but she offered to have someone call me back "in a jiffy."

A few minutes later, I got a call from a very professional sounding Human Resources Director named Phoebe something. It sounded kind of like Cates, but I was pretty sure the star of Twin Peaks was still acting. That would be depressing if she had to fill in as an HR Director while she waited for scripts to review.

Fighting off the anxiety that sometimes ruled me, I reminded myself to focus on the task at hand as she told me that our cameramen had only been working for them temporarily. She explained that their contractual arrangement did not allow them to share contact information. When I insisted that it was critical that I find out what the cameramen's names were, she hung up. I called back intending to have a chat with her supervisor, but the line was busy.

I didn't want to over-react, but I felt like I needed to warn the girls about my hunch of a possible killer, preferably before we all showed up in San Francisco. I strained my brain to come up with a name but came up blank. He wore a press pass like Rocky had, but I never got close enough to read it. I couldn't remember Rocky's last name, but I figured he might be a good connection to help me find the other one.

I tried Annika and Patricia's cell phones but only got "not-in-network" messages. Ninety-eight percent coverage didn't mean squat when you lived in certain parts of Texas or most of Colorado. Ironically, Annika and Patricia hailed from the outskirts of Fort Worth and Denver, so it wasn't surprising they couldn't be reached.

The following morning, my stomach churned again with my growing suspicions surrounding Tara's death. I hoped that riding my motorcycle up the coast would keep my mind focused on riding, rather than thinking and driving myself crazy. I planned on following the Pacific Coast Highway to San Francisco. According to MapQuest, my route would take ten hours, including several planned stops. I left by eight a.m. intending to arrive in the Golden City by six p.m. Annika and Patricia had agreed to meet for dinner so that we could map out our strategy for the races. But I had other things to discuss. I tried both of their cell phones for the second time that morning, but no luck. Next time, I would choose teammates who lived somewhere near civilization or, at least, cell phone towers.

17

On the other hand, they could already be aboard their respective airplanes, so I stopped obsessing about cell phone coverage for the moment.

My planned coastal stops en route to the Bay Area included San Simeon Beach, Big Sur, and Half-Moon Bay Beach State Park. I loved the beach, and it took all the discipline I could muster to continue north after taking in the hypnotizing smell of saltwater in the air and the thrill of watching the seagulls dive for their prey.

Having stopped at the other two beaches hours ago, I was only forty minutes from my final destination when I debated continuing on, but I parked in the parking lot for Half-Moon Bay Beach State Park. It was my favorite beach. I found it mostly deserted except for a few sandpipers. Fascinated with their tenacity, I sat for a few minutes and watched as they probed tiny holes in the sand for food, never caring how many times the water filled them back in. I climbed back on my Ducati, pondering the lessons most people could learn from sandpipers.

Chapter 4

A couple of minutes before six, I parked my motorcycle on California Street just a few blocks from the San Francisco Omni Hotel. An advantage of riding on two wheels was my ability to create a make-shift parking spot nearly anywhere. Sometimes they were even legal, but it was rare to get a parking ticket on a bike even when I pushed the limits.

Concentrating on my planned agenda with Annika and Patricia, I wasn't prepared for how impressive and beautiful the massive lobby was and how it bustled with activity. The Omni lobby was three stories of mahogany trim and crystal chandeliers, a high-end restaurant, and deep, comfortable-looking couches. The circular solid-granite check-in desk in the middle of the lobby was large enough to hold several customer service agents comfortably.

After check-in, I spotted Patricia across the lobby. She saw me at the same time and ran over and hugged me tightly. She was a different person than she had been in Boston. Her porcelain skin glowed against her jet-black hair, and she smiled in a way I hadn't seen since Aruba. She looked like she was going to burst with excitement.

"Miranda, I'm in love!"

"That's so fantastic! And I thought you had sworn off men permanently!"

"You remember that cameraman filming us at the top—"

"What?" My heart thumped. Should I tell her about my suspicions about him? Maybe this wasn't the right time. She seemed so happy. I couldn't break her heart. I tried to stay upbeat, but I knew I was failing. "Sorry, that's great, sweetheart. It is. I've got a lot on my mind right now. I'll see you at dinner."

She looked confused and hurt as I rolled my suitcase into the circular glass elevator and watched her as I ascended.

Room 1915 was expansive for a downtown hotel and nicely decorated with modern mosaics and art deco furniture. I ran the hot water in the oversized glass and marble shower and stripped out of my leather. While I waited for the water to warm up, I sat on the small stool in front of the mirror with my head in my hands.

"What do I do now?" I muttered to myself. "Who is this guy, and why would he kill Tara?"

Feeling cleaner after my shower, I was still confused. As I slipped into my black dress from Miu Miu of Beverly Hills, I continued the conversation with myself in the full wall mirror. I can't even remember his first name. Larry, Barry, Jerry? Was this God's way of telling me I shouldn't disregard people because they look homeless? Why am I talking to myself?

We had reservations at the restaurant off the hotel lobby. I would never have guessed a place named 'Bob's Steak and Chop House' would be elegant and tasteful but, with white tablecloths, bone china, sterling silver, and candles lit on every table, it was. As I walked in, I saw Patricia and Annika at a table across the room, whispering to one another.

Evident that they had been talking about me, they stopped as soon as I walked over. We gave one another obligatory hugs, but tension was in the air.

Never one for long silences, Annika spoke loudly, "So why are you trying to steal Patti's man?"

"What—"

Annika cut me off before I could get a word out.

"Or maybe you're trying to steal her joy. Maybe as long as you're happy, you don't care a thing about us. Maybe—"

Two could play that game. I stopped her short. "Now hold on a second Anni, or whatever it is Patricia calls you, I'm not trying to steal anything or anyone! Get off your high horse for a second, and maybe you could tell your rear end from a hole in the ground. I think he killed Tara!" I yelled too loudly.

People at tables nearby stopped talking and stared. Annika glared at me, and Patricia's face was beet red. She stood, knocking her chair over, then ran from the restaurant, without looking back.

Annika stood up. Her eyes flashed as the early evening sun shone through the huge window that looked out onto California Street. For a moment, I thought she was going to walk out too, but she set Patricia's chair up and sat down. Her previous flash of anger had softened into lines of concern on her forehead. "Girl, you'd better tell me what's up right now."

I took a deep breath both to slow my oncoming anxiety and to focus on what I needed to say. "The day Tara died was a blur for all of us, and the funeral wasn't much better. But since then, I've had some time to think. Since the Swiss authorities were publicly insisting that Tara's death was an accident, I figured they wouldn't have any problem sending her parachute to me. But they rejected my request stating that they needed it for evidence. The cameraman on the top—"

She interjected, "Larry?"

I pounded the table. "I knew it was something like that." Again, I was talking too loudly, and the couple at the next table glared at me. I lowered my voice. "He was helping Tara with her parachute, and he had almost unlimited access to the equipment the night before."

She took a long drink from her wine glass. "So?"

"So, I think he sabotaged the parachute. Think about it. He was the only one who left town after Tara died. That can't be a coincidence. Can it?" Maybe I was grasping at straws.

She sucked on a swizzle stick. "But why would he kill Tara?"

I leaned back in my chair. "I don't have any idea. I just put this together before I left to ride up here. Then, when I arrived, I found out he's dating Patricia. What the heck? I think she's in

21

real danger. We may be too. What did she tell you about how they ended up together?"

Annika seemed much calmer, drinking her glass of wine, and I was relieved she appeared to be over our earlier confrontation. "She hung out in Boston for a couple of days after we left, and she ran into him at the bar in the Ritz, drowning his sorrows. He had come to town for the funeral and opened up to her that he had fallen in love with Tara while we were all in Switzerland. She said that he seemed to be torn apart by Tara's death, and she felt sorry for him. They went for pizza and hit it off. They've been dating ever since. I thought it was kind of sweet." She had a dreamy look in her eye.

"What would a beauty like Patricia want with someone like him?" I cringed at my judgmental comment, but she let it pass.

"She said he was kind and brilliant. I'm not sure why he is working as a cameraman because she said he's like a physicist or something."

"Really? That's weird. Is he here with her?"

Annika chewed on her lip, which she often did when she was thinking. "No. She said he might join her later, though."

"We'd better find her." I stood up quickly, and Annika followed.

We bolted before our waitress could take my drink order, and she left a twenty on the table. Annika and I rushed out to the lobby and paced back and forth in front of the elevator, willing it to come. As we rode up, I could only think that Patricia was on her phone, filling Larry in on everything.

"She's in room 5015," Annika yelled back to me as we sprinted toward the end of the fifth-floor hallway. She was already knocking when I caught up.

"Go away!" Patricia sounded like she was crying.

At least she hadn't checked out or wandered out alone on the street.

22

Annika spoke in soothing tones, "Patti, can we please talk? Manda's sorry she upset you."

I gave her a piercing look.

"What?" she whispered to me.

She raised her voice again. "Honey, let us in, and we can get this straightened out."

We waited.

I begged. "Patricia, can we come in for just a minute?"

She hesitated, but the door opened to reveal Patricia in ragged sweats and a tee shirt. Her eyes were red and puffy, and she was blowing her nose.

"One minute! That's it." She blocked us from entering the room. Mascara ran down her cheeks.

Annika spoke softly but firmly. "Please let us in."

She glared at us but stepped back into the room. The room was a mess. She had thrown her clothes and everything else she could put her hands on. She looked beaten down. It hurt to see her that way, remembering all the times I had felt the same way over the years.

She flopped onto the bed. I sat next to her. "Patricia, I know you're hurting, and you can turn away from me, but you can't ignore me. I could be completely wrong, and maybe there is a logical explanation." She didn't respond.

"Remember how I requested that the Swiss police return Tara's parachute to me?"

She nodded.

"They denied my request because they are investigating the case."

She didn't look up.

"Patricia, look at me."

She turned but stared at the floor. "Larry promised me he had nothing to do with her death. He was just helping her with her parachute."

I tried to control my glare. "How did that come up?"

23

"I called him and told him you said he murdered Tara," she admitted.

I turned her face toward mine with my finger. "Why did you do that? What if he really did it? Now, he knows we suspect him."

She whined. "He would have figured it out. I was crying, and he knew something was very wrong. He's smart, Miranda. He invents stuff. You should see his house; it's like a laboratory…" The way her voice trailed off made me feel like I might be starting to get through to her.

"Is he planning on coming here during the races?" I asked.

Her eyes widened. "Larry said he had to go out of town on an assignment, but that he'll try to get back for the finals."

I considered our options. "Maybe we should change hotels. I'm assuming you told him we were staying here."

She stood up from the bed and nodded. "Yes, I told Larry we were staying here. I already gave him my room number in case he was able to get here earlier." She glared at me again.

Annika made her best attempt at being upbeat. "Okay, let's change hotels. We're probably not in danger right now, but I know I'd feel better if we moved. Besides, it might be fun. A friend told me that the Loews Regency, a couple of blocks away, was nice. Patti, you and I can share a room. Manda, you said that Heather was coming up tomorrow, so you two should share a room too. Then no one will be alone. We need to agree not to go anywhere alone this weekend."

I nodded. "I agree. We should use the buddy system and stay on our toes. Heather and I were talking about sharing a room anyway, so I'll let her know we are switching hotels."

I figured I might as well say this sooner than later. "You guys know that I'm not a big fan of the police after my experience on the force, but we may need to report our concerns about this Larry."

I wondered if I would ever recover from my time as a cop in North Carolina. Being shot in the face and multiple surgeries over two years didn't just fade from your memory. "I honestly don't believe there's much they can do at this point, especially today. I have to be down at San Gregorio Beach by 7:30 in the morning, and then the four of us will be down there all day. So, let's hold off on talking to the police right now. Are you guys ready to change hotels right now?"

Patricia stopped pacing, "No, Miranda! What if he didn't do anything, and this is all a misunderstanding? Maybe Tara freaked out and forgot to pull the ripcord. That's as likely as Larry doing something to her parachute."

Annika and I both stared, not knowing what to say. At an emotional level, I understood her hesitation. We didn't even know for sure that Larry was involved in Tara's death, but he seemed like the best suspect at the moment.

I spoke in a soft and soothing voice directly to Patricia. "Can you humor me and change hotels? Larry may be a great guy, but I'm experiencing a lot of anxiety about staying here."

Patricia was silent and wouldn't look at me.

Annika turned her attention back to Patricia. "I don't know what this guy, Larry, is capable of, but he sure went to a lot of trouble to get to Boston, and it was not a coincidence that you ran into him there."

Patricia stood firm. "Well, of course, he was in Boston. He loved Tara."

Annika picked up Patricia's clothes from the floor piece by piece and neatly folded them and put them in her suitcase.

"What did you say his last name was?" I asked.

"Lechter. It's Lechter."

I couldn't for the life of me figure out why that name sounded familiar.

25

Chapter 5

Within a half-hour, we had checked out of the Omni and dragged our suitcases the block and a half to the Loews Regency. We looked like an odd group, Annika and I wearing our dresses from dinner, and Patricia in her faded sweats. I was reminded of Cinderella with her two wicked stepsisters.

We entered the building lobby to find only a security guard and two ancient mirrored elevators. He rolled his eyes and pointed at a sign on the wall between the doors: 'Loews Regency Lobby 37th floor.' He yawned as if he had stated the obvious a thousand times, "The hotel occupies the top eleven floors of the building."

We nodded our understanding, "That explains it," I muttered under my breath. When we departed the elevator on the 37th floor, it was clear that the lobby was far less opulent than the Omni's. Behind the front desk, sat a balding middle-aged night manager reading the newspaper. He stood and shoved the paper behind the counter when we walked in.

"How can I help you this evening?" he said in our general direction while he straightened his bow tie.

I tried my best to sound upbeat as I sidled up to the counter. "We would be forever indebted to you if you could get us two rooms for the weekend."

His grimace concerned me. I knew we should have called ahead, "I'm so sorry, but we haven't had an open room for this weekend for months. The Giants have a weekend series with the Yankees, which only happens like once a decade."

I leaned over the counter and looked him in the eye. I smiled, hoping to elicit one from him. "You must have a couple of rooms you are holding out for special cases, right"—I glanced at his name tag— "Reggie?" I pulled a hundred-dollar bill from my purse and slid it across the counter in his direction.

His fingers tapped the computer keys, and a drop of sweat dripped from his forehead. "I'll tell you what. There's a hold on the 'Bridge to Bridge Terrace' suite and the adjoining room for a party who has not yet confirmed—"

I interrupted, "Thanks so much."

"I didn't say you could—" He attempted to correct my misconception.

I took out my AmEx Black card. "How about if we prepay through Monday?"

His wistful expression made me wonder if he had a commission arrangement or if the tip alone had been enough to seal the deal. He took the card, slid it through the reader, and handed me two sleeves with two keycards in each.

"Suite 4810 and Room 4809." He pushed two copies of the room receipt across the counter. "Please sign this one and fill in your personal information. The other is yours to keep."

I did a doubletake when I saw the amount. Even for San Francisco, twelve thousand dollars for two hotel rooms, three nights, was a little steep, despite being on the penthouse floor. "We owe you one, Reggie."

He beamed. "I discounted the suite by ten percent and threw in the other room," he said as if he had done us a huge favor.

I folded the receipt and put it in my purse.

Annika nudged me as we waited for the elevator. "What's our share of the damage?"

I smiled. "You heard the man. He comped your room. It's your lucky day!"

She hugged me when we got in the elevator. Then she held me out at arm's length, "Thanks, Manda. We're okay, right?" The lines in her face belied her smile.

I hit the button for the forty-eighth floor and then looked her in the eye. "We're fine, hon. I'm sorry if I went a little over the edge in the restaurant."

"I owe you an apology too, Miranda," Patricia said. "I should have known you were protecting me and not jumped to conclusions about your motives. I've noticed that guys are drawn to you, and the fact that you don't seem to care about their attention makes you even more appealing. I'll admit it. I'm a little jealous."

I was happy that my act was working. The fact was, I was scared to death to get in a serious relationship. I reached out for Patricia, and Annika joined our group-hug until the elevator door opened.

"There are plenty of men out there for all of us. I would never steal yours." I smiled, and Patricia kissed my cheek. We grabbed our bags and got off the elevator too late to notice we were still in the lobby.

Reggie, still smiling at the desk, yelled to us. "Oh yeah, I forgot to tell you, you need to insert your room key in the reader to get access to the penthouse floor. Just follow the instructions."

I hit the 'up' button, the door opened, and we got back in the elevator and tried again, this time with the room key inserted. We started upward. I still felt like I needed to clear the air with Annika and Patricia. "You two seem a lot closer since Tara died. In Boston, I felt a little like an outsider, and when I saw you two whispering in the restaurant, I started feeling the same way—"

The elevator stopped on the mezzanine level, and a well-dressed couple in their mid-twenties entered hand in hand, interrupting my speech. They were staring silently into one another's eyes. When they exited on the fortieth floor, I exhaled, "Wow, someday, that's the kind of adoration I'd like to find."

Annika smiled. "You and me both."

As we reached the forty-eighth floor and stepped from the elevator, Patricia's cell phone rang. Her screen read, 'Larry.' She shook her head and held her phone away from her like it was going to kill her. We hadn't prepared for this. "Answer it and act normal," I whispered.

She answered after four rings. "Hello. Oh, Hi, Sweetheart!" Her face tightened. "I'm sorry. I had to use the bathroom, and I left my phone on the bed." She shrugged at her lame attempt at a lie. Her face reddened. "No, Sweetheart. Anni's here. We decided to room together."

She shrugged again, asking us what to say. I motioned with my hand for her to continue. "It's okay. When you get here, we can get a room to ourselves. When are you coming?"

Her forehead lined with worry. "No, nothing like that. I want to be ready when you come. Larry, no. I want to see you too—" She held the phone away from her ear as he yelled. Then the phone went quiet. He had hung up on her.

She rubbed her eyes and dragged her suitcase in the direction of the rooms. "Larry's angry. He's never talked to me like that. I guess I blew it when I called and told him about Miranda's suspicion about Tara's death."

I hoped that wasn't the case. "Maybe Larry's just jealous. You two haven't been apart since you started seeing one another, right?"

"Either way, he sounded crazy. He's usually so gentle when we are together." She looked and sounded like she was going to cry.

"Let's get out of the hallway and try to figure out what to do," I said.

We walked to Annika and Patricia's room, slid in the key card, and went inside. Two king beds highlighted a large room decorated with modern art. I had been feeling guilty about taking the suite but felt better that they had two beds. I needed to address that with Jackie, my therapist. I paid four thousand dollars a night for these rooms for God's sake, and I still felt guilty.

Annika flopped on the nearest bed.

"Do you know where Larry called from?" I asked.

"He's in Seattle," Patricia said. "He said he's coming late on Saturday or Sunday morning. But I could see him dropping everything and leaving right now." Patricia spoke quietly and without emotion.

Annika, uncharacteristically quiet, lay with her eyes closed.

"Well, guys, we have a big day tomorrow," I said in the most positive tone I could muster, "so I guess I'll get going. We should be fine tonight. Even on the off chance that he decides to come tonight, he won't be able to find us. Let's come up with a game plan tomorrow because once he gets to the Omni and can't find you, he'll know something is up."

Patricia looked hopeful. "Maybe this whole thing with Larry is a misunderstanding."

Annika mumbled something.

I hugged Patricia on my way out. "Maybe it is. I hope so."

As I opened the door to leave, she approached me. "Miranda, I'm sorry you've been feeling left out. I felt that way in Boston at times, too, so I get it. Three is a tough number. I had two friends in high school who were very close, and I was the new kid in town. So, I know how that feels. I'll try to do better, and I'm sure Anni will too."

"Thanks. Hey, I meant to ask you, because I've always called you Patricia, do you prefer Patti or is that just an Annika thing? I know she has a way of changing everyone's name."

"Patricia is fine. Thanks for asking."

"Goodnight."

"Goodnight—Hey, as I said earlier, I'll be heading out early for tomorrow's race. I have to meet with Bernie. Then Heather is coming up with the sleds, so I'll meet you down there. Okay?"

"Okay. Goodnight, Miranda." She closed the door as I headed down the hallway.

I felt a torrent of relief pour over me. I hadn't realized how the tension between Patricia and me had colored my mood. My steps felt lighter as I nearly skipped down the hallway.

30

The Bridge to Bridge Terrace Suite, so named for the breath-taking views of both the Golden Gate and Bay Bridges, included an outdoor terrace running the full length of the outside walls of the massive suite. The stunning view of the lights across the city and the bay, emanating from cars, buildings, and ships in the harbor, made me briefly forget about our tenuous situation.

I was happy to have two bedrooms and two bathrooms. As close friends as we were, I was never a big fan of sharing a room with anyone. I guess that didn't bode well for getting married any time soon.

Despite the marble bathroom and kitchen countertops and floors, I couldn't believe the price tag, but I figured I shouldn't worry about that now. We were safe. That was all that mattered.

I glanced at my watch: barely eight o'clock. I felt way more wired than tired and thought briefly, again, about going to the police but decided we would be more credible if we went as a group. Besides, I knew the authorities wouldn't do anything based solely on hearsay. There was no proof that this Larry guy had any involvement in Tara's death. And the fact that the Swiss authorities were still investigating didn't necessarily mean that they were considering this a murder case. They could just be doing the obligatory investigation to confirm that it was an accident.

Besides, our fear that Larry might hurt or kill one of us was only conjecture. I figured they would probably take our statements, pat us on the head and send us away. My years on the force gave me a realistic view of the system. At one time, I believed my years of under-cover experience would give me more credibility with the police, but I had found that they more often resented me and distrusted me for rejecting their noble profession. I was an outsider with too much inside knowledge.

I considered going to bed, but I was hungry, and my growling stomach won the argument. I sauntered out of the suite to hunt down some bar food and a nightcap.

I stepped off the elevator at the mezzanine level. Live music echoed in the hallway. It seemed to be coming from the hotel bar, which was just down the hall, so I ventured in.

In my dress and heels, I felt a little over-dressed for a pub, but I looked darn good, so I figured what the heck? The aroma of stale beer, peanut shells on the floor, and subdued lighting made me immediately feel at home. As they say, you can take the girl out of the honky-tonk, but you can't take the honky-tonk out of the girl. Or something like that.

I ordered a cheeseburger and fries from the bartender on my way to a seat at a small table in a dark corner toward the back. I figured that way I could slip out undetected if I decided that I didn't want to listen to the singer, an attractive guy I pegged at around forty. The predominantly twenty-something female audience, particularly at the tables toward the front, clapped and sang along with every set, which was a mix of covers of the Eagles, America, Bob Dylan, the Beatles, the Rolling Stones, as well as some originals with country and southern rock overtones.

After a few songs, the singer took a break. I was surprised when he didn't stay in front with his groupies. He walked back to the bar and ordered a Sam Adams. He and the good-natured bartender, John, shared a few jokes.

After a few minutes, John brought out my food and a Guinness. Admittedly, a customary salad with oil and vinegar and a glass of red wine would have been more consistent with my training regimen for the race, but when I get nervous, my self-control goes out the window.

When I sat in the back of the room, as far from the stage as I could get, I hadn't banked on the singer coming back and sitting at a table facing me directly. About halfway through his beer, he stood and walked toward me. "Mind if I join you?" he asked, and I motioned him to the chair across from me.

"Feel free." I hoped I didn't sound too blasé. Jackie and I were working on me expressing my feelings, and I didn't mind him joining me. He was even cuter close-up. I was actually kind of lonely and feeling the need for male companionship, but I did have a critical race tomorrow. My internal voice reminded me that I shouldn't be staying out all hours of the night. But one beer couldn't hurt.

He stuck out his hand. "Jason Wall."

I smiled, looking up at the stage and the lighted sign behind where he had been playing, "So I gathered." I said with a touch of sarcasm. "Miranda." His handshake was firm and warm in mine.

He kept smiling as he sat. "Nice to meet you, Miranda. What's a nice girl like you—" He caught himself mid-sentence. "Well, you know what I mean." He shook his head as if he wanted to put the words back in and grinned.

"I could ask you the same thing." I winked. "Except for the girl part. Hey, now that you're here, maybe you can answer a question that has been in the back of my mind since I walked in. What's up with the teeny boppers? I mean no offense but, most twenty-year-old's won't give a forty-year-old guy the time of day. Forgive me if you're like thirty-nine, but you know what I mean."

"It's weird." He frowned. "I started in the music business twenty years ago. For whatever reason, the age of my audience hasn't changed much since then. I don't know if it's because I wrote most of my songs at their age, and they can relate to them or what. It's pretty much always like this when I play. But, if I tried to talk to any of them between sets, they wouldn't want anything to do with me. We have absolutely nothing in common. It's become an unspoken rule. On stage, they treat me like a rock star. Offstage, I'm like their embarrassing uncle."

I smiled and relaxed a little for the first time since he sat down. "That's a relief. I thought that they were groupies in every sense of the word. That was a little too much for me to picture. But I have to admit it took me back to when I was their age."

I continued, not sure why I was spilling my guts to this guy. "When I was eighteen, I ran away to North Carolina with a friend to join the police force. Ten years later, I left the force and moved to Vegas. I just wasn't cut out for it and needed a change in my life." I decided I didn't need to provide all the details about the two worst years of my life.

He smiled. "So, do you still live in Vegas?"

"Oh, no. I live in Malibu now." I almost continued with my life story but stopped myself. An awkward silence engulfed the table.

After looking at my beer, the table, the bar, and the door, I thought of something to say. "So, other than this, what do you do, Jason?" I hated small talk and could feel my face and neck turning red with embarrassment.

"I'm an operations manager for a small power systems manufacturer in Santa Clara. I play music for fun in my spare time. There was a time when I thought I could make a living at it, but I learned that millions of people have the same idea when they move out here." He shook his head, which I couldn't interpret. It appeared to be somewhere between humor and regret. Before I could ask, he continued. "So, what do you do now, Miranda?"

I sat back in my chair. "I'm the CEO of an internet-based surgical referral company." I avoided the 'cosmetic' before the 'surgery' since I had avoided that topic in my introduction. I attempted to keep it light.

While he pondered his response, I felt my phone vibrate in my pocket. Whoever was calling would need to wait.

He brightened noticeably. "Wow, that's cool. There's something special about a woman who can take care of herself. You have no idea how many women I meet who think I'm made of money because I'm a marginally successful musician with a day job and want to get their hooks in me and some of that cash. The fact is, I work for tips at most places I play. And like I said, my day job is with a small company, so I don't make much, but I like it."

He smiled again, and for some reason, I was instantly transported back to my first boyfriend the summer after graduation. He had the same penetrating blue eyes and boyish smile. I wasn't sure if he could see through me, but I felt like he could read my thoughts, especially the ones I wanted to keep to myself.

He spoke, and I snapped out of whatever spell he had put on me. "Hey, if you ever need a job, give me a call. You know, when this internet fad fades out." He slid his business card across the table. Our hands touched briefly during the exchange, and I felt an unexpected jolt of electricity.

I laughed to cover my embarrassment. "Very funny. I don't think that's happening anytime soon." I stuffed his card into my pocket.

He stood up. "Hey, I've gotta get back up there," he said, pointing at the stage.

I stood too. "Nice meeting you, Jason. I have to get upstairs and go to bed. Big day tomorrow. Street luge race."

"I'm impressed. You are a woman of many talents and mysteries. I'll be here all weekend, so stop by again if you get the chance." He half-waved as he turned around. Simultaneously, the lights went down, the background music went off, and the crowd started to cheer. I watched until he walked onto the stage, and I then I slipped out the back door. As I approached the elevator, I pulled out my phone to see who had called earlier. It was Bernie. I made a mental note to check my voice mail later.

Chapter 6

I woke from a sound sleep and could barely breathe. My hands were tied. I was gagged and blindfolded. I felt the gun barrel resting on my temple.

The phone rang. In a daze, I sat up in bed and grabbed it. "Miss Marquette, this is your five-thirty wake-up call."

My eyes slowly focused, revealing an empty room and, thankfully, no one with a gun to my head. This Larry guy brought up some ghosts for me. Jackie would have told me I wasn't feeling safe. Sometimes I wondered what I was paying two hundred and fifty dollars a session for if I always knew what she was going to say. But then again, one of my teammates had been murdered, possibly by the guy dating another teammate. And to top things off, he would be in town as early as tomorrow.

I still felt hazy as I showered in water as hot as I could stand. The bathroom was nearly as large as mine at home and adorned with a marble shower and vanities. The abstract paintings weren't quite my style, but they fit the décor. I dried with a plush white towel and I concentrated on getting my day started on a positive note.

I grabbed my watch and quickly dressed in my motorcycle gear, realizing I was running late. I grabbed a cup of coffee and a chocolate-chip muffin at Starbucks on the way out then jumped on my Ducati. Installing that cup holder was my best idea yet.

The nerves knotted in the back of my neck, and I reminded myself that if I didn't get my appetite under control soon, I'd gain twenty pounds before I finished racing. My trainer would have a cow if she knew what I was eating. I needed to stay on top of my eating and drinking for the rest of the week. Perhaps I'd start that food journal she was always pushing.

After fighting the typical Northern California traffic, the thirty-nine miles to the San Gregorio Beach State Park took over an hour. I was overjoyed at the surprise Bernie had for me, though. A huge banner hung in the parking lot flanking the entrance: Welcome First Extreme All-girl Sports Team (F.E.A.S.T. Your Eyes on Them!) with our new logo: a motorcycle ridden by a woman dressed all in black leather with her ponytail coming straight out the back of her helmet, based on a picture of me racing a few years back.

I found Bernie standing back and admiring the banner. "Bernie!" I shouted over to him. "I love it!"

The perfect publicist, late fifties and connected to everyone from network executives to movie producers to book publishers, he wasn't cheap, but worth every penny. This event would be the first in a well-orchestrated campaign to get our team some name recognition. According to Bernie, national TV was the quickest way to accomplish that, and ESPN providing pre-recorded coverage of the heat races and live coverage of the finals was an excellent place to start.

I got off my bike and hugged Bernie. "You're a miracle worker!"

He puffed up his chest. "This is the tip of the iceberg, Miranda. I've got twenty-five people planted in the crowd who will only cheer for you and the other girls. They all have signs and know how to grab as much airtime as possible. The airtime we get this weekend will be huge, and just what we need before the meeting with Bravo next week. You got my message, right?"

My face reddened a bit, realizing I never listened to the voicemail Bernie had left while Jason and I flirted at the bar. "I'm so sorry I didn't call you back. Things were a little crazy last night."

He nodded. "How are the other two girls doing? I know Tara's death hit you all hard."

I suddenly realized I hadn't kept him in the loop. "They're okay, Bernie, but we've got a problem. I have a suspicion that one of the cameramen from our Switzerland shoot killed Tara."

"I told you not to use that agency!" He glared at me.

"Seriously Bernie, that's all you can—"

He interrupted. "Sorry, Miranda, I'm trying to hold things together here, and that's not good news. I know it's not good news for Tara, but foul play is probably the best way to get Bravo to back out completely. They have already cooled to the idea of a series since her death. Well, to be more specific, their attorneys are concerned about liability. Their promo people could probably make a murder play well to the general public."

I glared back at him. "Bernie! Can you stop for one second! My friend and teammate is dead. Now the rest of us may be in danger. The alleged killer is dating Patricia."

"You've got to be kidding." He whacked his forehead with the heel of his hand. "When did you find that out? We've spent over a hundred thousand dollars of your money on publicity here, and one of your girls is running around with a guy who may have killed Tara? Do you have a death wish, or are you trying to kill me? I'm not as young as I used to—"

Once he and I got on a roll, complete sentences were a thing of the past. "This isn't about you. I know it's hard for you to fathom that there are other people in the world—"

"I'm trying to look after you, and I don't have anything left in the budget for bodyguards, but protection is clearly what you need most." He kicked the gravel in disgust.

"Okay, this isn't doing either of us any good."

His face softened a little. "Have you notified the police?"

"Not yet. I thought about it last night, but I figured it would make more sense for the three of us to go together. We switched hotels just in case this guy, Larry, gets into town and tries to find Patricia."

He smirked. "Come on, Miranda. Think! With all this publicity, how hard is it going to be to find you?"

"Okay. Good point. Larry called last night and told Patricia he would be here tomorrow night or Sunday. Unfortunately, she told him that I suspected that he murdered Tara."

"As I said, you girls are giving me an ulcer." He shook his head. "What's your plan? Do you even have a plan? Do you have any idea why he killed Tara?"

"I don't have a clue. None of this makes any sense. Larry and Patricia allegedly got together in Boston after Tara's funeral. He and Tara had been seeing one another before she died. They kept that a secret. I had some suspicions from the way they were talking just before she died, but I hadn't been able to confirm it . . ." The words caught in my throat.

Sensitivity was not Bernie's strong suit, and he hadn't noticed my emotional response. "He didn't waste any time moving on, did he?"

I didn't want to cry in front of him, so I tried my best to push through it. "Hey Bernie, we can talk about this later. I've gotta meet Heather and check-in for the race." I turned to go, then hesitated. "And don't tell anyone about this. It's all speculation at this point, and all we need is for the press to get a hold of this."

He grabbed my arm. "Miranda, you must focus on the races. Let the authorities handle the other stuff. I don't need to remind you how critical these races are to the future of the team. We—" He noticed my eye roll. "Okay, you have a lot of money invested here, but the payoff could be tremendous."

"And your cut of tremendous is, let me see, pretty darn good."

"I can't deny I have a lot riding on you, Miranda. Just don't forget who helped you get this far. When we first met, you were just a girl with some wild ideas. I don't want to see it all come crashing down because of some psychopath. Just be careful, Miranda." He was such an odd combination of a businessman and a father figure.

"I will." He was right, and I hated it. I was pretty sure if I pulled back now, the deal with Bravo would be toast, not to mention any book, movie, and merchandising rights that would naturally follow. If I played my cards right, Bernie's ten percent commission would be in the seven-figure range. I couldn't let Larry derail this. I wouldn't.

I headed back to my bike and rode toward the main parking lot near the beach, which they had transformed into a staging area for the race. I hoped to have a little time to spend on the beach after the races. I had been to San Gregorio Beach a couple of times, and the dramatic views of the ocean from the bluffs and cliffs that dropped hundreds of feet down to the beach were breathtaking.

Toward the north end of the parking lot, I spotted Heather with my old Ford pick-up pulling a trailer carrying our sleds.

I could always count on her. I yelled as I parked my bike, "Hey there! Thanks for bringing the sleds. I know I could've done it, but I needed that ride up the coast."

She walked over, and we hugged. She looked so young for her age, and I could have pegged her for late high school or early college based on her cutoffs and belly shirt.

I held her by the shoulders at arm's length. "Are you okay?"

She had an odd look on her face, which she forced into a smile. "I'm fine. The drive was a little stressful, and with the traffic, I wasn't sure I'd make it on time. There was an accident on nine, and the police diverted the traffic to two thirty-six, and you know how wild that road is, right?"

Two thirty-six was known for its hairpin turns and narrow stretches along with massive redwood trees flanking both sides of the road in several places. That stretch of road was treacherous even without pulling a trailer.

She seemed to recover quickly and shifted the conversation to me. "So, how was your night?"

"I went to the hotel bar and had an interesting conversation with the singer there. It was nice to get out." I smiled wistfully.

She laughed. "That's great, Miranda. Your luck with guys has been non-existent lately."

"Like you have to remind me! Have you seen Annika or Patricia yet?"

"Nope. I thought they might be with you."

I glanced around the parking lot where people had started to gather. "No. I had to come down early to meet with Bernie. What do you think of the banner?"

"It's awesome! I love the logo. But after all, it's a picture of you, right?"

I was suddenly a little embarrassed that I had moved forward with the logo for the team without their approval. "Yes, it's me. I'm not sure how the other two are going to like it, but, oh well."

Then, in a whisper, so the other racers who were starting to gather, couldn't hear, I said, "We switched hotels to the Loews Regency. You're not going to believe this. The cameraman, Larry, who I think may have killed Tara, is dating Patricia."

She gasped. "What? Does she know you think that?"

Continuing in a whisper, I said, "I told her last night, and even though she went along with changing hotels, she's still hoping it's a misunderstanding. I have a bad feeling about these races. What if he tries to mess with our equipment? It's almost impossible to keep an eye on it all the time."

"I'll do my best. But once the race starts, the racing staff controls all access to the sleds. You won't even see them until just before you start a heat," Heather said. She corrected herself. "Well, I'll have access to them, too, but I shouldn't need it unless you have equipment issues."

"That's good. I wasn't even aware of that." With so many thoughts in my head about the murder, the race, Heather's harrowing trip up the coast, and the meeting next week with

Bravo, I could barely control my anxiety. I closed my eyes and prayed for strength.

When I re-opened them, Heather was looking at me inquisitively but knew better than to ask what I was thinking.

I forced a smile. "Hey, I'd better sign-in. Can you take care of getting the sleds to where they need to go?"

She nodded her head as if she was already way ahead of me. "I'll take care of it."

I smiled a distracted smile, and my head was spinning. I headed for the registration tent.

With fifteen racers per heat, each one competed approximately once every hour and a half. Huge screens stood in the staging area visible from virtually anywhere you could find room to stand. The screens would show ongoing race results as well as which racers were participating in the next five heats. I was starting to worry about when my teammates were going to arrive. Luckily for them, they had drawn later heats. I was in the first race.

Within fifteen minutes, I had completed registration for the race. With little time to spare, I was on the shuttle bus to the top of the mountain. When I looked at the group of racers I was up against, it was clear that I was the only woman. Because I had been peripherally involved in street luge for the last couple of years, I was surprised I didn't recognize even one of my competitors.

I had heard some rumors that the luge purists from around the state were avoiding this venue because they didn't believe that the courses were safe, especially the last day, on Lombard Street in downtown San Francisco. I had to agree with them on that count, but I couldn't resist the publicity gained from the national coverage, and that was the bottom line.

This course was on a particularly steep and curvy portion of La Honda Road, which was a favorite of local motorcyclists, including myself, even though I wasn't officially a local. I

42

planned to get an early lead and keep it, so I didn't get tangled up with some well-intentioned amateur.

Everything was going like clockwork until I got to the top and waited for my sled. There had been a mix up with the sled numbers and it took twenty minutes to get it straightened out.

Finally, as we lined up at the start, I surveyed my competition. I didn't see anyone I didn't think I could beat. Things were moving fast, and I looked at my fellow racers one last time when the starting gun went off. That was the last time I saw any of them before the finish line. My strategy worked perfectly. I won easily.

As I made my way through the crowd of racers awaiting their turn for thirty seconds of fame, I ran into the young German, Felix Loch. We had just finished a pleasant conversation when Annika and Patricia arrived. Loch was a Winter Olympic luge hopeful trying to stay in shape during the offseason.

Annika whispered as she watched him walk away, "Hey, Manda, who's the hunk? He's cute!"

I just rolled my eyes. "He's half your age."

She winked.

I spoke to both of them, but Patricia was looking anywhere but at me. "I'm glad you guys are here. I've got enough to worry about without having to keep track of you two. You are so lucky that you were both placed in later heats. I already completed my first one. Not to brag, but I killed it!"

Annika raised her arms in a salute. "Of course."

Patricia said, "Sorry! We slept late. We were just in time for breakfast but missed the shuttle. We had to practically bribe a cab driver to bring us all the way down here. He didn't seem to mind the $120 fare, though."

"Hey, did you guys see the banner?"

"Yeah, awesome!" Annika said, then she poked me. "I'm not so in love with the logo, though. I guess you did put up the money for the publicity, so it probably makes sense that it's you, and you alone. on a motorcycle." Even though she said it in a teasing way, I knew I would hear about it later.

Patricia was brought back into focus with the mention of money, "How much did all this cost anyway? I feel bad that you are footing the bill for all this—"

It wasn't the time to talk about finances, so I changed the subject. "Hey, you guys better sign in. Annika, your first heat is in twenty minutes."

"So, Patricia?" I asked while she waited for her first race. I had avoided the topic since our arrival, and the timing was perfect, especially because Annika had just left for her heat. "What do you see in this Larry guy anyway? You are so pretty, and he's, well, nothing to write home about."

She scrunched up her alabaster face. "Why does everyone ask me that?"

"Because you could probably get just about any guy you wanted—"

She stood her ground. "I figured if anyone would understand it would be you."

I stared at her like she was a Martian. "What do you mean?"

"Look at all the pretty rich boys you have been with and where that got you, nothing but boredom or heartbreak." Patricia seemed stronger and more self-reliant than I had ever seen her.

"Okay, you've got a point," I said, although I wasn't totally convinced she was telling me the whole story.

Patricia got a far-away look in her eyes. "I know he's not the typical guy that most women would be attracted to, but that's part of his appeal to me. Do you know just how many times I've been cheated on over the years? Let's face it. Women aren't lining up to be with him."

I gave her an astonished look. "You mean you are with Larry because he's not attractive to other women? Now that's a new one."

"Granted, I wasn't in the best place when I met him, but I've come to appreciate the man he is. He's perfect for me." She blushed a little and bit her lip.

I force a smile, but I was still worried about her.

She picked up on my doubt. "I'm not afraid of Larry, Miranda. He loves me. If he did anything to Tara, he will tell me eventually. He tells me everything."

My head hurt. "Are you listening to yourself?" I shouted. Her expression told me I'd overdone it. I drew a deep breath and said, "Just be careful. We both know that things are not always what they seem. I'm glad that he's good to you, but what if he's manipulating you—"

She put her hands on her hips in defiance. "Now stop right there, Miranda. Why would he manipulate me?"

I wasn't giving up having gotten her attention for the first time since we arrived. "Men have their ways. They can be very clever that way."

She stared me down. "I know that, Miranda. And it's not that I haven't considered that Larry could be involved in Tara's death. Of course, I have. I have thought of nothing else since you told me your suspicion, and even before. I trust and respect you, and I know you have my best interest at heart, but I'm the only one who really knows him. I spent those days with him while he grieved her death. He loved Tara. You saw them together up on the mountain before we jumped. She trusted him, and I do too."

I bit my tongue before I was tempted to say what I was thinking, which was: 'That's why she's dead.' But, Patricia's heat started in a few minutes. So, I kept my mouth shut.

About five minutes after Patricia departed wordlessly, deep in thought, Annika returned. She looked anything but happy. "That darn German kid. You were right, Miranda, he's nothing but a child. He pulled a stunt out there, only someone his age would try. I think he should be disqualified!"

She had my attention. "What did Felix do?"

"We were three-quarters of the way down the track, and I was right behind him. Rather than speeding up like any real luge racer would do, he hit the brake, which caused me to have to swerve to avoid hitting him. The precious time I lost by swerving cost me the race. Basically, while he was blocking me, the rest of the pack raced passed us. I should have been at least second."

I tried to cheer her up. "You'll make it up in the next race."

She wasn't convinced. "I shouldn't have to. What a waste."

I figured I'd quit while I was ahead and changed the subject. I needed to bring Annika up to speed with my discussion with Patricia. "She still believes that Larry's innocent. I think even more now than ever. It's like she's under his spell. It scares me."

Annika considered this information. "I guess all we can do is protect ourselves and protect her as much as she will allow. I don't know the guy any better than you do, but he sure gave me the creeps in Switzerland. He never spoke two words to me, but I guess he was more interested in Tara. I've never known what makes some women go for guys like him. I haven't always had the best taste in men, but I've never been with a guy who looks like they spent the night in a homeless shelter. There are too many nice-looking guys more than willing to allow me to support them. Why mess with some Charlie Manson look-alike? It's pretty clear to me her relationship radar is all messed up."

I touched her arm, happy that she had put her anger about the first heat of the race aside. "I'm glad we are on the same page anyway. It makes me wonder what was up with Tara and him, but I guess we'll never know that at this point."

Annika caught the eye of a cute guy, and she was gone.

After a long day of racing and standing around waiting to race, the finals were next. I walked to the shuttle bus, assuming I'd run into Patricia, since she had made the finals also, and it was the only way to get up the hill. When I got on the bus, I was surprised to see Rocky, the cameraman on the ground at the Switzerland shoot. Seeing him brought back just how angry he

46

was that they had confiscated his camera. I made a mental note that he might have anger issues.

I sat across the aisle from him. He seemed to be lost in thought, or at least he wasn't paying any attention to me. I looked over at him. "Hi. Do you remember me?"

He had a blank look on his face. "To be honest, no."

"I'm Miranda Marquette." I stuck out my hand across the aisle, and a young racer nearly running toward the back seat almost knocked my arm out of its socket. "Hey!" I yelled.

"Sorry." He stammered and continued on with a smirk on his face.

Rocky looked directly at me. "Wait a minute. You do look kind of familiar. I'm Rocky Blanchard." We shook hands. He had a solid handshake and looked me right in the eye. He appeared to be the opposite of Larry in nearly every way. He was a jock with a great set of abs, at least from what I could tell through his black tee shirt. "So, where do I know you from?"

"Switzerland."

He looked at me again. "Oh. Oh yeah. That was your all-girl team. I didn't realize you were competing here."

I shrugged. "We try to partake in all extreme sports."

He appeared to be thinking back. "What a horrible trip that was. I still don't have my camera back." He hesitated and looked at his feet. "I'm sorry. I know you lost your friend, and here I am complaining about my camera."

"It was a bad time for all of us." After an awkward silence, it seemed like a good time to see if he knew anything. "Hey, remember the other cameraman on that job? Did you work with him much?"

He thought for a minute as the bus departed for the top of the course. "We worked together a couple of times before that. I haven't seen him since then, though. I didn't know him very well. He pretty much stayed to himself."

"Did you notice anything weird about him on that shoot?"

He chuckled. "Well, that's a loaded question. Larry was always weird." He then looked thoughtful with his hand on his chin. I wished he would hurry because the bus ride was nearly over. "Wait a minute. He and I got into a bit of an argument. It was customary for the senior man to have the choice of where he wanted to film. Since I was senior, I chose to work at the top of the mountain. Well, he went ballistic! I was shocked because the guy hadn't really said two words to me before that. Finally, after we argued for a while and it was clear he wasn't going to give up, I gave in. I didn't really feel that strongly about it. I regretted it later when the cops took my camera and all my footage. That stuff belongs to the network, and I'll be personally responsible for paying for it if I don't get it back." The bus came to a stop, and everyone stood up, crowding their way to the exit.

I handed him a business card. I knew they would come in handy. "I'm thinking of calling the officer at the scene with some questions. I'll ask about the camera for you if you'd like."

He looked at my business card. "Thanks. Give me another one so I can give you my number." He wrote his information down and handed it to me.

"Thanks! Hey, if you think of anything else about that day, could you give me a call? I'm still trying to piece together what happened over there."

He smiled. "Sure." Then he got off the bus carrying his ESPN-labeled camera and disappeared into the crowd.

I rushed to the sled distribution area. Ten minutes stood between me and the final. Each sled and rider had unique codes and a corresponding wrist band, which had to be scanned by the staff before the sled could be released to the rider. Somehow during the original registration process before the first heat, Annika and my sleds and wrist bands got reversed, but that was all straightened out now.

Many competitors complained about the complexity of the process, but I thought it was more than worthwhile while preventing the free-for-all that usually ensued at these events. At this point, anything that could prevent tampering with the equipment between races made me feel safer.

With only two minutes remaining, all ten finalists lined up across the road behind a white painted line. The views of the blue ocean in the distance were breathtaking, but I tried to focus on the task at hand.

I briefly pondered the danger I would be in over the next couple of minutes. Even though only a few racers sustained minor injuries during the preliminaries, there was always risk with any extreme sport. Street luge was considered moderately dangerous because of how small and unpredictable the sleds were. And when racing on a road as we were, catching some uneven pavement, running off the shoulder or into another racer, one could be catapulted off the course into a sign, a guardrail, or off a cliff.

Unlike auto racing, where a racer's starting position was improved by where one placed in the heat races, in a Street Luge final, all of us started together in a line across the road. In the final, all preliminary race results were wiped out, and it came down to one race for the top ten positions. The standings from eleven down were already determined for the day. So, the worst anyone in the finals could end up was tenth. After three days of racing, a tally of how each racer had faired in the heats and the finals would be combined to determine the champion. One tough day placed competitors at a significant disadvantage because there were only two other days to make it. The fact that Annika hadn't reached the final on day one wouldn't help her in the standings, but in a field of over one hundred, she had a chance to make it up with two good days. At least she had placed near the top of the group who didn't qualify for the finals.

As we lined up, ready for the race, none of the good-natured banter existed between the racers as it had in the earlier runs. Judging from the looks on their faces, some of the men took offense to the fact that women were competing. Earlier in the day, they had been polite if not a little standoffish. With the starting gun just seconds away, the condescending attitude of a couple of the racers turned downright aggressive.

The racer to my right spoke openly to the guy next to him about the class of people they had allowed to enter this race. I stood ready to rub their faces in it at the bottom of this course. If Patricia had lined up within earshot, I would have talked some smack with these Neanderthals, but I held my tongue.

Finally, the starting pistol sent us off. I jumped ahead of the pack immediately. After the first quarter, I still led but only by inches. Out of the corner of my eye, I saw a couple of guys veer off the course. I hoped it was those two losers to my right at the starting line. By halfway down, three of us were in a virtual tie. I could tell by the color of the sled that one of them was Patricia. I prayed that we could place first and second.

At the three-quarter mark, two more competitors were in place to grab the lead if one of the leaders should slip up. Because it was necessary to lie back while racing, I couldn't see much of what went on around me. I needed all my concentration to stay on the course and minimize over-steering and over-braking errors that would slow me down and cost me the race.

However, under-braking could result in an even worse outcome with the likelihood of flipping the sled due to centrifugal force. I was super excited as we approached the finish line. Patricia was still with me but just slightly behind. At the last second, with a burst of speed, someone passed me. I was kicking myself. It was that German, Felix Loch, who had knocked Annika out of her final heat.

While I was tempted to snub him at the finish line, I stood up and shook his hand. He grinned, which made me really want to slug him. He was lucky that he was just a kid. "Nice race, Miss Marquette," probably an attempt to make me feel old.

I gritted my teeth and smiled back. "You too, Mr. Loch. One down, two to go," and walked away.

Patricia finished third. She was excited in her quiet way. We hugged, and both held on for a long time. I could feel her tears on my cheek. "Maybe everything is going to be all right," she whispered.

I knew what she meant, but all I could say was, "Maybe. I hope so."

When we got back to the staging area, Annika appeared to have recovered from her disappointment, and she gave both of us a huge hug. "Nice going, guys! I'm gonna be there in the final with you tomorrow, I promise you that."

A guy hovered behind her in the background, and she motioned him over. "Tom, this is Miranda and Patricia." We all shook hands. "Miranda and Patricia, this is Tom Stringer. He's a world-class surfer who decided to try street luge to keep his life interesting, right, Tom?"

Tom had the blonde and built good looks of an L.A. surfer, and Annika was literally drooling over him. He seemed to enjoy her attention.

He grinned. "It's definitely interesting! I didn't make the finals either, but I had fun. Tomorrow's another day. Besides, if all that comes out of these races is meeting Annika here, then I'm already a winner." He whipped his hair out of his face, took her by the hand, and led her toward a yellow Corvette. My initial reaction was that he worked fast, but on second thought, it was more likely that she did.

By the time we got back to the hotel, my watch read seven-fifteen. After a full day of racing and standing around in the sun, I was exhausted. Heather and I went downstairs to Starbucks for a Frappuccino and a chocolate croissant. "I'll get back on real food tomorrow," I promised myself.

Heather's eyes twinkled. "Even your nutritionist said a little chocolate wouldn't kill you. Well, this might be a little more than she had in mind, but if eating bad is relaxing, then why not? Between the racing, the publicity and a possible killer on the loose, there's no point in getting more stressed than we already are."

Patricia messaged me that she and Annika were going to bed and that Larry had let her know that he probably wouldn't arrive until Sunday afternoon. Relief washed over me and reduced my stress more than eating chocolate ever could. I had hoped that he wouldn't be in the area for the second day of racing, and my wish came true if he could be believed.

Heather sat across from me at a tall table on the back wall of Starbucks. She looked fresh and energized in the sundress she changed into when we returned to the hotel. It was surprising considering she had driven eight hours with the sleds and stood in the sun all day while I raced. It reminded me of when we first met on Venice Beach. She had been sitting in the hot sun for hours but still looked like she just stepped out of the shower. We got to talking, and she told me she had just left her job as a waitress and was looking for something more challenging where she could utilize her degree in Business Communications. At some point in the conversation, I offered her a job as my assistant.

I leaned in to study her face. "I don't know how you do it," I said. "You're functioning on no food or sleep, and you look completely relaxed."

"I love to travel and be busy. This life is just what the doctor ordered. I couldn't stand the Midwest lifestyle in Michigan. I was bored to tears. I figure I can always catch up on some lost sleep. These days are priceless. Thanks for hiring me!"

"Believe me, hiring you was the best decision I ever made!"

Heather laughed. "Okay, then, I'm going to take my job seriously. You need to get upstairs to bed."

I mock pouted. "Really?"

Chapter 7

The site for day number two of racing was north of San Francisco in the Napa Valley. The parking lot registration area was the size of two football fields, at least twice the size of the one the previous day. Our Street Luge racing provided an opportunity for about twenty-five local wineries to set up shop for wine tasting and sales. It was great for the crowd of friends and relatives who would spend another day alternating between the excitement of racing and the boredom of waiting for the next one to start.

Before the racing began, I bought a couple of cases from smaller boutique wineries. During one of the breaks between heats, Heather helped me carry them to the truck.

The results from day two were significantly different from day one. While several of those who had placed in the finals on day one were also in the finals on day two, the majority were not. Patricia and I were exceptions. I placed fourth for the day, and Patricia was sixth. Annika placed second, so she was much happier than after her result on day one. Surprisingly, Felix Loch, the young German who led after day one, didn't make the finals on day two after clipping a guardrail on his first heat.

The Napa course had very different terrain than San Gregorio. Napa had more incline and tighter curves and favored lighter and more agile racers than the first course. Having superior sleds didn't hurt our chances as a team. Many of the competitors didn't make the kind of investment that we did in equipment because they considered this an off-season sport or a way to pass the summer and their sponsors were paying their tab. Because of our consistency between days one and two, I ranked second in the combined results, Patricia third, and Annika fifth.

As Heather and I rode across the Bay Bridge back into San Francisco, she brought up Larry for the first time since I had filled her in the prior morning. "Don't you think we should go to the police? I'm worried that guy's going to try something tomorrow. Even if the police didn't do anything, we'd at least be on record and have an open case, so they could hit the ground running if he did do something, God forbid."

"You're probably right. I'm gonna' talk to the girls tonight," I concurred. We rode the rest of the way in silence.

As we walked by Annika and Patricia's room, the sounds of a heated argument wafted not so subtly under the door. "*No, Ani. I had to tell him.*"

"Now, let me get this straight. You had to tell Larry that we switched hotels and what room we are in?"

"Yes! He made me." Patricia sobbed.

"Is he here? Now?" Annika asked.

"No, he's still not coming until tomorrow sometime. He just called to confirm the details for when he arrives tomorrow. I just couldn't lie to him, Ani. Not after how mad he got the last time we talked."

"We have to tell Miranda." The door opened in front of Heather and me. "Or, I guess we don't." Annika walked out of the room and pointed back toward Patricia and mouthed the words, "She's crazy." Then she called back to Patricia, who still sobbed in the room. "I'm going for a walk."

The three of us went down the hall to the suite.

Annika admired the view. "Wow, nice!"

I kept my voice low. "Let's go out on the terrace. Want coffee or anything?"

"My, aren't you the little hostess? No thanks. Let's talk," Annika said as she followed Heather and me outside.

The three of us sat at the concrete umbrella table overlooking the bay. The view of the city lights and the harbor was breathtaking. From our vantage point, we could see both bridges, Treasure Island, Oakland, San Francisco Bay, and San Pablo

Bay. The twinkling lights seemed to go on forever, like when you flew into L.A.

We all sat for a while, transfixed by the view and lost in our own thoughts. Finally, the suspense was killing me, so I spoke. "So, what happened?"

Annika exhaled dramatically. "I came out of the bathroom as Patricia was finishing up a phone conversation with Larry. It sounded like they were back to being all lovey-dovey so I asked her what she had told him. With some prodding, she eventually confessed that she had told him not only that we had changed hotels but also what rooms we had checked into. We don't even know if this guy is here in San Francisco now, for pity sake. How could she be so crazy? We need to go to the police. She honestly doesn't believe that he did anything or that he's dangerous. Even if we could get her to go with us, she would be of no use. I frankly don't even know what they can do for us, but we have to start somewhere."

As much as I hated dealing with the police, it seemed like our only option. "I looked it up earlier. The Central Police Station is just a few blocks up on Vallejo Street. Are you guys ready to go now?"

"Sure," they said in unison with more resignation than enthusiasm.

I leaned closer to Annika and whispered. "We better not tell Patricia at this point since she's told him everything so far. Although getting the cops involved might be a deterrent to most people, I don't think this Larry guy is like most people."

We slipped quietly down the elevator and headed up Sansone Street. The station was a bit further than it looked on my phone map, probably ten blocks, but none of us were all that excited about getting there, as evidenced by the less than lively pace we took.

Annika broke the silence after three blocks. "So, what exactly are we going to say when we get there?"

55

I thought for a minute as we walked somberly. "I guess we tell the authorities the whole story starting in Switzerland. That reminds me. I keep meaning to call Officer Brecker. I called and asked for him last week at around noon our time, so I guess it was nine p.m. there, but he evidently works days."

"Well, you met him during the day, right?" Annika said flatly.

"Yes, he was working during the day when we met, but I know that cops often work varying shifts from day to day or week to week. I used to be one, remember?" We were clearly getting on each other's nerves.

We walked a little further, and I continued. "I just keep wondering if Brecker would give me the straight story on Tara's murder investigation if I spoke to him directly. It's a long shot."

Realizing that I had ignored her question, I looked at Annika. "As far as the San Francisco police go, I guess we tell the truth and hope someone listens."

Heather responded. "I'm not sure there's much I can add since I wasn't there in Switzerland."

I tried my best to keep things light. "Just smile real pretty. That usually works to keep a guy's attention."

We walked the rest of the way in silence. The closer we got to the station, the more it felt like going to the cops was a mistake. We turned down a street lined with Chinese restaurants, and I suddenly wondered if we were lost. Within a few more steps, the white government-issue building came into view.

"Are you sure we should do this?" I said. "I feel kind of silly. What are we going to say? We think that our friend was murdered, but it might have been an accident, and our other friend is dating the guy we think might have done it, and we're afraid for our lives? What exactly are they going to do with that? I know what I would have done when I was a cop—circular-file it and then laugh about it with my buddies over coffee."

Annika's face looked unusually drawn and dark in the light of the sulfur streetlamps. "If you've got a better idea, I'm all ears."

Heather added, "Maybe it'll be better than you think it'll be. You are kind of jaded, Miranda."

"And you're way too positive for your own good, Sweetheart," I groused. We clearly were feeling the pressure, and I wanted to shove that back in immediately after I said it. She didn't respond, but her face showed that I had hurt her feelings. Jackie's said more than once that I purposely pushed those away who were closest to me. Maybe she was right. I reminded myself I needed to book a session when I got back to town.

Annika led the way, starting up the cracked and worn concrete steps toward the double doors of the precinct. She mumbled under her breath. "Come on, let's just get this over with."

We followed her into a small gray waiting room, filled with a mass of humanity—exhausted-looking mothers with skinny snot-nosed kids, tattooed leather-clad gang members, mini-skirted streetwalkers, and others that I couldn't classify as anything but scary. If this was the waiting room, I could only imagine what the holding cells looked like.

A plump mid-forties woman in uniform sat behind bullet-proof glass. In a surprisingly pleasant voice, she asked, "Are you ladies lost?" When I just stared at her blankly, she continued. "I'm sorry. It's been a rough night. Who am I kidding? Every night is rough here." She chuckled under her breath. "Can I help you with something?"

I figured there was no time like the present. "We would like to report a crime. Well, we'd really like to prevent a crime." She stared at me while I sputtered. "Could we just talk to someone? We believe we are in danger."

She said with a hint of sarcasm, "Bingo! There's something I can work with!" She handed me a clipboard. "Please fill out this form, then bring it back to me, and I'll get someone to speak with you."

Folding chairs were arranged in rows, evidently to maximize the seating capacity. We found the last three adjoining seats available and abruptly sat, Annika on my right and Heather on my left. Until I sat down, I hadn't realized my legs were shaking.

Heather's face crinkled with concern. "Are you okay? You're shaking, and you look pale."

I was relieved she wasn't angry with me after I had jumped down her throat earlier. "I'm cold," I lied, knowing my anxiety was building. "Let's just get this over with."

Five minutes later, we had completed the standard intake form with contact information and a general description of our complaint. I kept the reason for our visit brief, "We are in fear for our lives."

After a half-hour or so of rubbing elbows with San Francisco's underbelly, we were called back to a stark conference room by an attractive young brunette whose nametag read Stacy Intern. I figured she was either an intern or had an odd last name. The room smelled of smoke, sweat, and several other not-so-pleasant odors.

"Detective Morrison will be with you in a couple minutes," she told us and disappeared into the hall.

I stared into the two-way mirror, wondering if anyone stared back. This room brought back a period of my life I'd just as soon forget. The thin stream of sweat running down my forehead and my moist underarms clearly indicated that my otherwise calm exterior belied my anxiety level. I had avoided police stations like the plague since my accident.

Sitting in the interrogation room confirmed for me why I felt so ambivalent about reporting Larry to the police. I played out several possible scenarios in my mind, none of which ended in Larry's arrest.

Bernie had already told me, in no uncertain terms, that the Bravo Network executives had expressed second thoughts about our project since Tara's death. I felt more anxious, depressed, and helpless as we waited. My instincts told me to run, but I stayed put in deference to my friends.

Within a couple of minutes, a disarmingly attractive woman in her mid-thirties, with shoulder-length blond hair and a warm smile, walked into the room. My gut told me the commanding officer was male, but I had no way of confirming that.

She shook each of our hands before sitting on the opposite side of the table. "I'm sorry to have kept you waiting. I'm Detective Morrison." She flashed her badge. "It's a little bit of a zoo out there this evening, although, to be honest, it's no worse than usual." She spoke with a slight Irish brogue. She chuckled briefly then shifted into official cop mode. "So, what brings you girls out this evening? Your form indicates that you believe you are in danger."

I spent the next twenty minutes, providing the background information about Tara's death and Patricia's subsequent relationship with Larry.

When I finished, Detective Morrison sat looking thoughtfully for a second before she spoke. "Can I ask you this? Why is your friend, Patricia, you said her name was?" We nodded, and she continued. "Why is she not here with you?"

Annika spoke up. "She doesn't believe that Larry is responsible for Tara's death or is a threat in any way."

She smiled sadly. "You have no idea how often I hear similar stories, not including the BASE jumping and murder part, but situations where women feel that they are in danger, but no discernable crime has been committed. I believe every word you have told me, and I wouldn't doubt that this guy is dangerous. It sounds like he has more than his share of control over your friend. I wouldn't doubt that he is an abusive personality. That being said, until it can be established that he has committed a crime, I'm afraid there is nothing we can do."

I knew this would be the outcome. "Can you at least call the Swiss authorities?"

She nodded. "Yes, I promise I will do that. I suspect that the last thing they want is some Irish-sounding American cop mucking around in their business, but I've been wrong before." She stood. "Could you provide this gentleman's full name so I can at least see if he had any priors or has any open arrest warrants?"

I wrote Larry's full name on a pad of paper that she handed me. "Here is my cell phone number in case you find out anything. I put it on the intake form, but I thought this might be easier for you."

She smiled sincerely and handed her card to each of us. "Please, and I'm begging you, if you have any reason, while you are here in town, to believe that a crime has been or is being committed, or you have cause to believe that you or your friend are in immediate danger, call my cell phone immediately and 911." She opened the conference room door then stopped in her tracks. "Wait a minute, you said that you're racing in the street luge race tomorrow, right?"

We nodded.

"We'll be out in full force patrolling the area. There's supposed to be quite a crowd, and these days we need to be on the lookout for anything or anyone unusual. If you see anything suspicious, just flag one of us down." She thought for a second. "Hey, do you have a picture of this guy? We can e-mail it to the officers patrolling the area so they can be on the lookout for him."

"I can get one for you, I think. I'll email it to you," I said. "Thanks for all your help."

We all shook hands. Detective Morrison led us out the back door, so we didn't have to go through the waiting area. Annika spoke first as we all plopped down on the top step of the rear exit. "Well, I guess that felt pretty much like a waste of time. Now, what do we do?"

"We need to get back to the hotel," I said, trying not to sound demanding. "Patricia might be wondering what happened to you. There's no reason to tell her we went to the police, right?"

"No way! She would flip out." Annika stood up, towering over the two of us. "Let's tell her we went out for a drink. She hasn't tried to call or message us on our cell phones, so she's probably been on the phone with Larry. I'm sure he wants to keep pretty close tabs on her since she's been acting kind of squirrely with him."

We walked back to the hotel silently, lost in our thoughts. As we got out of the elevator on the forty-eighth floor, we could hear Patricia through the door of their room.

"No, Larry," she giggled.

I whispered, "Oh my God, he's here!"

"I can't wait to see you either," she said in a quieter voice.

"I guess he's not here." I motioned with my finger down my throat, pretending to gag. "Let's get outa here."

"I miss your kisses too, Snuggles." She giggled like a schoolgirl.

We couldn't get away from our end of her phone call fast enough, so we headed back to the elevator and down to the street.

Five minutes later, we ended up at the Wayfare Tavern on Sacramento Street, a couple blocks from the hotel. I had read in the hotel brochure that while it was relatively new, it had been designed to look like a turn of the century tavern. It matched the description perfectly. The bartender, Paul, seemed thrilled that we chose to sit at the bar and kept the stories coming while we shared a bottle of wine.

61

We shared stories about our extreme sports adventures and how we planned to take it all in the street luge tomorrow.

After about an hour, he said, "I hate to say it girlfriends, but this is the last call for alcohol."

I was shocked, "At ten-forty-five? You've got to be kidding!"

He washed glasses and good-naturedly barked orders like a mother hen. "You girls are racing in the big race tomorrow. You're lucky you stayed in the financial district where we close down early. I get the feeling you all could hold your own in a party town like this, but I'd imagine street luge takes some wicked concentration, especially down Lombard Street. You'd better get to bed."

He hugged each of us good-bye like he was an old friend.

The evening was warm, so the three of us strolled casually back toward the hotel. Annika wasn't quite ready to call it a night. "Look, there's the Tadich Grill. That's the oldest restaurant in the whole state of California. Let's check it out."

I moaned. "I can't believe you read the hotel brochure too. How can you even think about eating at a time like this? My stomach is in knots. Besides, you must have had three baskets of chips while we were at the Wayfare."

She took my hand and started dragging me. "Come on, it'll be fun. You're hungry, right, Heth?" She grinned sheepishly.

"Well, now that you mention it—"

Annika reached the door and pulled. "Darn! They're closed. I thought the windows were tinted, but I guess the lights must be out."

I felt so relieved, but I didn't want to appear to be a party pooper. "Man, this part of town does roll up its sidewalks early."

Heather mused. "Who had the bright idea to stay in the Financial District anyway?"

I laughed. "Ironically, Patricia."

Begrudgingly, we trudged back to the hotel and rode the elevator, although I was secretly relieved to be back. When we arrived at Patricia and Annika's door, all seemed quiet. Annika slid her key card in the door and opened it quietly. Patricia was asleep on the bed farthest from the door, her phone still in her hand.

Annika whispered, "Goodnight, guys. Get some sleep." She winked at Heather. "You're a lot of fun! I'm glad I got a chance to get to know you a little better. Manda is always trying to keep you to herself." They hugged.

Back in the suite, I collapsed on the bed in the larger bedroom. Heather waved and called, "Goodnight. Sleep tight," as she headed to the other room.

Chapter 8

I awoke with a start. Positive I had heard something, I strained my ears and heard nothing. I could feel my heart beating in my chest, and a drip of sweat glistened on my forehead. But the light streaming under the door from the suite didn't illuminate the room enough to see anything.

I thought I heard ragged breaths from somewhere on the opposite side of the room. Was that my imagination or just Heather snoring from the other bedroom? As much as I didn't want to know, I knew I had to turn on the light. Moving my hand slowly toward the lamp on the bedside table, I inched closer, careful not to make a sound. I felt the base, held my breath, and pressed the button. There was no one there.

I exhaled, not even realizing until then that I had been holding my breath, relieved that I was alone. I whispered to myself, "You have no reason to think Larry's after you." I just got a weird feeling whenever I thought about him, like I was missing something right on the edge of my conscious mind.

In what seemed like only a couple of hours later, the alarm erupted, waking me from another dream I couldn't remember. I glanced at the clock to confirm that it was six a.m. It felt so much earlier. My hand shook as I attempted to tame my toothbrush, still recovering from the early morning encounter with my imagination. The steaming shower made me feel nearly human, but the pit in my stomach wouldn't go away. I ventured out to the kitchen to make coffee, wearing a complimentary spa robe, then I sat at the island lost in my thoughts while it brewed. I nearly jumped out of my skin when Heather, who seemed to come out of nowhere, touched my arm.

She didn't mention my reaction but seemed hurt by it, so I figured I'd address the elephant in the room. "Sorry, it's not you.

It's me. I had a close encounter with Larry in my sleep, and I can't seem to shake it."

Heather's tight facial expression relaxed, and she hugged me. "Sorry, I scared you. We are all probably under more stress than we realize." She sat next to me, and we perched on the Italian leather bar stools in silence for a few moments. Finally, she stood up. "You made coffee! Thanks."

Happy that we cleared the air, I declared, "Sometimes I wonder if I like coffee a little too much."

She flashed a smile. "I'm not sure even coffee is going to save you today. You look terrible."

"Thanks," I responded with a minor touch of sarcasm. "Why do you always look so good in the morning?" It wasn't the first time I had wondered that.

"Clean living, I guess." She winked. "Hey, today's the day you win the final."

I crossed my eyes, trying to get out of my pre-caffeine funk. "Or get killed trying."

"Don't say that. On that course, you really could get killed. I don't know what the sponsors of the race were thinking of staging the final on Lombard Street." She sat at the marble counter, breathing in the aroma from her mug.

"I don't why they chose Lombard street either except that it's the most famous twisty urban hill in the world. The organizers probably needed to provide an element of danger to convince ESPN to cover the race. All I know is that I need to concentrate on winning this thing, so that I can show the Bravo Network executives that we are the real deal."

I took a long swig of coffee, pondering our plight. "Maybe we have all over-reacted to this Larry thing. Wouldn't it be crazy if Patricia was the sane one? She knows him a heck of a lot better than we do. I know one thing: I need to get him out of my head. I've had nightmares all week about him coming to get me, and they seem all too real. I can't wait until these races are over, so life can get back to normal."

"Tell me about it. You were talking in your sleep. I heard you from my room. I almost came over and woke you, but I couldn't resist a rare look into the complicated mind of Miranda Marquette." She giggled, "And by the way, who's Jason?"

I could feel my face turn a deep shade of red. "Oh, no one." I enjoyed our banter, but it was downright uncomfortable when she had more information about my dreams than I did.

Just then, my cell phone saved me from any further embarrassment. It was an international call. "Hello?"

A German-accented voice replied, "Miss Miranda Marquette, please."

"*Herr Offizier Brecker?*"

"Ja, this is he."

"Thanks for calling back. I had some questions about the accident."

"Yes?"

"I'm not going to have to interrogate you, right?" I laughed.

"No." No wonder they say that Germans are humorless.

Okay, have it your way, I thought. "Have you been directly involved in the investigation of my friend Tara's death? I mean, since you spoke to us."

"*Nein.* I summarized my interview with you and provided the information to Chief Detective Heinrich. He is in charge of the investigation."

"Is there anything you can share about the investigation?" I knew I was grasping at straws. "Do you think you are close to arresting a suspect?"

His voice was barely louder than a whisper. "I am not at liberty to discuss the details of the case."

My ears perked up. If Brecker couldn't tell me anything, why did he call me back? "Can you tell me anything at all?"

"There was DNA testing done, and they seem to be closing in on a suspect. That is all I can say." His voice trailed off.

I had to try. "Was it someone in our group?"

"I must go. I shouldn't have called. I'm sorry." The line went dead.

I flopped onto the stool next to Heather at the counter where she had just refreshed my mug with the nectar of the gods. "Darn! I had a bunch more questions prepared, but I couldn't remember most of them. I knew I should have let it go to voicemail so I could have let the caffeine kick in before talking to him."

Before I could continue my rant, loud voices in the hall interrupted me, and a loud knock rapped on the suite door. I didn't even need to look through the peephole to know Patricia and Annika were out there. When I reluctantly opened it, they barreled in, each trying to talk louder than the other. I suddenly felt like a playground monitor trying to sort out whose turn it was with the dodgeball.

Annika, as usual, won the loudness contest. "Miranda, tell her to get her head out of the clouds."

"Why did you go to the police? He is going to be so angry." Patricia pleaded like a sullen ten-year-old.

"That's not a reason not to go to the cops, Patti. He's got you so wrapped around his little finger." Annika paced around the kitchen like a caged animal.

Patricia's voice cracked, and her eyes welled up with tears. "He didn't do anything. Sure, I thought it was possible when Miranda first brought it up, but you two just don't know him like I do." She put her head in her hands, then spoke quietly and slowly. "He's going to be angry because he didn't kill Tara and now the police have been told that he did." She sat next to Heather at the counter and responded to Annika's statement as if she had just heard it. "And I am not wrapped around his finger."

Annika and I looked at one another. She rolled her eyes. I said, "Okay, honey. I honestly don't know what to think, either. I just found out that the Swiss Police are closing in on a suspect based on DNA testing. And let's face it, Larry's DNA had to be on Tara's parachute."

Patricia fought back. "I'm sure all of our DNA is on each of the parachutes. We all helped one another. That doesn't prove anything."

I nodded. "You've got a point."

Annika was determined to keep us on the topic of Larry. "He's still planning to arrive sometime today. He's been vague about his arrival time, which makes me wonder if he's already here." Patricia glared at her.

Anxious to move on from the Larry-go-round, I interrupted. "Hey, I almost forgot. Bernie wants us to be at a press conference at ten this morning at the top of Lombard Street. He said he's got some surprises for us."

I looked directly at Patricia "One positive thing that came out of our meeting with the police was the fact that they are going to be covering the race very closely. Detective Morrison emphasized that we must stay alert. If anyone notices anything out of the ordinary, they need to call 911. Patricia, that includes you."

I turned to address all of them, "All we can do is to stick together. I don't think this guy will try to take us all on at once. He will probably try to isolate one of us."

I turned to Patricia again, "I'm really concerned about you and Larry spending time alone."

Her face took on a far-away look. "I'm not."

Chapter 9

A half-hour later, the three of us were standing on a portable stage at the top of Lombard Street. It was probably ten feet deep and twenty feet long. There was a huge screen facing the crowd directly behind the stage. Bernie was about to address several hundred racing fans, the press, and other curious onlookers.

Reveling in the fact that the three of us placed in the top ten, Bernie puffed out his chest and stepped to the microphone. "The First Extreme All Girl Sports Team represents three of only five female participants of over a hundred competing in the Street Luge Nationals. The fact that they hold three of the top ten spots and each made the finals is a remarkable feat. Standing to my right, from left to right, are Patricia, Annika, and Miranda. You'll be seeing a lot of them over the next few days if you are anywhere near the Bay Area. F.E.A.S.T your eyes on the large screen behind me."

A full body shot of me in leather appeared on the screen. The caption read: "Hey, boys, two can play at this game, and I'm gunning for number one!"–Miranda.

Patricia was next with a pouty look on her face, in cutoffs, and a white crop top, high heeled white sandals. Her caption read: "I'm third. But watch out boys, I'm taking no prisoners."–Patricia.

Annika was last, with her long auburn hair flowing over an off-the-shoulder little black dress and a come-hither smile. "Only nice girls finish fifth. And I'm not a nice girl!"–Annika.

Our publicity shoot was months ago, but only Bernie had seen the proofs. I wasn't sure I would have approved of his dated and sexist captions had I known about them in advance. That was the advantage of having a gutsy publicist. Bernie talked for a few more minutes, and my face started to hurt from holding my smile for so long.

Annika whispered without moving her lips. "Did you know about this?"

I forced my smile. "No. Bernie only told me he had a surprise. You have to admit we made an impression."

"Don't you even defend him. The pictures are one thing, but those captions are embarrassing," I nearly laughed at Annika's attempt to whisper without moving her mouth.

"I agree, but if everything goes as planned, this will be a drop in the publicity bucket. We'd better get used to it." I stared straight ahead so the audience wouldn't suspect we were talking.

Annika spoke softly but in full voice, "I'm not sure I want to get used to it."

I didn't feel like arguing the point on stage in front of several hundred onlookers. That was when I saw a guy that I thought could be Larry. It was something about his gait when he walked that made me suspect it was him. However, everything else about him was different. His head and face were cleanly shaven, and he wore khakis and a blue golf shirt. I glanced over at Patricia to see if she had picked him out of the crowd. If she had, she didn't let on.

I tried not to stare, so he would think that his disguise had worked while continuing to watch his progress through the crowd. There was an area fenced off with a security gate marked Employees Only that he was quickly approaching. I was astonished when he flashed a card or badge of some sort at the security guard and was let through the gate. The fence was of the temporary chain link variety and was about six feet high. Two-inch strands of plastic were woven through the links, and I could not see inside the fenced area. He looked so different. I was already second-guessing whether that had been him.

I was jolted back to reality when the crowd began to applaud. Evidently, Bernie had finished his speech and, either everyone was really impressed with the team, or they were just happy he was done because there was an abundance of applause. I looked over at Annika, who wasn't fuming quite as much as earlier. I followed her gaze and noticed that she had connected with an attractive twenty-something in the audience. True to form, that was all she needed to get out of her funk.

Patricia was smiling a distant smile. She didn't seem to be looking at anything or anyone in particular.

I pulled out my phone and considered calling Detective Morrison but thought twice and put it back in my pocket. What if that hadn't been Larry? Whoever it was certainly didn't look like how I remembered him, so what was it that made me think it was him? Now that he was behind the fence, I doubted my initial impression.

Unsure of what else to do, I dialed Heather.

"Hi, Miranda! How'd the press conference go?"

The crowd had pretty much dispersed. Bernie was in deep conversation with a guy in a black suit. I didn't recognize him. I wondered if he was from the network. Annika had strolled into the crowd and was chatting with the guy she was making eyes at earlier. Patricia was texting on her phone. I could only imagine she was talking to Larry.

"Heather!" I said like I was surprised to hear her voice.

"Um, Miranda, you called me, remember?"

"Oh yeah, I did." My voice trailed off.

"Are you okay? You sound kind of strange." She knew me better than anyone did.

I hesitated. I wasn't sure if this was a conversation I wanted to have on the phone. "I thought I saw Larry, but he was dressed kind of preppy and clean-shaven. Do you think that's possible?"

Heather sounded distant as if she was multi-tasking. "I guess anything's possible, but that sounds kind of unlikely."

I wasn't convinced but decided to drop it for now. "You're probably right."

"Are you coming back before the race?" She sounded somewhat out of breath. I pictured her running around the hotel room, grabbing her purse, fluffing pillows, and straightening the sheets. She could do more in a minute than I could sometimes accomplish in an hour.

My mind was suddenly clear of my Larry-obsessed fog. "Yes! I need to come back to the room and get changed before the racing starts." I hadn't even thought about how soon the race was.

I was happy to hear the excitement in her voice. "See you soon!"

Patricia was the only one of our group left on the stage and was still texting.

I couldn't contain myself. "Patricia, are you texting Larry?"

She continued typing as if I didn't exist. Finally, when she was done, she glanced up at me from where she sat on the stage. "Well, if you must know, no." She pouted. "I haven't heard from him all day. I was texting my sister."

There was hope. Maybe my mind had been playing tricks, and he was still in Seattle. "I'm sorry to hear that," I finally said.

"No, you're not. But maybe it's for the best since the cops are on the lookout for Larry, thanks to you." Her words were clipped in anger.

All I could say was, "Maybe," and I headed back to the hotel. I was lucky to catch a cable car. Ironically, it had one of Patricia's promo pictures on the side. I guessed Bernie was right. People would be seeing a lot of us.

"God, I can't get away from her," I whispered under my breath.

The guy standing next to me obviously thought I was talking to him. He said in an oddly familiar voice, "Is there something I can help you with?"

I hadn't looked at him until he spoke. It was Jason Wall, the musician from the bar. I was, frankly, astonished, since I knew virtually no-one in this town. "Wow! You again?"

He flashed a brilliant smile. "I was hoping for something just a little more enthusiastic, but I guess that'll have to do."

My cheeks were hot with embarrassment. "I'm so sorry. I was really distracted. I race in a little less than an hour, and I'm not anywhere near ready."

His smile was unnerving, and I couldn't figure out why. "I kind of like seeing you not all put together. I guess you're human too."

I wanted to protest but finally smiled too. "It's a rare day when anyone gets to see me this vulnerable, especially before the first date." Suddenly I wanted to shove the words back in my mouth. What was I talking about? I barely knew this guy.

He opened his eyes wide. "First date? That sounds encouraging."

I stood there with my mouth open when the cable car reached my destination.

He hesitated. "Sorry, gotta go!"

I ran to get off before I said anything else that I might live to regret. I never looked back, hoping he hadn't followed me. Sort of.

Chapter 10

I was out of breath when I got back to the hotel room, and I looked like a nightmare. My hair had taken a real hit in the heat during the press conference.

I told myself my elevated respiration was because I was feeling the pressure of the race, and I was cutting it close timing-wise. I refused to admit that my encounter with Jason Wall on the cable car might have contributed to my breathlessness.

Heather was a welcome sight. She'd been an excellent substitute for male companionship. No complications, just a friend looking out for me. What more could I ask for?

I pondered what it was about this Jason Wall that made me crazy, but I didn't have time to think about it right now.

Heather, in her ever-efficient way, had my racing gear laid out on the bed. I changed into my one-piece leather suit. When the weather was cooler, I would wear Under Armour underneath, but it was just too warm for that today. I didn't mind because I had always liked the feel of leather against my skin dating back to my high school Goth days. There was something that felt wild and daring about having animal skin against my own.

Since Heather was going to watch the race, we left the hotel together when I was dressed and ready to go. It was fifteen minutes before registration closed for the race, and thankfully, we were no more than five minutes away from the registration desk, so my panic was subsiding.

Heather talked a mile a minute as we exited the hotel. "So, what was the press conference all about? What were Bernie's surprises? Were there lots of people there? Are you ready to race?"

I described the scene with the press, the crowd, the stage, and the giant screen. "Bernie had some amazing promo shots that he used to publicize the team. I was wearing what I have on now. He also had some awkward captions to each of them, but it was all pretty harmless."

She grinned proudly. "I can't wait to see them."

As soon as we crossed the street in search of a cable car, a bus with a picture of me on the side drove by. I gaped at it. "There I am now."

She gushed. "Wow! You're famous!"

I wasn't quite ready to admit that I had made it, but it felt special for Heather to believe that I had. "Thanks. You always know how to make me feel special."

We caught a cable car and made it with time to spare. Since there were so few finalists, we didn't face the long lines and chaos of registering the first two days. By now, the staff knew all the finalists on a first name basis, especially the three of us, since you couldn't go anywhere without seeing our faces plastered on something. It was impressive, if not a little unnerving.

When we reached the Participants Only sign, I jumped in line. Heather yelled, "Break a leg!" while she looked for a place to stand with a clear view. When I looked back again to wave, she was on her phone with a concerned look on her face. She then headed to the equipment area where all the sleds were stored before the race. I'd have to ask her what that was about later.

Unlike the other two days, at least this one wouldn't go on forever, but with the way they have the races spaced out, it would still take several hours for fifteen minutes of actual racing. I was looking forward to these races being over and getting out of this town alive.

With race start time edging ever nearer, I was feeling unsettled. I wasn't nervous about the race itself. With two days under our belts, we were in such good shape, I couldn't help but think we were going to take it all. I just didn't feel safe. I had to stay diligent and hope that I had been overly paranoid when I thought I saw Larry earlier.

Brigitte, who had staffed the registration table all three days, looked like she could barely keep her eyes open as I walked up. She was German, in her mid-twenties, really efficient, and very helpful. "You look like something the cat dragged in," I said and laughed.

We had talked quite a bit the first two days, and I knew this was her first trip to the United States. She planned on mixing a lot of pleasure with business, and from the look of things, she was succeeding. She groaned, and her English was even harder to decipher that usual. "Oh, Miranda. I knew I should have listened to you when you told me to take it slow in the bars. I had such a *gut* time *gestern*, I mean yesterday, evening but I'm paying now for it. So sorry about my English."

Thank goodness I took some German in high school. Her English wasn't terrible, but her pronunciation left a little to be desired, and it was a little like a German version of Spanglish. I mock scolded. "Did you drink water like I told you to?"

"*Nein*! This Coors Light tastes like water anyway." She laughed briefly, then held her stomach like she was going to throw up.

"Well, take some Tylenol and drink lots of water, and you'll be ready to get back out there in no time." I grabbed my wristband. "Gotta run! Wish me luck!"

"*Guten glück,*" she whispered, "I'm not supposed to say this, but I hope you win." She, at least, had some color in her face by the time I left the table.

Racing down Lombard Street presented all sorts of logistical challenges we hadn't faced in the other two venues. Just the fact that the race was taking place in the middle of a major city would have been enough, but when you added the roller-coaster-like course, traffic, massive crowds, food vendors, added security, and the media, it was more like a circus than a race.

I searched the crowd for any suspicious activity and saw Rocky, the other cameraman from our Switzerland trip, setting up to film the top section of the course. I reminded myself to seek him out after the race to see if he had seen Larry.

When I arrived at the starting line, they were removing the sleds from the locked fenced area that I had seen the guy I thought was Larry enter. Heather was talking to a staff member in the same area, and I wondered if there was a problem with our equipment. I figured she would tell me if that was the case.

I took several deep breaths and closed my eyes. Directly before the race started was not a good time for an anxiety attack, and I struggled to fill my mind with positive thoughts. I convinced myself that I probably hadn't really seen Larry earlier and that I was just paranoid. It wouldn't be the first time. While I attempted to pull myself together, I ran into the racer in front of me. "I'm sorry," I said before I looked up to see who I had nearly knocked down.

Felix Loch turned around and smiled. "Miranda, are you trying to injure me before the race even starts?"

We hadn't spoken since we competed in the finals two days earlier. So much had happened since then, I felt like that had been weeks ago. "Sorry, I wasn't paying attention. But I definitely don't want you injured so I can beat you fair and square." I gritted my teeth but smiled.

I had heard behind the scenes that he had been vocal about how disdainful it had been to compete with women. "We will see about that," he replied, frowning but then caught himself. "I mean, it is all for the fun of it. It looks like you've got a good chance of taking it all. Good luck!" He turned and walked away.

We had to wait a few minutes before they delivered the numbered sleds to the starting line. I grabbed mine and performed an inspection of the critical moving parts. It seemed to be fine, but you couldn't be too careful.

There were several loudspeakers set up near the starting line. "Racers, please take your places. The first heat will begin in five minutes."

Due to the narrow streets, even though there were only fifteen competitors left in the competition, we would only be racing five at a time. We'd each run three full heats and then a final with the five leaders, culminating in the highly coveted award ceremony and medals. I could almost taste first place.

Unlike the other venues, there were no shuttles from the bottom to the top. Once you reached the bottom and turned in your sled, you were on your own. With the multiple mass transit options, there would be plenty of time to get back to the top for the next heat, since they scheduled an hour between races and fifteen minutes between heats. It would be another long day of 'hurry up and wait.'

They had divided up our team, one per heat, so I wasn't racing anyone friendly. Patricia was in the next heat, and Annika was in the third. I hadn't seen either of them since the press conference, but that wasn't surprising. The last time I saw Annika, she was after some guy, and Patricia had been in a mood, so I figured a little space wouldn't hurt her.

As I approached the starting line, I forced myself to wipe all thoughts of Larry from my mind. The other four, all men, of course, were settling in their lanes. Street luge racers often preferred to line up on the outside. I, on the other hand, preferred to be as close to the middle as possible, especially on this course. Unfortunately, we hadn't been given a chance to practice on the track, so this first run was not likely to be a fast one since we'd all be feeling out the course and trying not to kill ourselves.

I closed my eyes one last time to silence the negative voices in my head about the course, about my competitors, about the impending reality TV series, and a thousand other things. Moments later, the starting gun sounded, and we were off.

I got a fast start out of the gate. Felix was on my right and, despite his poor showing yesterday, I still considered him the one to beat. The centrifugal force of the turns was much stronger than I anticipated, and I almost lost it on the first curve. Including the left onto Leavenworth, there were nine crazy hairpin turns in that one block down Russian Hill.

After I successfully navigated three turns, I felt like I was getting into a groove. I heard some commotion behind me as I headed into turn four, but there was no way I could look back without killing myself.

While it seemed like I was going painfully slow so that I could maintain my balance, no-one had passed me yet. This was another race where our superior equipment was going to work to our advantage. Cheaper sleds were far more likely to flip on these corners. Ours were heavier and, as a result, more stable than most of the others on the course.

By the ninth turn, I was heading down Leavenworth and gaining momentum. The block between Francisco and Bay streets was nearly as steep as Lombard, and I was well in the lead. The race officially ended at Beach Street, but it was likely my momentum would carry me all the way to Fisherman's Wharf.

As I coasted across Jefferson to the end of Leavenworth, I couldn't help but wonder what had happened to the rest of the pack. I couldn't have been that fast. I had the eerie feeling that I had taken a wrong turn and left the course, until a racing official directed me to the sled deposit area. Just then, I saw two sleds coming down the street, neck and neck. It appeared to be Felix and the French rider, Marcel Coty, who was miraculously leading after the first two days. In my opinion, he was not a great rider, and he had some lucky breaks.

As they coasted to a stop, I looked up the hill behind them and saw nothing. They both threw their helmets off in disgust. I approached them. "Hey, what happened up there?" I couldn't stand the suspense. I tried to hide my excitement and sound concerned.

Felix kicked the curb with his boot. "That darned surfer almost killed all of us." He must have been referring to Annika's friend. "He lost it on the second to last corner and took all of us out with him. He and the Czech were neck and neck, and they took the corner too fast and flipped. Marcel and I were able to brake to avoid the collision, but our momentum was completely gone." They both sat on the curb with their elbows on their knees. I wasn't sure if Marcel spoke English, and despite my heritage, my French wasn't all it was cracked up to be. Either way, he didn't say a word.

This would have been a lousy time to gloat, but I felt pretty good about my chances, especially since qualifying to make the final heat was based on the combined time of the first three heats. Even though these two guys finished, they would likely be way back in the standings after the first race unless a similar pile-up took place in the other two heats.

"I'll see you guys later." I waved as I left them alone in their misery and headed to Bay Street to catch the Powell-Hyde cable car line back up the hill. Granted, there was actually enough time to walk up, but I needed to save my energy for the next two heats, then, hopefully, the final.

Sure enough, within a few minutes, I caught the cable car. Sadly, it was adorned with a Coke ad. I was happy to be back at the top of Lombard Street within ten minutes. I reached the top, just as they announced the third heat, missing the second while I was making my way back. I hoped Patricia did well. I searched the crowd for Heather.

I saw a man standing against the Wells Fargo Bank building smoking a cigarette. He had jeans and a Harley t-shirt on with tattoos up and down his arms. I couldn't get a good look at his face due to the distance and sun glare, but I could have sworn it was Larry. I whispered to myself, "Now that proves it, Miranda.

You are losing your mind. Not everyone in this town can be Larry." A couple, walking hand in hand passed me, looked at me muttering to myself, their look confirming that my grasp on reality was in question.

I was about to move closer to get a better look at the guy when I spotted Heather. She was sitting in a portable chair and saw me about the same time I saw her. I couldn't read the confused look on her face.

She was standing by the time I made her way through the crowd. She seemed out of breath, even though she was just standing there. "You can use the chair. I'll stand. The vendor only had one." She forced a smile as she scanned the crowd. "I'm gonna try to find another one." And she was gone.

I was glad I had a place to sit, but I couldn't help but wonder why Heather wasn't happier that I had won the first race. She didn't even mention it.

Just then, the jumbo screens came alive because the third heat was just about to begin. "I wonder where Heather went?" I mused. I figured she'd be back eventually, hopefully with her own chair.

The camera showed the sleds on the starting line. Annika lined up in the middle lane as we had strategized. I hoped she could stay on task and keep her eyes off the guys she was racing. On camera, she fished her phone from her pocket. I almost immediately received a text. "Miranda, I need to talk to you right after this race. The sled is feeling kind of weird. I want you to take a look at it."

I returned her text. "Are you sure you should race?" But it appeared she had already shoved it back in her pocket. I hoped she knew what she was doing.

A voice came over the loudspeakers as the camera focused on the racers lining up at the top of the track. "Ladies and Gentlemen! Race one, heat three, is just about to begin. Please refer to your programs for the participants."

Despite her concerns about the sled, I was happy to see that Annika was all business and able to get herself set up in the coveted middle lane. The camera was focused directly on her as she maneuvered her sled behind the starting line. I suddenly had a pit in my stomach. What if Larry was behind that camera? C'mon Miranda, get a grip, I whispered defiantly to myself.

Just in time to be too late to worry about it, the starter's pistol fired.

Annika got a tremendous jump off the starting line. The camera focused solely on her because she led the pack by a significant margin. Remembering how slow my race had been, especially while getting the feel of the curves and the hill, I was starting to worry. We had discussed our strategy several times about the first heat, and we all came to the same conclusion: take it slow.

There were cameras strategically down the hill, and she was barely visible when she zipped past the next one. The network switched the view to a camera at the bottom of the twisty section looking up the hill. It was too far away to see the expression on her face, but I could tell something was wrong. As she approached the fourth or fifth turn, she had to be going at least fifty, nearly twice as fast as I was through that section, the left front of her sled caught the concrete wall on the left side causing it to go horizontal across the track and flip.

The crowd gasped as one as Annika went airborne and slammed headfirst into the wall on the opposite side of the track. The camera stayed on her long enough to see that she wasn't moving. Within seconds, the rest of the pack came around the blind turn and, by some miracle, was able to avoid running into or over her. The Jumbotron then switched to the camera at the finish line.

I stood up and looked frantically for the best way to get down there. I saw an opening and made a run for it. Still no trace of Heather, but I didn't have time to worry about her right now.

In what seemed like a lifetime of dodging parents pushing strollers, skateboarders trying to master the dangerously sloped sidewalks, lovers walking hand in hand like they had all the time in the world, and every type of annoying humanity I had ever encountered, I finally reached Annika. Patricia, who must have been watching the race from further down the hill, was knelt over her, sobbing. Annika lay crumpled on the pavement. Her helmet had shattered on impact with the wall and laid in pieces strewn across the street.

When Patricia become aware that I was there, she stood and hugged me as if holding on for dear life. I yelled to the crowd that appeared to be growing by the second. "Is there a doctor here anywhere?" A guy about my age in the front of the crowd yelled, "There's an ambulance trying to get up here, but the crowds aren't making it a slow ride."

I glared at him. "How do you know that?"

He spoke softly, pointing to the walkie talkie in his hand, "I'm an EMT."

I was losing it fast. "Well, *get over here,* doughboy!"

He picked up a small bag like it was a baby and held it tightly to him as he sprinted to Annika. He put his ear against her chest. He looked up at me with a grim white face. "CPR. Have you ever done it?"

I hesitated. "Well, yes, but that was many years ago.

He started chest compressions. "It's more effective if I do the compressions, and you do the mouth to mouth."

I was suddenly not feeling so bold. "Um, okay."

He had carefully moved her, so she was lying flat and timing his compressions. "Now!" He motioned for me to start.

I made sure her airway was clear and started mouth to mouth.

There was nothing I wouldn't do to save my friend, and I prayed with every breath. We went back and forth between compressions and mouth to mouth for what seemed like an hour but may have been fifteen minutes for all I knew. At some point in the confusion, we were relieved by several other EMTs, firefighters, and police.

I was dripping with sweat, sitting on the edge of a wall when Heather found me. She looked grim as she sat down with her arm around me.

At some point, they covered Annika's face with a blanket. She was dead. All I could think at the moment was that I would never know what she had wanted to talk to me about.

Chapter 11

Two hours later, I was sitting in an antique yellow cracked plastic chair in the dingy police station waiting room we had visited just yesterday. It still looked like it hadn't been painted since World War II. In fact, everything looked the same as it had yesterday, with every kind of humanity that you can imagine and probably several that you can't. I was dazed and exhausted. At this moment, I couldn't imagine anything ever seeming normal again.

Patricia sat on one side of me staring at, well, what appeared to me to be nothing. She was continually blowing her nose and wiping her eyes from the crying jag she had been on for hours. I couldn't tell if she was more upset about Annika's accident or the fact that Switzerland had issued a warrant for Larry's arrest for the first-degree murder of Tara. We practically had to drag her in to make a statement. Larry hadn't been in touch with her all day, so I felt like she was starting to believe that he might be involved in Annika's murder also. The fact that she was here and not wandering around looking for him was a testament to that.

Heather was on my other side. She was unusually emotional about Annika's death. I found that a little strange since she hadn't really known her before this weekend. She was sobbing off and on into a well-worn Kleenex but refused to accept a new one. She hadn't said much of anything since we got to the police station.

The sweat that had drenched my clothes from racing and then trying to revive Annika was starting to smell, which would typically have driven me crazy, but I didn't really care. While I believed I had done everything I could do to revive her, the guilt I felt about getting her involved in this race in the first place, was heavier than my eyelids were becoming after sitting here for what felt like an eternity.

Finally, Detective Morrison appeared and motioned us to follow her. Her warm smile had faded a bit since yesterday. Worry lines ran deep in her forehead and around her eyes. She carried a stack of files and paperwork and plopped them down on the table in a small and stuffy conference room. She motioned to the chairs around the table.

"Please sit."

Patricia sniffled and took out a Kleenex from her purse, blowing her nose and wiping her eyes.

Detective Morrison took her arm and helped her to the table. "I understand. It's a difficult time for everyone." She waited until we were all seated then picked up several documents strewn on the table in front of her.

The detective's upper lip was sweating. I couldn't help but think about how everyone showed stress and grief differently. Some people laughed. Some people cried. Some people became catatonic. At some point during the last hour, Patricia had displayed all three. Heather only cried.

The detective looked at Patricia but then turned her attention to Heather and me.

"Okay, I have draft statements for you to review based on our prior discussion and the subsequent events. They are only drafts, so you can mark them up, and I'll make the changes. I just figured it would be helpful for you to get a head start."

I breathed an audible sigh of relief. The last thing I wanted to do was rehash this whole thing again, especially since we had identified Larry to the police last night. I could tell that Detective Morrison felt terrible that she hadn't been able to protect us, even though we had asked for their help yesterday. Having been let down again by the police, I was hurt and angry. Probably sensing my hostility, she left us alone while we reviewed the documents.

"Take all the time you need," she said as she retreated for friendlier quarters.

I took five minutes to read them. Patricia had reverted back to her catatonic state, so at least she wasn't distracting me. I asked Heather, who was also staring off into nowhere, "How's it look to you? It looks pretty accurate to me."

She nodded. "Looks okay to me."

I nodded, even though I knew she hadn't read it. I rubbed my head and continued scanning my document finding it hard to concentrate on the words. I felt numb. As much as I tried to stay positive, I couldn't pull it off. I decided to try to work with Patricia since she was in even worse shape than any of us.

I moved to the chair next to her. She was staring at the wall. I turned directly to her, thinking it would be harder for her to avoid me. I spoke in my best 'mother speaking to a three-year-old' voice. "Patricia, honey, Detective Morrison is going to want to talk to you when she comes back. Since you were closer to Annika, especially since Tara, well, died . . ." She turned to look at me, which I thought was a good sign. I continued, hoping I had broken the spell. ". . . and you know Larry better than any of us, maybe you'll think of something that we didn't."

Patricia looked down at her phone. "I can't understand why Larry hasn't messaged me." Then she looked at me, or actually, through me.

I grabbed her shoulders and looked her straight in the eye. "Patricia! Wake up and smell the coffee! Annika is dead! The Swiss police have put out a warrant for his arrest. And it's just a matter of time before the San Francisco Police do the same. You're just lucky to be alive!"

Patricia didn't respond right away. Then she whispered, "He can't go away now because I'm pregnant." Then she burst into tears.

I didn't know how much insanity I could withstand in one day. "Patricia, how did this happen? Well, I know how it happened. Didn't you use, well, you know, protection?"

Patricia looked at the table. "Yes, of course. Well, there was that one time."

I felt like the mother of a wayward teen. "It's always that one time—"

She looked me in the eye, pleading, "Miranda, I love him, and I want his baby."

This wasn't the time to hit me with romance and flowers. I was barely holding it together. I just gave Patricia a pitying look, shook my head, stood, and walked out of the conference room door.

I heard Heather say, "Miranda?" as the door was closing, but I didn't turn around. I needed air. I needed sanity. I needed to be anywhere, but here. I remembered where the rear exit was from last night and sprinted to the door. I rushed past people in the hallway, nearly knocking an elderly woman over and almost colliding head-on with the largest black man I had ever seen.

Finally, I made it to the door. As I pushed it open, I felt a rush of air escape from my lungs. I hadn't even realized I was holding my breath. I collapsed on the top concrete step and tried to get my bearings. Panic attacks were becoming an all too familiar part of my life. The world was closing in around me. My breathing was fast and shallow. My heart was beating so fast it hurt my chest. Sweat poured from every part of my body, but I was freezing at the same time.

I closed my eyes for a long time, just wishing the world would go away. After what felt like hours but was probably only a few minutes, my symptoms started to dissipate. As I sat quietly, listening to the sounds of the city; sirens, car horns, people talking to one another on the sidewalk as they passed, babies crying, trucks and motorcycles revving their engines, my heartbeat slowed to a reasonable pace. I opened my eyes and did my best to think about nothing. There would soon come a time when I would need to think about everything, but this wasn't it.

I watched the traffic go by and the people rushing to wherever they were going for a while longer until the door opened. I turned around to see Heather, who had made a remarkable recovery from when I had last seen her in the conference room. The worry lines on her forehead belied her faint smile. In very Heather-like fashion, she didn't let on how worried she was about me.

"There you are. I had a feeling I might find you here." She sat next to me and put a reassuring hand on my knee.

We sat quietly for a few more minutes. It had probably been a half an hour since my meltdown. I finally felt a little better and asked Heather, "So, how are you doing? You seem better."

She said, "I'm fine. I had to get a grip when you left me alone with Patricia." She smiled, sensing that I was venturing back to reality after my most recent panic attack. "Detective Morrison returned soon after you left and, remarkably, was able to get Patricia to a better place. No offense, but your relationship is far too parental to be productive."

I laughed out loud, remembering my encounter with Patricia. "God, I sounded like my mother!"

She stood up and offered me a hand then opened the door and led me through.

"Let's get this over with, so we can get out of here. I'm not sure how appropriate it would be to have fun this soon after Annika's death, but if she's up in heaven looking down on us, I'll bet that's what she would want us to do." She smiled, encouraging me to do the same.

I obliged and tried to lighten up my tone. "Annika was a trip. I feel so guilty, but I'm going to say it anyway. I couldn't stand the way she never called anyone by their full name. Seriously, has anyone ever called you Heth in your whole life?"

My attempt at humor backfired as I began sobbing when the reality of her death hit me again like a punch in the gut. Heather hugged me, and I held on to her for dear life as we leaned against the wall outside the conference room. Finally, I collected myself enough to go back in.

Patricia and Detective Morrison hovered over a document near the end of the table furthest away from the door. They spoke in hushed tones as if they were conspiring together to take over the world. Heather was right. She had worked wonders with Patricia. I remembered the day Tara died when no-one could get her to talk at all.

Happy to see that things were under control, but not wanting to break the spell she seemed to have Patricia in, I spoke quietly to the detective, "Detective Morrison, if you are finished with us, I think we are going to call it a day."

Morrison glanced up, clearly not wanting us to undo any of the work she had done, "Thanks, Miranda. You too, Heather. We'll be in touch." She smiled and went back to work. I felt guilty leaving Patricia with the detective, but it felt like she and I needed some space.

Heather and I slipped out the door of the conference room and walked down the back hallway and outside. Breathing in the late afternoon air revived me even more than a Starbucks could have.

We walked in silence almost all the way back to the hotel. We stopped on the sidewalk, waiting for the light to change. She turned to face me. "Miranda, what are you going to do now?"

I didn't know what to say, so I was silent.

She continued. "I don't know what's going to happen. I feel like changes are coming. Your team is basically done. So that means either your reality show is toast, or you will have to start over with a new team. I've always been good at predicting when major changes are coming in my life, and they are coming. I don't know exactly what they will be, but I'm determined to enjoy my time working for you as long as I can."

I smiled weakly and touched her arm. "Don't write me off just yet. The company's gonna be fine." I chose to ignore the subject of the repeated requests from the Feds for information over the past few weeks.

We crossed the street silently and entered the hotel, in many ways, changed from who we had been when we left this morning. We would never be those exact same people again. Part of us died with Annika.

Chapter 12

I pulled the covers over my throbbing head. No matter what I did, I couldn't sleep. I looked at my watch. 6:30 a.m. I reached for my pillow and pulled it over my head, but there was no denying it. I had to get up.

I pulled on my Victoria's Secret short sleepover robe. I had shivered through the night, but I wasn't sure now if that had been fear and anxiety or the temperature of the suite. It certainly felt warm now with the steady stream of sunlight coming through the window, so I couldn't stand the idea of a heavy cotton robe that hung down nearly to the floor.

The kitchenette boasted a Braun twelve cup coffee maker, which was unusual for a hotel, where they usually made you suffer with those one-cup pods that tasted like dishwater. There was a three-pound bag of Starbucks Pike Place beans in the refrigerator and a Cuisinart grinder on the counter next to the coffee maker. The sound of the coffee beans being pulverized was annoying, but I was compelled to stand there until it finished. Somewhere in my mind, it was a metaphor for hanging in there through the aftermath facing me in the next few days.

I had no idea what today would bring. Heather and I had been so exhausted when we returned to the room from the police station, I didn't call Bernie or Patricia to see if there was anything we needed to do. I knew Annika had been taken away in an ambulance, but never gave a thought to where they would take her, whether her family had been called or any of the details that needed to be dealt with when someone died.

Although it was early, I punched in Bernie's number and got his voice mail. "Call me, Bernie, when you get this." I heard the exhaustion in my voice. "Thanks. Bye." He was always calling me at odd hours, so I figured turnabout was fair play. If I knew Bernie, he would already be formulating a plan, and I knew if I got someone on the phone who was the least bit sympathetic, I would burst into tears. I definitely couldn't call my mother or my sister Sabine although they were likely to hear about Annika sooner or later. For my own sanity, it would be better if it were later because I just couldn't talk to them right now. It was too raw.

I hoped we didn't need to hang around in San Francisco any longer than we had initially planned. The finals had been canceled, or at least postponed, due to safety issues. I doubted they would be rescheduled. I couldn't even think about the marketing dollars I had expended on this event, and now we had plenty of notoriety, just none of it any good.

Just as the coffee was brewed and smelling heavenly, Heather, in an oversized pink ribbon breast cancer awareness tee-shirt and a pair of terry shorts, crept out of the bedroom. Her outfit made her look even tinier than usual. Her eyes were puffy and red. She had been crying again. Her lack of eye-contact told me she didn't want me to ask about it.

She groaned, "Coffee. Bless you," and slithered to the cabinet to grab a mug and sat on a stool at the counter, staring at the coffee maker as it slowly filled the pot.

When the pot held barely enough for two mugs, she poured both of us coffee and motioned me to sit next to her. We sat staring straight ahead for a few minutes until she broke the silence. "It's gonna be a tough couple of weeks, so anything you need me to do, let me know. I feel horrible about Annika, but I didn't have the kind of relationship with her that you did. I guess what I'm saying is, it's okay to lean on me." She smiled weakly.

I pondered what she had been crying about since she didn't seem particularly broken up about Annika, but I didn't ask. As much as she appeared to be an extrovert, she was a very private person. We both sat sipping coffee, lost in our own thoughts for a few minutes. Finally, I said, "Thanks. I don't even know what I'm feeling right now. Mostly numb, I think."

Tears streamed down my cheeks, but I forced a smile. She wiped a tear from my cheek and hugged me. I hugged her back, happy that she seemed to be back to her old self. She was acting really weird yesterday from the point I had returned from my first and only race.

My cell phone vibrated on the table. I looked down for the number and saw that it was Bernie. "I'd better take this." I wasn't sure I could hold it together and didn't want to have another breakdown in front of Heather. I motioned that I was going to take this in the bedroom.

"Hello?" I said, not really knowing what else to say.

"Hello, Miranda, I'm sorry about Annika." He sounded harried, busy, and uncomfortable.

I knew he didn't have a place in his life for emotion, so I tried to keep it business-like. "Thanks." I hesitated, pushing back the tears. "So, what do we do now?"

He also hesitated but, like a typical man, didn't want to touch the topic of Annika. He changed the subject. "It'll be a while before we know about the race and whether or not they'll reschedule the final. It's complicated working with the sponsors, the TV networks, and the city trying to salvage something of this mess. It'll be weeks or months before it's all straightened out. By then, they might as well wait until next year and just let the whole thing settle."

He kept talking, probably not wanting to leave any space for me to react. "There may be one piece of good news, though. I spoke to Tony at Bravo, and it looks like the negotiation meetings are going to move forward. Probably next week."

I couldn't even think about a reality series right now, but I had no idea how I would feel next week. "Honestly, I'm surprised. I figured the series died with Annika," was all I could think of to say in a monotone.

He didn't take the bait. "I don't have a solid date for the meeting yet, but I'll let you know. Talk to you later." He hung up.

I sat on the bed for a few minutes wondering what was going to happen regarding Annika. I imagined the family would have the body shipped back to Dallas. It felt so cold of me to have reduced Annika to a body. I was emotionally shaken and again wondered if I'd ever feel normal again. My stomach hurt, I had a headache, my eyes hurt from crying, and I was exhausted. I also couldn't help but feel responsible. After all, it was my idea to create this all-girl team in the first place. Now, two of them were dead.

One thing was clear, though. It was time to get out of this town. Then it hit me like a hammer. She had texted me that she thought something was wrong with the sled. I should have stopped the race right then. I might as well have killed her. I chose to ignore the sweat under my arms and ear ringing, which were often my first telltale signs of an anxiety attack.

I meandered into the kitchenette and perched on a stool next to Heather.

She was somber. "Everything okay with Bernie?"

I squirmed a little in my seat. "Oh, just business stuff. Nothing on Annika." I was lost in my thoughts about the sled and how I could have stopped the race and saved her life. One thought led to another, and I cursed myself for not trusting myself when I thought I saw Larry go through the employee gate. It must have been him. I just stared straight ahead.

I took my last swig of coffee and headed back to the counter for a refill. When I spoke, I could tell I sounded exhausted. "Are you ready to head back today? I don't see any reason to hang out here. I thought there might be some loose ends to tie up, but it doesn't look that way."

Heather sighed. "I wish I didn't have all that equipment to haul back. I can barely see out the windshield anyway, but watching the trailer in the rear-view mirrors is nearly impossible."

I thought for a couple seconds. "Hey, maybe we can get my motorcycle into the trailer. Then we could make the trip back together."

A smile curled up just slightly on her otherwise serious face. "Thank you, Miranda. I didn't want to ask."

I tried to sound stern. "You really need to tell me what you want. I'm not the most perceptive person on earth, so just speak up. If I don't want to do something, I'll let you know, but I can't do what you want me to do if you don't ask."

"I'll try. I'm not really good at expressing my needs," Heather said as she headed toward her bedroom, "I guess I'll pack. I'm glad we can ride back together. I was really dreading that drive."

I headed to my room to pack my toiletries in one of my already packed suitcases. I usually choose to keep my clothes in my bag to avoid the possibility of bed bugs. It probably wasn't as likely here as in a cheap motel, but you couldn't be too careful.

I felt a little better having chosen to take some action rather than sitting around moping.

Chapter 13

We took our time getting ready to go and had another cup of coffee before we checked out. I had a brief internal debate about whether to make another pot or blow this town. Leaving won in a landslide. We were both ready to go. Besides, in a caffeine emergency, there were Starbucks nearly everywhere these days.

We had left the truck and trailer across the bay in Oakland to avoid the complication of trying to park in San Francisco. Oakland wasn't much better, but at least we were able to find a Walmart, so we were set for overnight parking. Neither of us was looking forward to a six-and-a-half-hour trip on the 101 but taking the PCH would add at least an hour and a half. We opted for the 101 to save time, motivated by the fact that we could soothe our aching muscles in the hot tub when we got back.

I took the motorcycle to meet her in Oakland after we loaded all the bags into a cab. I hoped she remembered the address of the Walmart where we parked. I was pretty sure I remembered the route. I was relieved when I saw the Walmart sign on the 880 just south of Oakland in San Leandro. I had to cross four lanes of bumper to bumper traffic, but I made it. I could see the truck and trailer in the distance and was relieved they hadn't been ripped off or towed away over-night despite Walmart's liberal policies regarding overnight parking.

When I pulled into the parking lot, Heather was nowhere to be found. I figured I got a jump on her thanks to lane-splitting, the practice of riding a motorcycle down the line between lanes on a multi-lane road. As far as I knew, California was the only state that allowed it and, no wonder. It was incredibly dangerous. But, without it, motorcycle riders would often sit in traffic for hours, and that would discourage their use for transportation. While you could argue the safety of a motorcycle, you couldn't beat the gas mileage.

I decided to use the bathroom, which was the other thing Walmart was good for. Although, it wasn't smart to take merchandise in there. I knew that from experience back in my Goth days. Probably the black lipstick and pierced lip didn't help me to look like an innocent shopper at the time. I groused at the embarrassing memory of being taken into custody by The Walmart police and the fight I had later with my mom.

When I got back to the truck, Heather was still missing. I wasn't too worried yet, considering the bumper to bumper traffic that defined the Bay Area. When we had devised travel plans, I hadn't planned initially on loading the motorcycle, since motorcycling was always my preference, but I always kept a ramp in the trailer for that eventuality. You never knew, even in California, when the next torrential downpour was coming. At times like these, I was happy I rode a manageable Ducati, which was probably a third the weight of a Harley touring bike. I'd never have been able to get a hog up that ramp.

I was debating whether to ride it or walk it up the ramp when Heather's taxi pulled in. She looked a little less put together than usual. I decided to wait until the cab driver drove away to ask for details. She sat on the edge of the trailer as if she needed to sit on something stationary.

I joined her. "What happened to you?"

She spoke slowly. "Oh, it was fine. I just figured I would die and not have to worry about a thing after that." She stood up and paced and flailed her arms as she spoke. "First, getting out of the city was just a nightmare. He was literally riding on the bumper of several other cabs. What is wrong with this town? Do all the cab drivers have a death wish?"

She took a deep breath and continued, "It was stop-and-go, but mostly stop all the way. And every time he went forward, I didn't think he was going to stop in time. The worst part, though, he was trying to talk to me with such a heavy accent, I couldn't even guess what most of the words were. I just nodded and smiled through the whole ordeal. It was terrible." She buried her face in her hands.

I could count on one hand the number of times I had seen Heather's feathers get ruffled. It was rare, so I knew her ride was even worse than she had described. "Do you want to take a break before we get on the road?"

She begged, "No, please, Miranda, can we just go? The sooner we get home, the sooner I can take a shower. That cab was disgusting."

I was happy to go. "That's fine. You want me to drive?" I figured she did, but I was trying to be empathetic. Jackie would be so proud.

"Yes, please drive. I'm way too stressed right now to take the wheel." She strode toward the passenger-side door, and I jumped in the driver's seat. I was about to drive away when I realized I hadn't secured the motorcycle to the trailer or pulled up the ramp. I rolled my eyes at my lack of concentration. I whispered to myself, "Just get me home, Lord."

I turned to Heather, who was settling into the bucket seat. "Hold on, I've gotta take care of some things back there. Just close your eyes for a minute. You'll feel better."

It took less than ten minutes to make sure nothing was going to bounce around while we rode. A tear slipped from my eye when I realized only two sleds were returning home with us. The others had been retained for DNA testing. When I got back in the truck cab, Heather was asleep. Heather could fall asleep at the drop of a penny. Most of the time, when I tried to sleep, I would just lay awake and plot out how I was going to take over the world. It was a curse; a brain that never turned off.

She was lying with the seat reclined. I didn't have the heart to wake her up to tell her that her snoring was driving me crazy.

After about an hour and a half, we stopped for lunch at the Steinbeck House in Salinas at Heather's insistence when she, thankfully, woke up about a half-hour before we stopped. I wasn't aware that John Steinbeck was from Salinas, much less that his childhood home was a restaurant and museum. Having recently read *The Winter of our Discontent,* I felt very much at home in his.

Heather was over the top with enthusiasm, and it made my heart happy to see her bubbling with excitement. Her improving mood made me feel fewer pangs of guilt about Annika's death if I happened to laugh or smile.

"I can't believe we are in John Steinbeck's house. I have read all his books. Back in high school, I had a dream of being a writer because of him."

I was surprised. "I never knew you wanted to be a writer. Did you pursue it?"

She laughed. "I wrote some poems and short stories in college, and I was even published in the annual UCLA creative writing publication, but I made the mistake of taking Professor Story's Novel Writing 101 class. She had us write several book chapters in various genres, and she provided us with feedback. Her critiques were so brutal, I felt lucky to get through the class alive. I had no desire to write professionally after that."

I was surprised after all that we had talked about since we met, that I had never learned this about Heather until now. I conjectured, "Maybe she was just a harsh critic so that her students would get to be better writers, or maybe she was just full of herself."

She grunted. "Oh, she definitely was, or worse. I set up a meeting with her because I was so surprised that she hadn't liked my writing better, and she proceeded to provide me with endless examples of how poor my writing was. She really seemed to enjoy herself ripping my writing apart, and I just wanted to sink into the floor."

"Do you still have anything you wrote?" I wondered.

She put her finger in her mouth as she thought. "I think I do somewhere in a box of school stuff."

100

I was excited at the idea of getting a glimpse into the inner workings of Heather's mind, probably as much as she had enjoyed listening to me talk in my sleep. "You should dig it out. I'd love to read it."

Her face reddened, and she avoided my gaze. "Oh, I don't know, Miranda. What if you hate it?"

"I'm sure I won't. Besides, your professor already has you believing that you can't write, so what do you have to lose?" I willed her to look me in the eye.

Suddenly, she was aglow with anticipation and on the edge of her chair. "Really, Miranda? Would you read it for me?"

"Of course, and I'm sure it'll be great." I retreated to the menu and my thoughts smiling a satisfied smile. Maybe everything was going to be okay.

The service and food were excellent at the restaurant. The servers were volunteers working for free to benefit the restaurant and museum. Our waitress, Stacy, couldn't have been more than twenty, and it surprised me that she had the inclination to work for free. At that age, I wouldn't have been caught dead working without getting paid.

When she brought our check, my curiosity got the best of me. "Stacy, can I ask you a question?"

She smiled. "Sure, I'm an expert about the house and the museum, so ask away."

I spoke in hushed tones as if this was a huge secret. "You've got to be college-age at the most. You're a volunteer, right?"

She nodded.

I continued, "What possessed you to decide to work for free?"

She shrugged. "It's a long story, but the short version is an adorable guy who was volunteering here, asked if I wanted to also. I, of course, said yes." Her full smile turned to a sheepish grin. "Then he left, and I would have felt like an idiot just quitting, so I stayed on. That was three years ago, so I guess I stay now because I love it. My parents think it's great to get work experience while I'm in school, so they help me out with spending money."

I patted her hand. "That's a relief. At least you're human. I never would have done anything so philanthropic at your age. But now that I found out you did it for a guy, I feel better." I slipped her a $100 tip.

She started to protest, but I put my finger to my lips. "Just don't tell your parents."

Lunch had taken longer than planned, although the food and company were well worth it. But if we wanted to get home before dark, we were going to have to step on it. Since I was driving, I had every confidence that we would make it, barring any traffic jams, speeding tickets, or earthquakes. Welcome to California.

As we left town, I was amazed when 'Me and Bobby McGee' came on the XM Radio. It was a cosmic moment because of the reference to Salinas in the song. Heather and I sang along just like Janis, Bobby, and the truck driver in the song.

Four hours later, we pulled through the gate of the ranch. I was so relieved to be home and felt a sense of calm come over me as soon as we pulled up to the house. Heather and I hadn't talked much for the last couple of hours. We sang along with the radio for a while. Then she fell asleep again while I was lost in my thoughts.

The breeze off the Pacific made it a perfect early evening temperature of 74. I ran around the house opening windows to get the stale, closed-up-house air out, and the fresh air in. Heather was unpacking her suitcase as I barged into her room to get her windows.

Before she could put her unworn clothes back into her drawers or closet, I grabbed them. "Hey, where are you going with my clothes?"

I yelled behind me, "Just a precautionary post hotel bedbug cleaning."

I could hear her protesting, but it was too late. I was determined to stuff anything that had touched a foreign dresser or closet into the laundry with hot water.

In no time, I was back in my bedroom. It was going to feel so heavenly getting into my own bed tonight. I could barely wait to sink into my foam mattress and feel the coolness of the freshly washed linen on my skin. But it wasn't even seven yet, so I'd be up for several hours. I got in my bathing suit, anticipating the one hundred-and-two-degree temperature of the crystal-clear water in the hot tub. When I first moved here, I wasn't so particular about wearing a suit in the hot tub, but multiple package deliveries and unexpected guests had tamed my wild ways.

Heather was still in her room when I slid quietly down the stairs and out to the deck. I lifted the cover off the hot tub, turned on the jets, and lowered my weary body in. It would have seemed trite to say that all my troubles melted away as soon as I was submerged, but it was entirely accurate. It was twenty minutes of heaven where no-one could demand anything of me. There were days when it was the only twenty minutes I had to myself. I closed my eyes and savored the moment.

I was surprised when the automatic timer stopped the jets. I must have fallen asleep. Good thing I didn't drown. There was no sign of Heather whom I had expected might join me at some point. In my haste to get in, I had forgotten my towel. So, I did a couple of laps around the deck, dripping off before I went inside.

Still dripping, I made a beeline for the downstairs bathroom. Although it had a tub and shower, they virtually never got used except when we entertained multiple people overnight, which was rare. I took off my suit, dried off, wrapped up in a towel, and threw the suit in the dryer, which was in the laundry room adjoining the bathroom.

I figured that Heather must have fallen asleep upstairs, and I peeked through her bedroom door, which was partially opened. Yup, she was. I crept in, turned out her light, and shut her door quietly.

I ran across the hall to my room and donned exercising shorts and a tee-shirt, not because I was planning on exercising, but because they were comfortable and happened to be in the first drawer I opened. I didn't care how I looked as I wasn't expecting company. Of course, that was when people usually dropped by.

I went down to the kitchen, powered up my laptop, and spent the next hour catching up on work emails. I had answered the most urgent ones from the road, but anything that could wait had waited. The business was running really smoothly right now with Heather to keep things organized. I had many happy customers and many happier contracted doctors who shared their fee with me for the referrals that I was providing. My only worry was this CMS investigation that was continuing on. I had figured we would give them some documents, and they would review them and go away, but that wasn't the case so far.

It seemed the more I provided them, the more they asked for. Demanded was more like it. The IRS had better manners than these people. We had just barely made their last submission deadline, and they were already requesting more. Hopefully, Heather and I would get them what they needed again before the deadline. With Annika's death still weighing heavily on me, I wasn't in a place where I could concentrate all that well.

I opened a bottle of Cabernet and pondered my future.

Chapter 14

I woke exhausted and disoriented, with covers strewn from one end of the bed to the other, one pillow at my feet and another with the pillowcase surgically removed some time during the night. The guilt and anxiety that I had tried to mask with a bottle of wine came rushing back with a vengeance in the form of a massive headache. Annika's death weighed heavily on me.

Walking to the bathroom felt like I was trying to run a marathon with fifty-pound ankle weights. Until the recent arrest warrant issued for Larry by the Swiss, I had held out hope that Tara's death was an accident. I could reconcile that in my mind as an isolated incident. However, Annika's death confirmed, once and for all, that there was foul play involved. I couldn't think straight, and before I kicked the cat by mistake or over-watered my house plants, I decided I had to get out of the house. I threw on the same shorts and tee-shirt I wore last night and a pair of beat-up running shoes. I left a note for Heather on the counter and dashed out the front door, locking it behind me without putting on make-up or running a brush through my hair.

Just as I pulled my key from the deadbolt, my cell phone vibrated. Detective Morrison's name popped up on the screen. I was shocked to hear from her so soon. I pounded the green phone icon in anticipation.

The detective wasted no time getting down to business. "Miranda Marquette please," she sounded like I was another thing to get off her 'to do' list.

I smiled, hoping to improve both my mood and hers. "Yes, detective, this is she."

She spoke quickly and suddenly just above a whisper. "Oh, Miranda, thank goodness it's you. I must have had your number wrong, so I finally tapped into a database after calling ten variations of the number and scaring the crap out of several people."

I was happy that she felt comfortable telling me that story but was still dying to find out why she called. "Well, I'm glad you finally got me. I hope I gave you the right number."

She groaned. "I don't think it's you. It's the third time I've done something like this just this week. I'm wondering if I'm developing dyslexia."

I flashed back to my days as a cop. "I'm sure you're just rushing. I don't think people develop dyslexia. They're born with it. Just overworked, I'd guess. I used to do the same thing when I was in your shoes."

She sounded grateful. "You're very kind."

It was satisfying to know that my empathetic side was improving. My therapist and I had been working on that for a couple of years. I hesitated, as I could hear the shuffling of papers in the background.

"So, what can I help you with, detective?" I finally inquired

She almost immediately shifted gears, and her voice took on a less conversational tone like she was reading. "First of all, I need to inform you that this call is on a recorded line. Please acknowledge if that is acceptable by stating 'Yes' or 'No.'

I sat down on my front step. "Yes."

She continued, sounding like a pre-recorded message. "As of 8:05 a.m., this morning, July 13, 2008, Lawrence Lechter was arrested for the murder of Tara Androsio. Per the Extradition Treaty of May 14, 1900, with the Swiss Confederation, and the Supplemental Extradition Treaties of January 10, 1935, January 31, 1940, and November 14, 1990, the defendant must be surrendered to the foreign nation, in this case, Switzerland, no later than thirty days after incarceration. Do you understand the information that has been provided via this telephone call?"

My mind was racing with questions. I had no idea if I could ask questions on this official, recorded call, or if I should have an off-the-record conversation with the detective later. I had nothing to lose, so I took the chance. "Yes, I understand. Can I ask questions?"

She waited a minute to respond. I was pretty sure from the waver in her voice that she didn't deal with this type of thing every day any more than I did. "I'll try to answer your questions, but there are no guarantees."

Her lack of confidence encouraged me to proceed. "Well, just where did you find Larry to arrest him? When do you think the trial is going to take place? Do you think I'll need to testify? Do you know where it will be? How will this impact the case regarding Annika Bloom?"

Detective Morrison laughed. "Whoa, Miranda. Hold on. I don't have a clue about anything having to do with the Tara Androsio case. We will be giving your contact information to the Swiss authorities, and they will be in touch. That's all I can say about that situation. As far as the Annika Bloom case or Mr. Lechter's arrest, I can't comment at this time since there is an active investigation underway."

I felt like she had let the air out of my balloon, even though I wasn't shocked at her response. "Well, you can't blame a girl for trying." My heart sank, but my mind was racing. I had as many questions for myself as I did for her. Would I be able to afford to take the time away from the business for an extended trial in Switzerland? I didn't have any idea how the court system worked there, so I needed to get educated quickly. It seemed wrong for our country to extradite Larry to Switzerland for trial when he could very well be responsible for Annika's death as well. What will happen if he is convicted there, and then a warrant for his arrest is issued here?

I decided that I could drive myself crazy if I didn't stick to my guns and take a moment to relax. Switzerland, Larry, and all my questions would be here when I got home.

I hadn't taken the time to unload the sleds from the trailer last night and didn't feel like doing it now. Since I had loaded the Ducati last, it was easy to set up the ramp and back it down into the driveway. I was ready to go in about five minutes.

As I pulled out of my electronically controlled gate, I waved to my next-door neighbor, Andrew, as if I didn't have a care in the world. He was working on the bougainvillea at the end of his driveway. He and his wife had no children and had, sort of, adopted me as their own since I moved here. They usually provided me with valuable insight when I was in a quandary or didn't know where to turn next. It was great and rare having neighbors like that. I needed to stop and see them soon.

I debated my options and decided to take a quick ride to Tuna Canyon Park, just south of the city limits. As I experienced the first time I rode up here from L.A. five years ago, the views of the beach were breathtaking. There were plenty of hiking trails, which would allow me to clear my head. Whenever I felt like my life was going in circles, walking around the Labyrinth, the high point of the park, grounded me.

The Santa Monica Mountains were among my favorites to climb because they were beautiful and accessible. When I turned onto Topanga Canyon Boulevard, Fernwood-Pacific, and finally left on Tuna Canyon Road, a calmness settled over me. My stress level since leaving Malibu for the Bay area, over a week ago, had been through the roof until I breathed in the fresh mountain air. When I first relocated to L.A. and had no idea where anything was, this was the first park I found to escape the hustle-bustle of the City of Angels. I had come back here many times over the years.

The memories of my experiences in the mountains came rushing back as I climbed up to the same clearing I had reached so many times before. I suddenly realized how far I had come in my life since the first time I hiked these trails. At that time, I was still recovering from being shot in the face and losing my partner

108

just weeks after we had left North Carolina and our jobs as undercover cops.

Back then, I never dreamed I'd be unbroken enough to make my business this successful. Malibu was too much to hope for, but here I was. I looked at the clear blue sky and thanked the higher power for everything I had survived. I had no idea if the higher power's name was God, Jehovah, Buddha, or Mickey Mouse, but after I survived my accident, I was convinced for the first time in my life, that our existence here on Earth was more than just a series of meaningless, random events. That was a significant leap for me after years as an agnostic.

I walked for a couple of hours, stopping frequently to take in the views or to watch a hawk gracefully soaring over the trees in an endless search for subsistence. As I approached my bike at the trailhead parking lot, my head felt clear and focused.

Riding the high of my nature hike, I was not quite ready to go back home, so I decided to head to the beach. Living as close as I did, I took the ocean for granted and virtually never came to the shore unless someone visited from out of town. That needed to change.

Topanga beach was right at the bottom of the mountain and had restrooms, showers, and changing facilities. It wasn't the most fantastic swimming beach with lots of rocks along the shore, but who swam in the Pacific anyway other than surfers in wet suits?

I often had, in the past, charted my future sitting on the beach. Staring out past the calming ebb and flow of the waves pounding the shore made my problems seem smaller somehow. I spent a couple of hours running through the next several weeks in my mind. I needed to get educated on the Swiss court system, what I should expect in court, what the timing of the trial would be, and make a plan. I then needed to get with Bernie to strategize the Bravo Network meeting and how this trial might impact the reality show. I felt like everything else could wait, and Heather could cover the business for me and take care of the CMS requests. I was so thankful for Heather.

But first and foremost, as much as I hated funerals, I needed to go to Annika's. I hoped her family wouldn't blame me for her death as Tara's had. Since I hadn't connected with Patricia since we left the police station in San Francisco, I had no idea if she would attend or not. She had been close to Annika, especially since Tara's death, but she and I were not in the best place the last time we were together. Deep inside, I knew it would be best for everyone if we reconciled, especially because Larry had been arrested. She had to be freaking out. Maybe the funeral would provide us an opportunity for a new start.

My phone rang. My iPhone screen announced it was Bernie. As I got used to everything the new phone had to offer, I was happy to have finally retired my Blackberry earlier this year. "Hey Miranda, how are you?"

He sounded a little more relaxed than the last time we spoke, which was still considerably more wired than your average bear. "I'm good, Bernie. What's up?"

He said, "I'm FedExing a contract for next week's meeting. I already have my attorney reviewing it, but the meeting should be a formality, more like a meet and greet."

I was confused. "I thought we were far from a deal. What changed?"

He continued. "My contact was pretty pessimistic, but his boss couldn't sign the deal fast enough."

I was incredulous. "That's odd." Suddenly something wasn't adding up for me.

He sighed. "What's odd?"

I continued. "A couple of days ago, the whole thing was falling apart because Tara and Annika were dead. Now they are ready to sign? Listen, I'd love to do this reality series more than anything, but what am I missing?"

110

I couldn't see his face, but I knew what expression he was wearing. It was that 'I told you so' smirk that I couldn't stand. We had a classic Love-Hate relationship. I was sure he saw dollar signs when he looked at me, but he also saw unlimited liability. "Let's review the contract and have the meeting. I'll be on the lookout for any signs of anything that raise red flags in the contract. My gut tells me it was you they were after all the time, and the team was complicating matters and making the reality TV show a much more expensive proposition."

I chewed on my thumbnail as I often do when I'm nervous. "Thanks, Bernie. That would be amazing if we can pull this off. I could kiss you right now."

He tried to laugh, but it ended up sounding like a cough. Either way, he completely ignored my comment. "The meeting's on the seventeenth, a week from Thursday, in their Hollywood offices. Do you want to meet there or go together?"

"We can meet there, Bernie. Let me know if you or your attorney have any concerns about the contract, and I'll let you know if I see anything I can't live with."

We hung up and I crossed my fingers the meeting wouldn't conflict with my upcoming travels, either to Texas for the funeral or, most likely, Switzerland.

Chapter 15

Heather and I eased back into a regular work routine. I was confident I could leave town for a couple of days with no issues. If anything, we seemed even more in sync than we had before we left for San Francisco. She seemed far more confident to be left alone, which I was relieved to see.

After dreading it since we got home, the day before Annika's funeral arrived. As much as I would have liked Heather to come with me, we both agreed it was better that she stay behind and tend to the business, since we had finally caught up from our last trip out of town. I spent a productive day helping Heather address the non-routine emails or making direct calls to customers where necessary to smooth ruffled feathers or address issues regarding services provided by our physician network. I often found that a partial refund or a complimentary spa weekend were effective deterrents to written complaints to the Department of Health and Human Services. We preferred to stay under the federal government radar.

Late in the afternoon, I went upstairs to pack my bag for the trip. A few minutes later, I slogged down the stairs feeling unprepared, guilty, needy, and sick to my stomach. I had even debated not going, but I owed it to Annika and her family. It was time to get myself out of the way and suck it up.

Heather looked at me, quizzically. "Are you okay?"

I tried to be upbeat. "I'm fine. Just not looking forward to the trip." She knew me better than anyone. "You know how I feel about funerals."

She came over and hugged me. "Yes, I do, and I hope it goes better then Tara's did."

I smiled weakly. "I do too. I'm also dreading seeing Patricia now that Larry has been arrested. I'm sure she'll find a way to blame me."

She nodded, but there really wasn't much she could say.

I felt a Migraine coming on. I rarely got Migraines, but when I did, they were debilitating left untreated. Thankfully all I needed to accomplish today was a flight to Dallas, and I knew I couldn't delay any longer, so I pushed myself toward the door and waved. "See you in a couple of days." I forced a smile as I swallowed a couple of Imitrex.

Dallas was a doable three-hour flight from LAX, but with the change in time zones, it would feel late by the time I arrived. What would have been seven to ten p.m. in the same time zone, became seven to midnight with the shift from Pacific to Central Time. My decision to fly tonight was made for me when the flight I wanted for tomorrow morning was full. The funeral wasn't until tomorrow at two, so at least I had plenty of time to get some sleep and collect myself.

I parked the convertible in the short-term parking garage because I hated waiting for a shuttle, packed with sweaty tourists and screaming kids. That was the excuse I used for the fact that I didn't like to relinquish control of my timeliness to a shuttle driver who had gotten his CDL license through a correspondence course.

I arrived an hour before my flight was scheduled to leave. I laughed to myself as I passed the security line, which stretched around the inside of the building for as far as I could see. I couldn't believe how many people were leaving LA on a Wednesday evening. Was there an earthquake scheduled that no one had mentioned? Leaving the poor suckers to wait in line, I headed for the first-class passenger area.

I hoped by taking a last minute flight I might avoid the press once I landed in Dallas. They had been harassing me day and night since Annika's death. At some point, an intern at CNN had made the connection between Annika's and Tara's deaths and me, as well as the death of Sabine's ship captain back in New Orleans. So suddenly, I was news, which was the last thing I

113

wanted. I hadn't missed the irony that just a few days ago, I would have done anything for the kind of publicity I was getting now.

My strategy for this trip had been to secure a hotel as close to the airport as possible and to worry about where the funeral was in the morning. The Hilton was close to Dallas Love Field, so that was perfect.

The flight was nothing short of a dream. As the only passenger in first class, the steward, a mid-forties, muscular black man, Gregor, was at my beck and call, serving gourmet food and anything I wanted to drink. I opted not to have a Cabernet even though the 1999 Altamura sounded heavenly. However, the escargot soufflé was spectacular.

Once we landed, I struggled back to the reality of negotiating the Dallas Airport. I dreaded the car rental counter because I knew if something could go wrong, it would. Over the past five years, I had blown through all the major car rental agencies, including Hertz, Avis, Budget, National, Enterprise, and Dollar, hoping for better customer service, only to be let down time after time.

There had not been one of them that lived up to my expectations. It didn't matter if I made a reservation in advance, rented an expensive luxury car, rented a convertible, or a minivan, there was always an issue. It was something different every time: they didn't have the car that I reserved, they had my vehicle, but it would take an hour to prepare it for re-rental, there was no vehicle in the space number they had indicated, or there was no space with that number. It was always something. My expectations were so low at this point; if I got a car that ran and didn't smell like someone had transported their drenched Great Dane, I'd be thrilled.

After I grabbed my suitcase from the carousel, I was drawn to the Thrifty counter, probably because this was the only car rental company I hadn't used yet. One person stood at the

114

counter. Two agents worked behind it, so I immediately felt like it was my lucky night. Jose, the free customer service agent, seemed excited to serve me. Figuring people treated you better when you have dressed appropriately, I liked to travel well dressed. I wore a red skirt with a matching blouse. They were expensive, tasteful and told the world that I meant business.

Jose took the time to explain which vehicles they had available and what the costs were, with and without that outrageous insurance that no-one actually needs if they own their own vehicle and have insurance. After the typical ten minutes it took for him to print my documents and for me to review and sign them, he pointed out the window to the well-lit parking lot. My apple-red Cadillac CTS was in the first row and matched my outfit perfectly. I hoped it wouldn't be disrespectful to show up to a funeral in a red car, but it was too late to consider that now.

It took me two minutes to get to spot A-22 and my vehicle. It was definitely my lucky day. The key lay on the front seat, and the Caddy roared to a start when I pressed the start button. I pulled out of the parking garage with no-one stationed by the gate to check my paperwork.

Finding the hotel was a piece of cake, especially with the built-in GPS. As I parked the car and headed to the front desk, pulling my suitcase with my carry-on stacked on top, I felt nervous anticipation about the funeral tomorrow. All sorts of questions ran through my mind. Will Patricia be there? And be civil to me? Will the family blame me as Tara's had?

My stress level was confirmed when I grabbed three freshly baked chocolate chip cookies at the check-in desk. Bob, the night manager, didn't seem to mind. If fact, he asked if I wanted a couple more. I couldn't tell if he was sarcastic or not, so I left well enough alone.

Chapter 16

I tossed and turned all night. The room was too warm, no matter where I set the thermostat, so I wore an oversized t-shirt and workout shorts to bed. I woke up freezing in a cold sweat from a very frustrating dream that I couldn't remember. I looked at the clock: 3:03 a.m. I awoke again at 4:07, 5:42, and 6:36. I finally decided to get up.

Before I stepped into the shower, I glared at the mirror. My hair was a matted mess, my face was red and puffy, my eyes were bloodshot, and I looked, quite frankly, scary. If I'd been wondering why I hadn't attracted any decent men recently, the answer was right in front of me. With the possible exception of Jason, but I couldn't think about that right now.

I stood in the glass and tile shower with the water as hot as I could stand it running over my head, hoping that I'd suddenly feel awake and alive. It wasn't happening. Finally, I gave up and stepped gingerly from the shower, being careful not to slip on the tile floor. I toweled off, mindlessly blow-dried my hair then pinned it into a low knot at the back of my head. I then dressed in a conservative black dress and medium heels. For jewelry, I remained conservative, wearing simple gold studs in my ears and a plain gold chain necklace. My Rolex was gold already, so matched.

Visiting hours were from ten to noon. I hadn't planned on attending, but since I wasn't able to get the morning flight, I was here much earlier than expected. So, I decided it was the right thing to do.

I called the front desk to see if they knew where the funeral home was. The funeral turned out to be in a suburb of Fort Worth and was a half-hour to forty-five minutes from here. I didn't mind since I was dreading it anyway.

I popped into the Sports Page Grill adjacent to the hotel for breakfast. I sat staring out the window engrossed in my thoughts about Annika, the funeral, and everything that had led me here to Texas.

I'd been seeing one therapist or another, off and on since before I left the force in my late twenties. I like to call my present one, Dr. Ruth even though her name is Jackie, is about my age and doesn't speak with a German accent. She had encouraged me to see this trip as an opportunity as opposed to the torture I had feared it would be. I hoped and prayed it went better than Tara's.

After downing my scrambled eggs and toast, I put the plastic cover on my coffee and jumped in the car and drove to Benbrook, Texas. It got surprisingly rural quickly when you got outside of the city limits. In L.A, I was used to having to drive forever before suburbia turned rural, which usually meant desert or something less hospitable.

The modern brick funeral home had a huge parking lot and yard, bordered by corn fields on three sides. It looked more like an office building or a doctor's office, but the sign in front confirmed it was Winscott Road Funeral Home. I hadn't anticipated the TV news vans when I pulled in. Bernie and I had spent so much time and money, well in advance of that last race; I shouldn't have been surprised that the press had picked up the story. After all, the crash had been filmed live, reported on the major news networks, and went viral on the internet.

I attempted to slip in the side door of the funeral home and had nearly made it when one of the reporters recognized me from the publicity pictures. He held up a microphone attached to a boom the size of a baseball bat and chased me, yelling, "Ms. Marquette, Sam Smith, WFAA-TV News. Do you feel responsible for your teammate's death?"

Had Bernie been out here, he would have told me to say, "No comment," and shoved me through the door. I was so offended by the question, though, I couldn't ignore it. I didn't see what harm answering his inane question would do.

"I feel horrible about Annika's death, but I do not feel responsible. We were all adults on the extreme-sports team and made our own decision about luge racing. We were all doing what we loved, and she was aware of the risks."

Since I had made the mistake of responding, the one reporter had been joined by ten others yelling their names and call-letters, along with as many cameramen and women.

A tall, statuesque Hispanic woman got my attention first. "Rachel Rodrigues, WFTW. Ms. Marquette, how do you respond to your teammate, Patricia's, allegations that you pushed them all to enter events they didn't want to enter?"

My face burned, and I knew I wouldn't be able to control my anger much longer. As I was about to answer, a hand came from behind me and pushed the microphone away.

Bernie said calmly, "No more comments. Please allow her privacy during this difficult time." He wrapped me up and led me inside.

I hugged him when I composed myself. "Thanks so much, Bernie. I couldn't stop. They made me so angry. Who are they to question my motives and my practices with the team?" Then it suddenly hit me. "Hey, what are you doing here? You didn't even tell me you were coming."

He winked and spoke in hushed tones with his back to the viewing. "Let's keep you out of the limelight." He walked me to the other side of the room, out of earshot of the other mourners.

I whispered, "I guess Patricia's not very happy with me right now. And she doesn't even know she's fired from the team even if I decide to continue having one."

Bernie continued, "The team isn't mentioned at all in the Bravo contract, so maybe you're better off not mentioning anything to Patricia. You are who they want. She was too private a person for a reality TV show anyway."

118

I noticed people were staring at us. I figured it wasn't polite to hold a business meeting in the middle of a viewing, so I waved Bernie off and walked in the general direction of the receiving line. I was thankful I had traveled alone.

I spotted Patricia sitting by herself in the chapel and decided to take a detour to talk to her before wading through a line of relatives I had never met. I sat next to her. She stared straight ahead. We both sat like that for a couple of minutes.

"It's all your fault, Miranda," she said quietly.

That was not a positive start. "I didn't force you or Annika to race. You answered the ad. How is that my fault?"

She looked at me like I was from Mars. "Not that. Larry's arrest is all your fault. If you hadn't gone to the police in San Francisco, they wouldn't have had a clue who or where he was."

I debated whether to try to talk logic to someone who was no-doubt crazy and decided against it. "I'm sorry you feel that way, Patricia. I was hoping we could move past that, but if we can't, we can't." It seemed like a good idea to take the first step toward giving her the message that our extreme-team days were over too.

She broke into tears. "What is our child going to do without a father?"

"I hope he's innocent. Maybe being tried in another country where there isn't so much publicity will be a good thing."

Her body language said it all. She crossed her arms on her chest and said nothing.

I immediately stood up and left toward the receiving line again. I was apprehensive after what happened at Tara's funeral and had no idea who any of the people were, but at the very end it was a couple in their seventies who I identified as Annika's parents. I said I was a dear friend of Annika's when I got to their place in line.

119

Her mother was first to speak. With tears in her eyes, she smiled when she saw me and took my hand in both of hers. "You are Miranda, right?"

I nodded apprehensively.

She continued, "I'm so happy to meet you, Miranda. We have wanted to meet you for such a long time so that we could thank you. I don't know if Annika ever told you, but she was severely depressed when she joined your team. Meeting you turned her life around. She had attempted suicide three times the year before she joined you. It was a very dark time. Being able to travel and compete, she felt like a part of something for the first time in a long time. She had been very much a loner before that."

I was dumbfounded and fumbled for the right words. "Are we talking about the same Annika? She was the life of the party. She made everyone smile no matter where she went."

Her mother frowned. "She had been that way before her depression took over, probably five years ago." She looked down the line of people. "I guess we'd better move along, but I'd love to talk to you later. Can you come back to the house after the service?"

I hugged her. "Of course. I'd love that."

I wiped tears from my eyes as I found some empty chairs in the back of the room, far away from Patricia and the other mourners. Annika's mother's reaction had been so unexpected that I could barely hold back more tears. I was so thankful that I had helped Annika but was very confused about why God had chosen now for her to die when she finally had something to live for.

Between the viewing and funeral and the afternoon at Annika's parent's house, I had made two huge decisions. The first was that I was checking out of the hotel today, even if I had to pay for another day, rather than staying another night. The second was that I was going to fly to New Orleans for a few days to spend some time with my family. Remaining true to my vow, I booked a charter to New Orleans.

My promise to my family to visit more, after I was there last, had come up empty so far. And planning a trip from California seemed like much more of a commitment than the hour and a half it would take from here. On the way to Annika's parents' house, I had called my mother to make sure she and Tom were home and that the house wasn't full. They had friends from across the country who often came for days or weeks at a time. Having spent their whole lives in New Orleans where people loved to visit, they had amassed a large and diverse group of friends. I couldn't envision myself ever being that popular.

I landed in New Orleans just before 9 p.m., and my mom picked me up at the airport. Because it hadn't been that long since my last visit, there was only limited guilt-tripping from her about visiting more, which was a significant relief. The last time I visited, we didn't get out of the airport before we started bickering about something or other.

We had seen each other several times on my last trip down, even though I had stayed with Sabine, my sister. But something looked different about Mom. She looked older, and more lines streaked her face than the last time I had seen her, which caused me to wonder, "Mom, is everything okay, with your health, I mean?"

She couldn't meet my eyes.

"Mom?"

A tear dripped down her cheek. "I have breast cancer."

Good thing I wasn't driving. "What? How long have you known? What stage is it?"

I knew the news had to be grave because she was discussing it rather than brushing it under the table. "Stage three. It has spread to the lymph nodes in my neck. I start chemo next week."

Despite wanting to stay stoic for her, I couldn't control my river of tears. "Oh, mom—" I couldn't form any words. I wanted to say I wished I hadn't moved away. I wanted to say I would move back and take care of her. I wanted to say I knew that she'd be okay. But they would have all been lies.

We rode to the house in uncharacteristic silence.

Tom waited at the front door, which I had never seen him do. He came out and hugged me when I got out of the car, which was also unusual. My typically stoic stepdad, grabbed my suitcase and carried it upstairs for me. It seemed like he just wanted to take action of any kind, probably to take his mind off Mom's cancer.

My mom rarely stopped talking when she had company, but things had changed. When Tom came down from taking my suitcase up, he started asking me a barrage of questions. How was the funeral? What was up with the Extreme Team? How were negotiations going for the reality TV show? How was Heather? I was surprised because I never thought Tom had that much interest in me and my activities. Maybe he could never get a word in.

I didn't talk that much about myself because it seemed like a distraction from the thousand-pound gorilla in the room.

"When did you find out, Mom?"

She thought a minute. "Just two weeks ago today. We've been spreading the word slowly. It's not something you want to tell people."

Tom spoke up. "We've been looking on the internet, and the survival rate of stage three is going up all the time. There are always new drugs in the works."

Mom chuckled. "Probably with my luck, they'll cure it by the time I'm dead."

"Mom! Don't talk that way," I scolded.

Mom smiled. "It's okay, dear. I'm not going to be here forever, but I'm hopeful that we will beat this. I wish it were discovered sooner, but it's way better than stage four. Let's have a good time while you're here. How long can you stay?"

I frowned, feeling guilty about being here and leaving Heather to run things and about my mom's cancer. "I need to be back by Friday."

"Well, then we have a couple of days. That's great!" Mom hugged me.

Who was this woman, and where was my mother? There had never been a time when I had stayed long enough or been good enough for that matter. I pushed those thoughts down and decided to be happy I was home. Sabine had moved close-by since she sold her shrimping business. I had been a little taken aback when she sold it, after I tried to help her save the company and nearly ended up in prison for murder, but I decided it was time to put that behind me.

I texted her. "Hey, are you around?"

Since she sold the business, she was semi-retired but only three years older than me. I figured she would start to work again at some point, if only for something to do, although she was spending a lot of time with Mark Peterson, my friend and defense attorney, lately. It sounded like their on-again-off-again romance was going strong, and I couldn't help but wonder if there were wedding bells in the air. Mark had wanted to date me back in high school, but I had no interest in having him as more than a friend. Ironically, if Sabine weren't in the picture, it wouldn't be out of the question now.

My phone buzzed. "Are you?" It was Sabine.

"Yes, I'm at Mom's house. Can you come over?"

"On my way," she responded.

I put my phone in my purse, trying to stay in the moment as my therapist had strongly suggested. She had recommended that I get rid of my cell phone entirely, but that wasn't happening. I needed to figure out how to maintain a balance without having to stop using it.

I hadn't seen Sabine's new house yet but based on the address she had sent to me, I knew it was within walking distance.

Within a minute, her red Corvette convertible was in the driveway. Her medium-length brown hair looked perfect, as if she had been at the hairdresser when I texted, but that was just how Sabine was. Her flowered cotton dress and white sandals had a European flair reflecting the fact that she had lived in France until her sixteenth birthday when she moved in with Grandpapa. At that time, I thought she was my cousin, but due to a set of strange circumstances that I hadn't known until recently, she was, in fact, my sister.

"Ma Belle, Miranda!" She pulled me close.

I held her for dear life. My friend and teammate had died, and my mother had cancer. The world, as I knew it, was falling apart. But, no matter the miles or the years, Sabine had always been my closest person on earth. We survived many ups and downs together as teens. She was my mentor and my idol. She came and sat in my hospital room for my recovery from my many surgeries when I was shot in the line of duty and stayed for weeks at a time. It wasn't until recently that we started functioning as nearly equals in our relationship. But there were times when she felt parental toward me, and I sought her approval. I wasn't sure how I felt about the change in rolls.

She spoke softly. "How are you holding up? Losing another teammate must have been horrible for you."

I had tried so hard not to think about Annika since leaving Dallas, grief came rushing back, and tears streamed down my cheeks. "I'm okay. It's hard to believe she's gone. I feel so guilty sometimes about what happened. The press was ferocious at the funeral. I wanted to crawl into a hole."

She held me until my tears subsided.

I whispered to her, "And did Mom tell you she has cancer?"

Sabine whispered back, "She just told me today. I don't think she wanted to, but with you arriving, she couldn't very well keep the cat in the bag." She switched back to full voice. "How long are you staying?"

I cringed, anticipating her reaction. "Until Friday."

She laughed. "That's longer than I predicted. I guess I lose the pool."

I stood with my hands on my hip. "Seriously, you are betting on how long I would be staying? What kind of family is this?"

Mom chimed in. "One that likes to see you, honey. That's not so bad."

I couldn't argue.

I stuck close to Mom for the first twenty-four hours of my visit, trying to pick up on any apparent changes in her health: balance issues, headaches, or unexplainable pain anywhere in her body. She seemed to be staying positive, which was good. I was still worried.

On Thursday, I visited Sabine in her new house, which I admired as much as her last one. She was decked out in a black and white polka-dotted bodysuit and skinny black jeans. I wasn't sure I had ever seen Sabine wear the same outfit twice. Her clothing budget must be tremendous.

She took me on the grand tour, leaving no details to chance. She had completely gutted and redone the house, built in haste after Katrina. At the time, people just wanted a place to live and hadn't given much thought to the finishes. Her kitchen counters were granite, her floors a combination of imported artisan tile and hardwood. There were en suite bathrooms in each bedroom. The decorating was tasteful and modern with no particular theme, but everything just fit together. She had the eye.

"So, what else is going on in your life, Miranda?" She tried to sound casual, but I could tell she was intensely interested by her direct stare and penetrating eyes.

I sat for a minute, collecting my thoughts. "Wait a minute; I didn't even tell you my big news! The guy suspected of killing Tara has been arrested and is being extradited to Switzerland for trial. That probably means a trip to Europe sooner than later. I've been studying the court system over there, and they do things differently, and far more quickly than we do."

She glared at me in a pleasant-natured way. "Just when were you going to tell us that? You really don't focus any more than you did as a teenager. Remember that night you stayed out until 3 a.m. playing video games. You forgot to tell anyone where you were."

I cringed at hearing that 'remember that night' story so many times over the years and chose to ignore it. "I'm not sure how it'll work if he's convicted over there, and then a warrant for his arrest is issued here for Annika's death. I'll have to ask Mark about that." A tear dripped down my cheek and I brushed it away.

She wrung her hands. "Just be careful, Miranda. For whatever reason, two of your teammates are dead. I worry about you."

I could feel a drop of sweat running down my back. It was unlike Sabine to give me anything but support, so I knew she had to be really worried. I said softly, "You don't have to worry about me."

She reached for my arm. "I'm sorry, Miranda. I usually don't let you know how much I worry about you."

I reached out and hugged her. "I love you, sis."

A tear glistened on her cheek too. "I love you too." Then she changed the subject cheerfully, trying to lighten the mood, "So what else is new?"

I responded quickly. "Nothing much. Heather's been holding the business together while I'm trying to hold myself together. We've got this federal investigation of the company going on, which I didn't think was a big deal, but they don't seem to want to go away." I thought for a minute. "And the Bravo Network still wants to talk about a reality TV series. Bernie and I meet with them next week."

She looked at me askance. "Are you still thinking of doing that? Exposing every personal detail to the world? You wouldn't catch me dead doing something like that."

I sat with my elbows on her kitchen counter and my head in my hands. "I don't know what I want anymore." I paused for effect, then look directly into her nearly black eyes, "Do you have any wine?"

We both laughed, which broke the building tension. "Of course." She opened a glass door to an under-counter wine cooler. She poured two glasses of Cab Sauv. I was sure it was French, and I had no idea of the winery. French Cabs were usually drier and a little heavier than their California counterparts. Sabine smiled. "You and I can be so alike but so different. Just do what makes you happy. You'll know what to do when the time comes."

She always made me feel good about who I was, even when I left home at eighteen. I believe that deep inside, she knew it was a wrong decision for me. She never judged me or gave me a hard time about my choices. I always loved her for that. "Thank you." I hugged her again.

"For the wine?"

"No. For always supporting me even when I make bad choices."

"You have always done the same for me. After I put you through hell to help me save my shrimping business, and then I sold it, you were very gracious," she said with a broad, sweeping gesture.

"I learned from the best." I was relieved we wound our way through that conversation still on good terms.

I spent the night at Sabine's and woke up early so that I could have some quality time with Mom before I flew out.

She was having coffee with Tom at the kitchen counter like a thousand other times. But there was a peace surrounding her that I had never seen.

I was curious if she felt it too. "Mom, I have to ask you something." I had to think for a moment because I didn't know precisely how to word my questions. "Do you feel good about having cancer?"

She looked directly at me. "Of course not, but when I got the diagnosis, I made a decision. I wasn't going to be one of those whiney cancer patients looking for sympathy, especially while I was still feeling fine. There may come a time when I can't put on a brave face. If and when that time comes, you will know it's because I'm in pain, not because I'm in a bad place mentally. Besides, should this not go the way I want it to, I want your most recent memories of me to be loving and peaceful. You deserve that."

I hugged her. "Thanks, Mom. I love you."

"I love you too, Sweetheart."

We had several more hours of reminiscing, laughing, and crying. It was one of the best times I had ever had with my mom. Because I left home so young, I hadn't developed an adult relationship with her. Jackie credited that decision with my inability to grow up. She and I had agreed to disagree on that one. I left for home feeling at peace with whatever happened to us in the future. I believed that we could handle it.

Chapter 17

I arrived home just before 3 p.m. on Saturday. Even after fighting the L.A. traffic, I felt as relaxed and human as I had in a while. While I was still grieving for Annika and burst into tears at the drop of a hat, after her parents were so kind to me at the funeral, and my mother was at peace with the world, I felt grounded after my trip. Heather was M.I.A., so I laid down on the couch, intending to get a catnap. I slept uninterrupted until five when the cat woke me up wanting dinner. After I fed her, I dragged myself upstairs and fell right back to a dreamless sleep.

I woke up before just before 6 a.m., still tired. I wished I could sleep longer, but after fourteen hours, it wasn't in the cards. I grabbed my laptop and caught up on some work emails until I got out of bed at ten.

I was making coffee when my cell phone vibrated. According to the screen, it was an international call from Thun, Switzerland. This was probably the call I had been waiting for. I pressed the green telephone on the screen, then the speaker button. "Hello?"

A woman's voice came through clearly. She had a mild German accent but spoke excellent English. "May I please speak to Miranda Marquette?"

I had been practicing smiling when responding to a telephone call to sound more welcoming. "Yes, this is Miranda. What can I do for you?"

She sounded like she was practicing the same. "Miranda! I'm so happy that we could connect. This is Gretchen Schmid. I am what you, in America, would call the court clerk from the Thun criminal court in the Canton of Bern."

I glanced at my watch. It was 10:15 a.m., which meant it was 6:15 on Sunday evening in Switzerland. "Gretchen, I'm happy to hear from you, but isn't it Sunday evening there?"

She laughed. "Yes, it is. I was on vacation last week, and a co-worker let me know that the judge had wanted some calls made before Monday and that he would give me a day off if I made them over the weekend. After I agreed, my husband reminded me that we had a full weekend planned, so I ended up working tonight. I hope this is a good time for you."

I was impressed with her dedication.

I was dying to know everything she could tell me. "It's a great time for me, thanks."

She hesitated briefly. "Before I start, I wanted to send you our condolences. I understand that you recently lost two close friends and teammates."

I swallowed hard. Accepting that Tara and Annika were dead was difficult enough but having a complete stranger address it so eloquently made tears well up in my eyes. "Thank you," I managed to say. "You're very kind."

"You're welcome," she responded. "I always try to put myself in the shoes of those I call. Sometimes, it's easy to become callous when faced with tragedy every day. I try not to be that person."

I did my best to pull it back together, but my tears reminded me of how fresh my wounds were. "I really appreciate it."

She took a deep breath. "Okay, now let's talk about some less depressing things." She seemed to enjoy her job and jumped into our conversation with both feet. "I don't know, Miranda, how much you know about the Swiss justice system."

I wasn't sure if she was asking me if I knew anything about it, so I responded. "I know a little. I've done a few internet searches, but to be honest, there was far less written about it than I thought there would be."

She laughed. "Yes, we aren't as public about everything like you are in your country. Let me tell you the crucial details, and you can ask me questions afterward. First of all, Switzerland is organized a similar way to the United States, even though we are only the size of your states of Vermont and New Hampshire combined. We don't have states, though. We have Cantons. Each one has its own government and court system, similar to your states. Before you ask, I spent five years in the United States, that's how I know so much about it."

I laughed. "I was wondering about your knowledge of the U.S., and your English has a very Western feel despite your accent."

"Thank you. I work on it every day." She took a breath and continued. "Our court system has been going through a transition with the goal of all Cantons having the same rules and procedures. The government's goal was to have this completed two years ago, but it will probably take another year or so. The good news is that Bern, where your crime took place, already had rules similar to the ones the government is putting into place. Some of the others are so far off; it's going to take them years to make the changes."

She spoke in a hushed voice as if she was telling me a world-altering secret. "The most important thing for you to know is that we do not have a jury system like you. Many people find that shocking, but with DNA evidence turning over so many cases decided by juries, we are very comfortable not embracing it. We have opted to use a combination of elected judges and a panel of experts in the area of criminal law appropriate to the case. So, for example, in a murder case, we might have two additional judges who are experts in forensics, DNA, and evidence gathering, to assist the presiding judge with his decision."

I wanted to let her know I was listening at this end. "I had no idea. This is all very fascinating."

She was on a roll and didn't seem to want to stop any time soon. "The other important difference between our systems is that most cases are all but decided before the trial begins. All the evidence will have already been presented to the panel of judges. There is also no cross-examination by a defense attorney like you have in your system, although the general public is allowed to pose questions to the panel of judges so that salient points of the case are not missed by the prosecution. The defense attorney's role is to make sure that all evidence presented by the prosecution has been fairly presented and within the law. All in all, our system is under-stated, efficient, timely, and not a spectacle like in the United States."

I nearly reacted defensively to that last comment, but when I thought about it, I realized she was probably right. So instead, I queried, "So how does this all affect me?"

Gretchen was patient to a fault. "Don't worry, dear. We will get to that. But do you understand everything I have told you so far?"

I nodded, even though she couldn't see me. "I think so. It does sound very different than our spectacle." I laughed at my attempt at humor.

It went right over her head and she continued. "Now, I'm not saying there won't be any press coverage, but we do our best to discourage it. This will be the first murder trial that we have hosted in several years, and the fact that both the accused and the victim are from the United States may have an impact on the level of worldwide interest, but that remains to be seen. Either way, we expect a quick and fair trial."

I pushed down the feeling that she was avoiding giving me unpleasant news. "So, what are the next steps at this point?" I forced a smile so I wouldn't sound as anxious as I felt.

Gretchen exhaled. "So, we are still working with the City of San Francisco to get the defendant transferred to our jurisdiction, but we don't believe it will take long. Then, we'd like to start the trial as quickly as possible." She hesitated again. "We believe it would be to everyone's advantage for you to travel here for the pre-trial exchange of information and for the trial itself. Do you think that is something you would be able to do? We have a program that could help to assist with your expenses if that is an issue."

This was all happening so fast; I was struggling to process it. I was sure I sounded distracted as I made a checklist in my mind of things I needed to do before I left. "Um, no, that's not an issue. Wow, how soon do you need me to come out? I didn't expect this to happen so fast. It's usually months here before a trial is scheduled."

She jumped right in. "Well, you're not in Kansas anymore," then giggled hysterically. "You have no idea how long I have wanted to say that. I was confused for years when people said that to me until I saw the movie." She took a moment to contain herself. "Sorry. Anyway, I won't have a solid date until the extradition takes place, but we wanted to give you a heads up so you can plan accordingly since your testimony is critical to the process. I will be calling you back as soon as we nail down the timing, probably later this week."

I barely heard her as I plunged deeply into my own world. "Thanks. I look forward to hearing from you." I hung up the phone and retreated to the couch with the all too familiar tightness in my chest and short staccato breaths. My ears were ringing, and the room closed in around me like a straitjacket. Engulfed in sweat, I fought my nervous system to regain control.

My panic attacks were becoming more frequent despite stepping up my therapy to twice a week again. I sat on the couch with my knees pulled to my chest for a long time, maybe a half-hour or perhaps an hour. I have no concept of time when these things hit me. When it finally subsided, I was just happy I could breathe normally again, and the feeling that I was going to die had passed.

I grabbed a cup of coffee and dragged up the stairs to the shower. The steaming water helped to clear my head and make me feel normal again. It was getting harder and harder to figure out what my 'normal' was anymore.

Needing a distraction, I meandered over to my tall dresser after I dressed in skinny jeans and a black crop top. On the back of the chest was Jason Wall's business card. I'd been saving it for a moment like this.

When I met him, I didn't know whether I was coming or going. I knew that I liked him, and maybe that was all it would ever be.

I surprised myself when I got out my cell phone and picked up the business card. What day was this? Sunday. I imagined that he wasn't working today, so it should be safe to leave him a voicemail at work. I figured that would be easier than an awkward conversation if he picked up the phone. Then if he called me back, I would know he was interested. Good plan.

I dialed and immediately connected to his voicemail, which suggested that I leave a message after the tone. I smiled, hoping it projected through the phone. "Hi, Jason. I'm not sure you remember me. This is Miranda Marquette. We met at the hotel bar in San Francisco. I thought I'd see how you're doing. Give me a call when you get a chance." I left him my cell phone number.

I had no idea what I was doing, but I had no social life since I started the extreme team. I was completely unattached and had been for quite a while. The fact that I had left Jason a message confirmed one thing: I was listening to my therapist. She suggested that I needed to reach out if I was ever going to develop lasting relationships. Judging from my present state, that was an understatement.

I stood staring at my wet hair in the mirror, realizing that I needed to start the blow-drying process, or I'd have a real mess on my hands.

Once I had tamed my curls, it hit me that I had absolutely nothing on my schedule. My meeting with Bravo wasn't until the end of next week. My house was empty. I didn't want to ride my horses. I didn't want to ride my motorcycle. I didn't want to drive my car. I was restless and dying to do something, but I didn't know what. I opened the sliding door and walked out on the deck. My gorgeous ocean view didn't even calm my restlessness.

My phone rang. I didn't bother to check my caller I.D. figuring it must be Heather filling me in on where she was.

I hit the speaker button. "Hello, is Miranda Marquette in?"

The voice was vaguely familiar, but I couldn't place it. "Yes, this is she."

"Miranda, this is Detective Morrison." You could have knocked me over with a bendable straw.

"Yes," I replied.

She continued when it was evident I had nothing else to add. "Miranda, I've been assigned to the case relating to the murder of Annika Bloom. I wanted to see if we could get together and chat so I can pick your brain. You had already built a pretty good case, at least based on what you knew at the time, so I thought you might help us hit the ground running."

Immediately, my mistrust of cops kicked in. "Do I need to bring an attorney?"

Her answer was predictable. "An attorney? Whatever for? You're the furthest thing from a suspect."

I knew she wasn't stupid and had attended the police academy as I had. For that matter, anyone who watched even an occasional Law and Order rerun knew the most likely suspect was someone who knew the deceased. If someone also had motive and opportunity, they were the prime suspect. While I had no reason to kill Annika, there was no way for the detective to know that. And I was one of a handful of people who had touched her sled during the days before her death, and I was also one of her closest friends, according to her parents.

I tried not to let my paranoia take over. "Sure, I'd love to. Just name the time, and I'll be there."

Detective Morrison breathed a sigh of relief through the phone. "Thank you, Miranda, I didn't want to have to compel you to come in. I know this may not work for you, but is there any way you can get up here tomorrow? Monday's are usually my quietest day, and I'm in the precinct from at least 8 to 6."

I had been so bored just moments ago, and now I was questioning whether I had the time to go to San Francisco. I knew it was nothing more than apprehension and fear. I decided to be brave. "Tomorrow works for me. How's noon?" I figured I could either leave this afternoon and stay overnight or leave early and arrive by noon. Another motorcycle trip up the coast was never a bad thing.

"See you then," she said. If she was setting me up, she was a great liar. Of course, no one knew better than I did that being a good liar was a significant asset if you were a cop. I hoped she was enthusiastic because I had just made her investigating job easier.

I made a conscious decision as I hung up my phone to keep my thoughts positive. I had no reason to believe they suspected me. As far as I knew, Larry was still their prime suspect even though he was due to leave the country at any time.

I wracked my brain for anything that might be helpful to the case. But other than the fact that he had filmed us in Switzerland and was dating Patricia, there was nothing I knew of to tie Larry to Annika. She hadn't given him the time of day.

Chapter 18

Morning came early on Monday. Heather's bedroom door was closed, and I could hear her snoring behind it, so I figured she had come home late. It was unlike her not to text me, call me or leave a note, but she was a big girl, so I gave her the benefit of the doubt. I did wonder what she was up to, though.

Figuring Heather was the least of my worries, I focused on my trip up to the Bay Area. I had decided against traveling yesterday because I didn't want the hassle of packing and strapping a bag on my Ducati. If I ended up having to stay somewhere on the way home, I'd figure it out then. It wouldn't be the first time I had washed my underwear in a hotel room sink and bought a toothbrush.

When considering my route, since I was time limited, I decided to take the Five North, even though it wasn't as scenic as the Pacific Coast Highway. I would probably take the PCH home if I could make the timing work. I knew of a couple of vintage motels on the coast, which were perfect for a short night's stay if I needed one. I would worry about that later.

I left just before 6 a.m. as the sun was coming up. I savored the smells of the strawberries, grapes, onions, and tomatoes as I passed through the fields of Oxnard. It had been a while since I had come up the Five, and I had forgotten about the cattle yards at Harris Ranch Road, about halfway to San Francisco. The stench of the cattle yards seemed to extend for twenty miles in either direction. I finally pulled over and tied a rag from my saddlebag over my mouth and nose. Note to self: take the scenic route home.

After hitting the typically impossible traffic from Santa Clara to the Bay Bridge, I pulled in front of the police station with fifteen minutes to spare, saved only by the lane splitting law. I debated running into one of the many Chinese restaurants up and down the street but opted for a hot dog and some fries from a street cart. I still had a couple of minutes left before my appointment after I wolfed it down but opted to go inside because I felt vulnerable on the street.

Having come through the same door for the third time in as many weeks was not a particularly comforting feeling. But I was relieved to see that the city's underbelly was still asleep, or at least not here. The waiting room was empty.

There was a young man with multiple tattoos I didn't recognize behind the counter. "May I help you," he said. I could barely hear him through the bullet-proof glass.

I yelled, probably louder than I needed to. "I'm here to see Detective Morrison. I have an appointment."

He checked a sheet in front of him. "Ms. Marquette?" He pronounced it 'Markay,' which was an unusual mispronunciation. 'Market' was the most popular, followed up by 'Markwet.' He was overthinking the year of French he took in high school.

"Marquette," I corrected him with the emphasis on the correct syllable.

He blushed under his tattoos. "Detective Morrison will be right with you."

I calmed myself by playing solitaire on my phone, but I was a bundle of nerves inside. I was about to make a move when my phone rang.

It was Heather. I pushed the answer button. She started talking immediately. "Hey, where are you? I've been worried sick. It looked like you might have been here, but I wasn't sure, and then I started to worry and—"

I interrupted with a snarky attitude in my voice. "Heather. Hold up just a second. I was home on Saturday and Sunday and never saw you once. Where was your note?"

There were a few seconds of silence. She wasn't used to me calling her out on anything. Her tone of voice let me know I had hurt her feelings.

"I didn't even know you were home or when you were coming home. You didn't text me after you left Texas when you got to New Orleans, so I thought you might be staying for a while with your family."

I suddenly felt terrible. "I'm sorry, Heather. You're right. I'm not your mother, and I know you're a big girl. Sometimes I just worry about you. Forgive me for going from zero to . . ."

She already sounded better. "No, you were right. I should have let you know I wouldn't be home for a couple of days. I went to visit friends in Venice Beach on Friday night, and suddenly, before I knew it, many bottles of wine later, it was Sunday. It was fun, but I'm too old for partying." She groaned and then shifted gears. "So, where are you anyway?"

I smiled to myself, relieved that we were back to normal. "I'm in San Francisco. I got home on Saturday and got a call from Detective Morrison yesterday." I figured I'd take on one topic at a time and tell her about my Switzerland call later. "She wanted to compare notes about Annika's murder. I'm a little paranoid that she considers me a suspect, but I'm trying to keep an open mind."

Heather giggled. "Like that's likely, you killing Annika. How about Larry? Now that he's being sent off to the Alps, do you think they'll put out a warrant for his arrest him here?"

Just as I was about to answer, the door opened, and Detective Morrison walked out.

I interrupted Heather and spoke quietly. "Hey, the Detective seems to be ready for me. I'll give you a call later."

She sounded disappointed. "Okay. Let me know how it goes. Bye."

"Bye." Her mood changes made me wonder if there was more going on with her than I was aware of, but I couldn't worry about that right now.

"Miranda, how nice to see you again." The detective approached me and extended her hand. "Thanks for coming up on such short notice."

I forced a smile, trying to look sincere, and spoke as enthusiastically as I could under the circumstances. "Glad to do it. It gave me a chance to take a nice long ride." I pointed to the motorcycle helmet in my other hand. I thought better of leaving it with the bike in this neighborhood where it would probably be sold on the black market before the detective was finished with me.

She smiled. "Well, I'm glad it wasn't all work and no play." She led me to the same conference room we had used last time and the time before. I sat with my back to the two-way mirror again, so whoever was watching on the other side couldn't read my face. She sat across from me.

I wondered as we settled in if she was going to prep me, make me sign an affidavit, or anything, but she just started talking.

"I remembered from our other conversations that you used to be a cop. That, to me, means that you are a trained observer of clues and details that other people might not notice. I'm hoping that maybe you noticed something, maybe something that you didn't even think twice about, that might assist with our case."

I nodded, not wanting to speak too soon or too much. I was still nervous and apprehensive but was trying not to show it. "Where should I start?"

She motioned with her hand. "Back to the beginning, when you were in Switzerland." She had a small notebook in front of her and started to write as soon as I opened my mouth.

140

I settled back into my seat and folded my hands. "I can't remember how much I told you before."

She stared straight into my eyes. "Don't worry about that, Miranda. More is better."

I closed my eyes briefly, putting my thoughts together. "Since my near-death experience, I have been a thrill-seeker. It was a wake-up call that life is too short. After I moved to Malibu, I hired a promoter and publicist to help me develop the first all-female extreme sports team. He had the idea that one or more of the new television networks popping up every day might be interested in doing a reality TV show about us. Have you ever seen 'Keeping up with the Kardashian's?'"

She nodded and rolled her eyes.

I started feeling more comfortable about her motives, and my thoughts were flowing freely. "I know. It's pretty crazy, but it's incredible what people will watch on TV these days and how much advertisers are willing to pay for the millions of viewers who want to live vicariously through these reality show 'stars.' So, I put together this team of financially independent women who had similar interests, wanted to travel, weren't tied down, and quite frankly, were attractive enough to garner a substantial audience if we were able to secure a reality TV show."

I could tell by her glazed look that she was aware of most of this, so I moved on. "Anyway, the four of us took a trip to Aruba to see how we got along on the road. It went great, and we planned out several events, the first being a BASE jumping expedition in Switzerland, which was a warm-up for our first nationally televised event, the street luge race we were involved in here."

Detective Morrison put her hand up. "Before you go on, I know these extreme sports are second nature to you, but what exactly is BASE jumping?"

I was happy that she was interested in my sports. "BASE jumping is the sport of flinging yourself off a stationary object with a parachute on. The word 'BASE' is actually an acronym for Building, Antenna, Span, or Earth, which really means Cliff, but BASC wouldn't have been as good a play on words." I realized this could take all day if I didn't speed it up, so I tried to focus. "Bernie, my publicist, got the idea at the last minute to hire cameramen to document our trip to Switzerland. He figured he could get some airplay on TV, YouTube, or possibly a documentary. As it turned out, we never saw any of Larry's film, and the other cameraman's equipment was confiscated by the police. As far as I know, they still have it."

She perked up. "There was another cameraman with you in Switzerland?"

I strained to recall his name. "Yes, Rocky, something. Um, Blanchard, I think it was. Yes, Rocky Blanchard. He was here filming the luge racing too."

I wasn't sure what it mattered, but she almost seemed more interested in this other cameraman than Larry. "Did you speak to him while you were here?"

"Yes, for a second. We were on a shuttle bus together on the first day of racing. I asked him a few questions about Larry. He had worked with him a couple of times but didn't know him well." I knew there was something else he had said but couldn't remember.

She was furiously taking notes even though I was pretty sure we were being recorded. "Did Rocky say anything else?"

Suddenly I remembered. "Yes, Rocky said that he and Larry had gotten into a bit of a quarrel. As the senior on the job, Rocky had the right to choose where he filmed and chose the top of the mountain. When he told Larry, he got belligerent and told him that he would be working up there. Rocky wasn't happy about it, but he let Larry have his way."

She chewed on the eraser end of a number two pencil. "So how did you and your equipment, like the parachutes, get to the top of the mountain?"

"There was a cable car that ran from Lauterbrunnen to Murren, which was our entry point. Most people buy them after they get overseas and leave them there, but we had planned on doing several other BASE jumps as well as some skydiving, so we bought them at home and took them with us. Similar to skydiving, each jumper is responsible for their equipment, taking care of it, keeping it in good condition, making sure it was ready for the jump, that sort of thing."

It had been a while since I had thought about our trip to Switzerland back when we were all hopeful and ready to take on the world. It seemed so long ago now. I held back tears that I didn't want to show to the detective.

She didn't seem to notice and continued. "Let's talk a little more about the people on the trip?"

I nodded.

"You said that Tara and Larry had developed a relationship."

"Yes."

She scanned the previous pages of her notes. "How did you know?"

I put my finger on my chin and thought for a minute. "I thought I noticed a spark between them just before I jumped, and I was going to ask her about it, but I never got the chance. Then Patricia confirmed it for me when we met up here before the luge race."

She continued writing. "How did Patricia know Larry and Tara had developed a relationship?"

This question and answer session was feeling more like an interrogation than I had expected, and I was starting to sweat ever so slightly under my arms. "Well, I didn't ask, but I assumed that Larry told her when they talked at length in Boston after Tara's funeral. That was when she and Larry got together." With a touch of sarcasm in my voice, I said, "Anything beyond that, you'll have to ask Patricia."

She looked a little surprised at my tone but responded with a slightly sharper tone than previously, "Oh, I plan to. Believe me."

Realizing that the conversation was becoming adversarial, the detective took a few breaths, closed her eyes, and restarted the questioning in a calmer voice. I recognized the tactic, having used it many times when I was on the force.

"Did you ever see either of the cameramen or anyone else for that matter, messing with the parachutes?"

I shifted back into a less defensive posture. "We stored the equipment in a closet in the hotel. It was more like a Bed and Breakfast than a hotel. I didn't realize just how small Lauterbrunnen was until we got there. It was pretty much a train station, the make-shift hotel, a pub, and a few houses. The hotel had an owner and maybe one cleaning person who had access to them, but otherwise, just the team and Larry. I guess Rocky could have accessed them if he knew where they were. We all walked to the cable car from the hotel, except for Rocky, who was filming from the bottom. I'm not sure how he got there."

The detective pursued this line of questioning further. "So, Rocky didn't take a cab from the hotel since he wasn't taking the cable car to the top?"

I glared at her. "This was barely a town. I'm pretty sure they didn't have any cab service." I was getting annoyed, and I'm sure it showed in my voice. "As I said, I don't know how he got there."

She gave me a sympathetic look. "Why don't we take a little break?"

I blushed, realizing that I was getting irritated. "I'm sorry, Detective. Being in a police station always puts me on edge. Is there a water cooler around?"

She smiled. "No problem. Happens all the time. There's water just around the corner."

"Thanks." I stepped out the door as quickly as I could without looking at the detective. I had hoped to keep a grip on my anxiety level, but it seemed the more she questioned me, the more I felt like a suspect. I knew that sounding defensive was the worst thing I could do, yet I felt the resentment bubbling up from inside. I took a couple of deep breaths and slowly drank some water.

After a few minutes, I strolled back the conference room as if nothing had happened. The detective sat taking notes as if I had never left.

"Feeling better?" she asked.

I nodded. "Yes, much. Thanks. I have just a touch of an anxiety disorder that rears its ugly head now and then. So, thanks for noticing that I was uncomfortable."

She smiled warmly. "Okay, I'll try to be quick. I have a few more questions, and any details you can provide would be great. It is standard procedure to get everything I need while you're here. I'd hate to have you take another six-hour trip, to answer more questions that I forgot to ask the first time."

I tried to relax. "Okay, I'm ready."

She stood and approached a whiteboard on the wall. "Now, how long did you stay in Switzerland?"

I continued, "I only stayed one night. Several of them came a day or two earlier to see the sights, but I'm not completely sure who. The plan was to stay two days after the jump and then go to Germany, but after the accident, we all decided to go home."

She started writing on the board, names in boxes, arrows pointing from one person to another. "I'm interested in the relationships between your team and your entourage. If everyone arrived a day or two apart, it doesn't seem like there was much time for relationships to develop. Do you think that Tara knew either of the cameramen before the trip?"

I thought for a moment, not wanting to jump to conclusions. "Unless Tara kept it a secret, she didn't know either cameraman before the trip. She attracted men like flies to flypaper, though."

She turned to look at me after writing my name on the board. "So, you had never met Larry before this trip to Switzerland?"

I shook my head. "No."

Her stare penetrated my eyes. "No?"

I hesitated like a first grader who just gave the wrong answer to 'one plus one.' "No, I had never met him before."

She shuffled some papers in front of her. Some of the pages had been paper clipped. She flipped to the first section. "We've had a chance to speak to Mr. Lechter, and according to him, you two go back quite a way. And I quote 'I'm originally from just south of New Orleans, Chalmette, to be exact. That is just north of Meraux, which was the original stomping ground of Miranda, Marquette. We went to school together. I'm sure that's why she requested me to film their BASE Jumping in Switzerland."

I felt my face getting hot and, no doubt, red. I struggled for words. "Can I see that?" I motioned at the papers in front of Detective Morrison.

She didn't touch them. "I'm afraid not. This is classified police business, plus I have my notes on them." She hesitated as if she expected me to say more.

I found myself staring at the wall behind the detective. I imagined that Larry claiming that he knew me wasn't good news, but I had no idea how bad it was.

The detective was growing tired of the silence. "He claims that you killed your teammates."

I stood up quickly. "What?" I started pacing on my side of the table, sweat running down my back.

Her eyes followed me.

I glanced at her, trying to see if she was bluffing. "You don't believe any of this garbage, do you? You and I both know the lengths a criminal will go to, to get off. This story is ridiculous!

146

I don't know this guy from Adam, and I certainly didn't kill Tara or Annika. That is outrageous!"

She smiled, but I didn't think it was particularly sincere. "Okay, calm down. We're not accusing you of anything. It just seems odd that this guy is so sure he knows you, and you continue to deny it. It just makes me think. I'm sure you'd do the same in my position. Of course, we checked the records of Saint Bernard Parish Schools. I believe that's where you attended. Right?"

I nodded.

"Larry was a year ahead of you. He told us that he was quite fond of you at one time. Claims he even asked you out."

I wracked my brain for the slightest hint of recognition.

She stood and grabbed the papers in front of her. "I'll be right back. It seems like you need a moment." She slipped out the door.

I sat down with my head in my hands, my ears starting to ring. I felt like I was in the twilight zone. This Larry guy didn't even sound remotely familiar, and it wasn't like guys were breaking down my door to ask me out back then. I couldn't keep up with the questions running through my brain. Was I a suspect? Was she playing with my head? Were they going to detain me?

Detective Morrison returned with another detective. I couldn't help but think this wasn't a good sign. They both sat across from me. "This is Detective Johnson," she said.

He nodded in my direction but didn't speak.

She continued, "It's very early in this case, but you have to understand that this new information puts a shroud of doubt over anything you have told us so far, including your written statement. In light of Mr. Lechter's story, we are going to need another statement from you."

She looked me straight in the eye. "And please, Miranda, don't lie to us. We are pretty good at detecting crap. After you provide your statement, we will decide where we go from there."

She left me with the other detective. I wasn't sure why, but there was a reason. He was a post-armed forces looking guy with short brown hair, blue eyes, and a square jaw. Not my type but attractive in his own way. He had some papers in front of him. Referring to them, he said, "First of all, is there anything you would like to change from your original statement?"

I answered immediately. "No. Everything I said was true and correct."

He produced several blank pages. "We will append your statement, then, with your response to the statements made by Mr. Lechter. Do you mind if I use a tape recorder?"

"Of course not." I tried to sound confident, but it was a challenge. Why didn't I go with my gut and insist upon an attorney? Granted, I didn't do anything, but I sure felt like I had, and more importantly, it seemed like they are assuming that I was hiding something. This, after I rode six hours to share what I wasn't even legally compelled to provide.

He turned on the tape recorder. "Ms. Marquette, could you please respond to the allegations provided to you by Detective Morrison from Mr. Lechter's statement."

I spoke slowly and clearly, trying to sound unemotional but truthful. "I do not know Mr. Lechter other than the fact that he was assigned to film my team in Switzerland by an LA agency. I have never met him in the past and never had the opportunity to speak with Mr. Lechter. He is either gravely mistaken or a liar."

Johnson spoke matter-of-factly. "Is that your complete statement?"

"Yes."

He turned off the recorder. He stood and appeared like he was going to leave and then stopped. He leaned on the table and spoke. "I don't know you at all, but you seem like a nice person. Let me tell you one thing off the record. I'm pretty sure this guy does know you from the past, maybe even junior high. He told me a story about where he asked you to a dance in front of a couple of your friends. You laughed in his face and called him 'Larry Leper' and, evidently, that name has stuck with him his whole life. It was quite traumatic for him, and he holds quite a grudge against you. That's the only reason we aren't holding you right now. We suspect he may be killing your team-mates to get back at you."

"Why didn't Detective Morrison tell me that?" I asked.

"She wanted to hear your statement first. She wants to believe you, but this complicates our case. We understand that it may be hard to remember an incident dating back to junior high, especially since it was likely more meaningful to him than it was to you. On the other hand, it's certainly plausible that you could have known him, which the defense will certainly exploit." He headed toward the door again. "Detective Morrison should be back with you momentarily."

I caught his attention before he made it out the door. "Detective Johnson, thanks for leveling with me."

He smiled a put his finger to his lips. "Remember, loose lips sink ships."

I had no reason to rat him out to Detective Morrison, but he had no way of knowing that. I wondered if he regretted sharing with me. I put that thought out of my mind, stood and paced the room. I felt like my head would explode as I tried to process everything I had heard within the last fifteen minutes. My anxiety was at a fever pitch, and I took slow even breaths to slow my pulse down.

I understood now why Detective Morrison had asked me back here. This wasn't something she could do on the phone. I wasn't even sure they hadn't been planning on arresting me as an accessory, depending on how I responded to their questions.

I sat down and forced myself to focus on junior high. You would think being asked out for the first time would have been memorable, but I was drawing a complete blank. I didn't even remember a Larry Lechter or Leper for that matter, and there were only five hundred students in our high school. I realize that I was very self-absorbed, but how could I have ruined this guy's life and not even remember who he was?

Detective Morrison came back a couple of minutes later. She seemed to have perked up. "Sorry for all this in and out. We just got Mr. Lechter's statement moments before you arrived, since he'll be leaving the country soon and we may not get another opportunity. The detective and I were trying to process the information pretty much at the same time you were. For now, I'm going with my gut and believing you. If you set this guy up and then turned him in, I guess I'll pay the price for that later. And I guess you will too." She smiled, but I didn't know why.

I pondered standing, getting my helmet and getting ready to go but didn't want to assume she was done. "Is there anything else you need from me?" I tried to sound sincere but felt a bit sarcastic.

She spread her hands in a "we'll see" manner. "Well, I can't very well tell you to stay in town since you don't live here, but I strongly suggest you stay in close touch with us. We will do the same if we get any breaks in the case."

I stood up and shook her hand. "It was good to see you again." I started to walk out and stopped. "I don't know if you really believe me or not, but I had nothing to do with the deaths of either Tara or Annika. They were my friends and teammates. My gut says Larry's responsible for both, but if I should find out otherwise, you'll be the first to know."

She grasped both my hands in hers. "Keep in touch, Miranda. I'd rather have you on my team than on the other side for sure."

Chapter 19

I headed back through the nearly empty lobby and out the front door. In this neighborhood, I was relieved to see my motorcycle hadn't been stolen or taken apart. I was about to strap my helmet on when my cell phone rang. I didn't recognize the number, but I took a chance that it wasn't a random marketing call.

"Miranda Marquette, can I help you?" I figured I'd be formal in case it was a business call. Sometimes Heather gave my cell number out if there was something I needed to handle.

"So, there you are," from the phone came a male voice that I didn't recognize.

I responded coolly. "I'm sorry. Do I know you?" I held my finger over the hang-up button.

He laughed and eased my building tension. "This is Jason Wall. Sorry, I thought you might recognize my voice, but that didn't happen. Maybe I should have sung."

I wanted to eat my words. "Jason, I'm so sorry. It's nice to hear from you. I'm glad you got my message."

"Are you in Malibu? Is everything okay, or was it just a social call?" He sounded a little out of breath and very concerned about me. It felt good.

I hoped he'd be happy with my response. "Nope, I'm in your neck of the woods. San Francisco right now. But I am about to head south."

He hesitated, sounding a little unsure of himself. "How about lunch before you head back?"

I couldn't think of a reason not to; in fact, I was concerned I sounded a little too enthusiastic when I responded, "Sure! Where do you want to meet?"

He hesitated briefly. "How about BJ's Brew House on De Anza Boulevard right off the 280?"

151

"Sounds perfect. I can be there in an hour or so depending on traffic."

"Great! See you then." I was relieved to hear the excitement in his voice, but then almost immediately felt sick to my stomach.

I strapped on my three-quarter helmet and let my ponytail trail behind me. The ride down was unusually smooth with just a couple back-ups here and there, which were solved by lane-splitting. I arrived about fifteen minutes ahead of schedule, which gave me a moment to collect myself, take out the hairband holding my ponytail in place and brush my helmet hair so it hung down to my shoulders. That was a better look for me and didn't make my facial features seem so severe, and the shadows did an adequate job of hiding the hairline scars across my face. I rushed into the ladies' room, and I dabbed on what little make-up I usually wore. I checked myself in the mirror over the sink and decided I passed.

Just as I was strolling out the door to see if my 'date' had arrived, a blue Chevy Silverado pulled into the nearly empty parking lot. Three o'clock was a great time to get a table since it was after the brunch crowd and before dinner. Jason looked just as I remembered him, wearing faded jeans, a classic flannel shirt, and cowboy boots. He didn't look Californian at all, which was fine with me. I had had it up to my ears with guys who couldn't stop looking at themselves in the mirror as they passed one. Back in San Francisco, he didn't strike me as one of those, but I'd be paying closer attention now that I had a personal interest.

We walked silently side by side as we approached the restaurant, and I was starting one of my negative inner dialogs. "Oh my God, he's having regrets. He hates me. Why can't I think of something to say?" Sweat ran down my back, and I concentrated hard on turning my internal conversation around.

The hostess brought us to a table near a window overlooking Apple Headquarters. I hadn't ever seen it from this angle. It was huge. As I stared out the window, I could feel his eyes on me. "What?" I laughed nervously, sounding like the Valley Girl I tried so hard not to be.

"Can I say something?" Lines crossed his forehead.

"Sure," I replied, and he held my gaze.

He chose his words carefully. "Other than a couple of brief encounters, we don't really know one another, right?"

I nodded with a growing pit in my stomach.

"We appear to be an eligible bachelor and bachelorette." He rolled his eyes at the corny phrase but continued. "As far as I can tell, we find each other attractive and have enjoyed the limited time that we've spent together, right?"

I motioned him to keep going. "Okay, Cowboy, what's your point?" My goal of controlling the conversation had failed miserably.

He was on a roll and was no longer waiting for me to respond. "I've tended to move things along fast in relationships. They get hot too soon, then they crash and burn." He bit his lip, gazing over my shoulder before he continued.

I took the opportunity to interrupt. "At least you crash and burn. My relationships have tended to flash and fizzle. I would kill for crash and burn! At least I'd know I was alive."

"Be careful what you wish for. I don't really recommend it. Anyway, without sounding lame, I was wondering if we can be friends. Maybe it will turn into something after that, but I'm probably my best at the friend stage right now." He turned his eyes away when I met his stare.

I immediately internally scolded myself for moving too fast and coming on too strong. I had already scared him away.

We shifted our attention to the curvy forty-something waitress who brought out ice water, paper placemats, and silverware. She winked at Jason. "What can I get you, dear?"

He ordered a burger and fries.

Her expression turned sour as she addressed me between gum chews. "You?"

I had no idea what was on the menu, so I improvised. "How about a salad with vinaigrette?"

She tapped her pencil impatiently on her pad. "Italian okay?"

I glared at her and wondered why Jason wasn't doing anything to intervene. "Fine."

Oblivious that I had been mistreated, he continued. "Now, where were we?"

I winced as I bit the inside of my cheek. "I'm sorry if I gave you the impression that I'm desperate." He had hit a nerve, and I wasn't even sure which one.

He looked surprised and troubled. "Whoa! Hey, I think I misspoke there. I wasn't saying anything about you at all. My last few relationships haven't ended well, and I'm just saying I'm probably not relationship material right now."

I cringed, having jumped down his throat two sentences into our conversation. "I'm sorry. I'm a little bit sensitive right now. Starting as friends would be great," I lied.

He seemed intent on changing the subject, probably afraid my head would explode if we continued with relationship talk. "So, what brings you to this part of the world so soon after your races?"

I was happy to change the subject too. "I was at the police station. I wasn't sure if you had heard about my teammate's death."

He nodded and blushed slightly. "I wasn't really sure what to say, so I didn't bring it up. Sorry."

I was coping a little better than I had been earlier, but still mourning to the point that I couldn't bring myself to look him in the eye. "That's fine. I'm okay." I hesitated, my words not coming together. I finally met his eyes and then looked away, surprised at how attractive he was now that he had no interest in

154

me. I'd have to mention that to my therapist. He seemed to be waiting for me to say something else.

"I was in San Francisco, providing the police with a statement. I left there feeling like a suspect."

He did a double take. "You? That's ridiculous! Why would you kill your teammate?"

I was having a hard time hiding my concern, unaware that I was shredding my napkin until I noticed the pile of white paper in front of me. "I must have one of those guilty faces." I grimaced and crossed my eyes, trying to lighten the moment.

He smiled. "Well, if it makes you feel any better, I know you didn't do it."

We sat in silence for a minute; then I put my hand on the table near to his. "Sorry, Jason. I'm a little out of practice having an intelligent conversation with a man."

He nodded and smiled but didn't respond.

The waitress brought our food without comment, and we ate in silence for a few minutes and spent the rest of the meal struggling to keep the conversation going. I was surprised when I looked at my watch to see it was 4:30. It seemed like we'd been here for eight hours. "Oh, my God. I can't believe it's this late already. I have got to get on the road."

He looked disappointed. "So, our first date is over so soon?"

I blushed at the mention of the "d" word. "I guess so."

He picked up the check, which I thought was a nice touch, then walked me to my bike. He briefly hugged me like I was his great aunt.

I laughed as I got my helmet on. "I guess you were serious about this friend thing."

He appeared about to say something, but I hit the gas and was gone. I figured I might as well leave him wanting more.

Chapter 20

It was nearly 10 p.m. when I pulled into the driveway. I was happy that there were still lights on, and I could see Heather sitting at the kitchen counter. I unlocked the door and walked in. "Are you still working?"

She looked up. "Yes, I've been answering emails all evening. I'm not sure what is up with people, but suddenly everyone wants cosmetic surgery."

I moved to the couch with the cup of coffee she poured me when she got her own. I smiled at my fortune that the business was booming.

She inquired with an air of distraction, "So, how was your trip?"

I stared at my coffee cup. "Do you really want to hear about it. You seem kind of busy."

She took that as her cue to get away from her computer screen and she sat on the edge of the sectional facing me directly. "Start at the beginning."

So much had happened in the last week, I hardly knew where to start. "Okay, Texas was a surprise. Well, not completely. The press was brutal. Evidently, Patricia had spoken to them and blamed me for everything, including Annika's death."

Heather bit her lip. "How awful!"

I continued, "Thankfully, Bernie saved me from a confrontation with them and got me inside before I did too much damage. Before I entered the viewing room, I saw Patricia sitting alone in the chapel, so I figured I'd try to bury the hatchet with her. Well, she was having none of that. If anything, she seemed angrier and more resentful than she had before we left San Francisco."

Heather, always the positive one, said, "Well, at least you know where she stands."

I snorted. "You could say that! There was a pleasant surprise. Annika's parents were extremely gracious and had nothing but nice things to say to me. Her mother told me that Annika had been very depressed before she joined the team, and she credited me for bringing her back to her former self."

She met my stare, "That must have felt good after your experience with Tara's parents."

I nodded. "It really did. I was so glad I decided to go. So, then I decided to go to New Orleans on the spur of the moment. I figured I was so close; I should see my family." I started to tear up, remembering my mother's news. I tried to speak but got choked up. "My mom has breast cancer."

She came over and put her arms around my shoulders. I couldn't talk at all for a while, but I finally caught my breath. Heather just kept whispering, "It's okay, it's okay, it's okay," over and over again, and I finally started to believe her.

I sat up and tried to pull myself together. "She's stage three. I'd be totally freaking out if I were her. But she seemed to be the most peaceful that I had ever seen her. She wasn't talking just to fill space. She even let Tom get a word in edgewise a couple of times. It made me realize just how much I love her and miss her. She was like the mom I used to have before our world came tumbling down when my dad left." I smiled wistfully. "She's starting treatment next week, and the doctors are cautiously optimistic about her prognosis."

Heather nodded. "That's great to hear. I hope you decide to see her more often. I know she drives you crazy sometimes, but you only have one mother."

I started to tear up again but forced them back. "I got home on Friday night, and you were nowhere to be found! I guess you'll have to give me the rundown of what's up with you after I'm done."

She grinned sheepishly. "I told you on the phone, a wild partying weekend. I'm getting too old for those for sure"

I gave her a sidelong glance, but she wasn't giving anything else away. "So, as I told you on the phone, I got the call from Detective Morrison yesterday and decided to ride up there today. Remember how I was a little paranoid? Well, it turns out that just because you're paranoid, it doesn't mean they're not out to get you."

Heather scrunched up her face. "Uh-oh. What does that mean?"

I continued, "Well, it started okay. The detective asked me a bunch of questions about Switzerland and the cameramen, both of them for some reason. Then more specifically about Larry. It was all going okay, I thought, then she asked me if I had known Larry before Switzerland. I, of course, said that I didn't. Then she got an odd look on her face and told me that Larry said that we did know one another and that I had killed Tara and Annika."

Heather looked like I had just woken her up from a nightmare. "What? You've got to be kidding me? What did you say?"

I tried to keep calm, but I still couldn't believe it either. "I said that I had never met Larry before. At that point, Detective Morrison left the room, and a couple of minutes later, she returned with another Detective. Johnson is a really ex-military looking guy. So she said that he's going to take my statement and left me with him."

Heather protested. "You already gave her your statement."

"Yeah, I know, but they were thinking I was going to change it based on their revelation. But I told him the same thing I told her. So, here's the weird thing. He stood up and was packing up to leave, and he sat back down at the conference table next to me. He seemed concerned about me and told me he wanted to fill me in. He then told me that Larry told them that he grew up in Meraux and knew me in school."

She started pacing around the living room. "No way!"

I grimaced. "Wait, it gets worse. According to Larry, he asked me out in Junior High and, not only did I say 'No,' but I called him 'Larry Leper,' causing him extreme embarrassment and anguish in front of his friends. And, to make matters worse, the name stuck with him. He's never gotten over it."

Heather shook her head. "Kids can be so cruel."

I nodded, "Yeah, including me."

"So, do you remember him?" She stopped pacing and sat next to me.

I shook my head. "No, I don't. I've wracked my brain even to remember anyone asking me out in junior high, but I've got nothing."

Heather thought for a minute. "Maybe this works in your favor. If this Larry guy holds a grudge over you, doesn't that make him a non-credible witness, especially if he's accusing you of being a murderess? It sounds to me like he doesn't want to go down alone, so he's grasping at straws. But I wonder if he has any eyewitnesses to your 'dis' of him back in the day."

I felt deflated despite Heather's attempt to cheer me up. "He probably does or can pay one off."

She continued, "But, wait a minute, so what was the point of giving you all this information? Do you think they thought you'd break down and confess?"

I thought for a minute. "God, I don't know Heather. I was so paranoid by that point, if Detective Morrison had come back with a uniformed cop wielding handcuffs, I would have just put my arms behind my back. I was just happy to get out of there with my freedom. I figured I'd make sense of it later, but I haven't been able to, despite a six-hour ride back. I'm baffled."

Heather put a finger to her lips. "I hate to say it because it always means more work for me, but it looks like you're going to have to put on your amateur detective hat again."

I chuckled. "Don't even say that. The last time I tried that, I almost did end up in prison for good."

"Oh, don't be so modest, you cracked that case." She shifted in her seat, and her voice got quiet. "You're pretty sure this Larry guy killed Annika, right? You wouldn't have to find a lot of other witnesses to testify?"

I mumbled under my breath. "I don't know what I think anymore."

She chose to change the subject. "So, did anything else interesting happen while you were up there?"

I rolled my eyes. "Well, one little thing?"

She stared me down. "Dish girl! This sounds like it might be good."

"Well, it could have been, but it fizzled out before it got started."

She looked at me and motioned with her hand for me to continue. "And?"

I continued, "Well, I kind of called that Jason guy's office and left a voice mail just before Detective Morrison called. You know the guy I met in San Francisco?"

She clapped her hands. "Wow, that was unusually bold of you."

"So, anyway, he called me back right after I left the station, and we decided to get together for lunch."

She was on the edge of her seat.

"To make a long story short, we went to lunch, and it was pretty awkward. The bottom line, he told me he wasn't relationship material and wanted to be friends. I was kind of embarrassed like he thought I was desperate, so I cut the lunch short and took off on my motorcycle without looking back."

She cringed. "Maybe that was premature. With a little patience on your part, it could grow into something more."

I brushed her off with a wave of my hand. "It's not meant to be, at least not at this point in our lives. I still have his number, so maybe I'll call him again someday."

160

Suddenly exhausted from my very trying day, I said, "I'm going to bed. Hopefully, things will seem better in the morning." I had planned on telling her I would probably be going to Switzerland sooner than later, but tomorrow seemed like a better day for it.

Chapter 21

I awoke earlier than I had planned when my vibrating phone finally annoyed me awake at seven-thirty. I stared at the iPhone, wishing it to go to voicemail, but it stopped ringing. I put my head down, and it started again, so I figured it must be urgent. I picked up the phone and glanced at the screen. I had four missed calls, all from Thun, Switzerland.

There was a familiar voice on the other end through some static. "Miranda Marquette, please?"

I immediately sat up so I wouldn't sound drowsy. "Gretchen! I didn't expect to hear from you so soon." I tried to remember what day it was, and I determined it was only Tuesday. "What time is it there anyway?"

I could tell she was smiling, and I was happy we had developed a good rapport in such a short time. "It's 4:30, and I'm leaving after this call, so let's make it fast." Gretchen giggled. She paused, and I could tell she was leading up to something.

"I have good and bad news. The good news is that things are progressing much faster than we expected. The judges have already interviewed the defendant and defense witnesses, and they are ready for the prosecution. There are a couple of locals that won't take long, and then we need you. That's the bad news. We need you out here as soon as you can get here."

I had figured it wasn't a social call, but I thought maybe next week or the week after. I regretted not giving Heather a heads up about having to travel again so soon, but she seemed to roll with the changes. At times, it seemed like she was happier without me around, but maybe it was just my insecurities coming through. I figured I might as well cut to the chase. "So, when you say, 'soon,' you mean . . ."

"Tomorrow."

There was total silence as I processed, and she, probably, held her breath. Finally, I said, "I need to testify tomorrow? I don't think there is a plane fast enough to make that happen."

She exhaled loudly. "No, you just need to arrive tomorrow so that you can testify Thursday morning."

I calculated the nine-hour time difference and the eleven-hour flight in my head, and with any luck, I could catch a plane this evening, that would get me there by late afternoon tomorrow. Things seemed to be moving so fast; I took a couple of deep breaths to slow my heart rate down. I finally forced out the words.

"Oh my God, I have to get moving if I'm going to make that. I need to get plane tickets, pack, book a train, book a hotel, and figure out just where I'm going when I get there."

She picked up on my panic. "Miranda, hold on. Yes, you need to pack. We will take care of the rest. My Administrative Assistant will call you with all the details. Her name is Renate, and she's very efficient. She will coordinate everything from your front door to here in Thun, and I'll meet you at the train station here."

With her assistance, my heart rate was nearly back to normal when we both hung up. Within minutes Renate had called me with all the details including a limo to the airport, a first-class seat on a non-stop flight to Zurich on Swissair, leaving LAX at 7:20 p.m. today and arriving at 3:15 p.m. tomorrow. By 8:30, I was packed, showered, dressed, made up, and ready for my day and my week.

I hadn't heard a peep from Heather, and without opening her bedroom door, it was hard to determine if she was still here, went out last night and never came back, or left early this morning. Heather had become far more evasive and mysterious than she had been when she first moved in. I wasn't sure if she had met somebody, was sick of living with me, or was plotting to take over the world with her homeless ex-friends living on Venice Beach.

With everything that was going on, I hadn't paid attention to the finances in a couple of months. Occasionally I checked the bank balance to make sure it was around where it had been the last time I checked it, but it would be smart of me to regain control when I returned from Switzerland. I figured Heather couldn't do too much damage while I was away, even if she had hooked up with some shave-headed Buddhist, tattooed from head to toe with vipers and dragons.

"You're letting your imagination run wild," I whispered to myself as I tried to figure out how to blow the next five hours. I didn't want to work because I was so out of touch. I figured I'd let Heather take care of it. On the coffee table was the novel my ex-boyfriend, Paul, finally got published. I had avoided reading it so far, assuming there would be some character roughly based on me, and I'd have to spend the next week trying to figure out if I was right or if I was projecting something on him that he never felt for me.

Three hours into it, I had identified no less than five characters I was convinced were at least loosely based on me. It was exhausting, so I stopped reading a couple of hours before my limo was due. Heather never appeared, so I assumed she never came home last night. Since this was out of character, I was worried about her. I thought she could take care of herself, but I still worried. There were signs that things were changing with her and between us, and I told myself that this was a normal part of the evolution of our relationship. In short, the honeymoon was over.

I couldn't shake a feeling of uneasiness as I prepared to leave. I did a quick check of the bank accounts and the company's customer service email account and found nothing out of the ordinary. "Don't get paranoid," I admonished myself. "Heather's just going through something."

I wrote an extended note and left it on the counter, explaining that I would be out of town, in Switzerland, for the next few days or up to a week. I told her to contact Bernie if she had any issues since my time zone would be nine hours later than hers. Even as I wrote, it felt oddly impersonal compared to what I would have written to her a month ago. I reminded myself to talk to my therapist about these feelings when I came home.

~*~

As luck would have it, it took less than an hour for the limo to get to The Tom Bradley Terminal. TSA PreCheck was a blessing except that I breezed through security in five minutes. I nursed a glass of cabernet in the first-class lounge since I had at least two hours before boarding. It was feast or famine at the airport. I was either ripping off my heels to make better time, racing with time and sprinting on-board, out of breath and dripping with sweat or sitting around watching people. The latter was often scarier.

The last thing I did was to shove Paul's book into my bag as I was walking out the door. I figured that if I could stop trying to interpret his character's personality and how they related to me, it might be an entertaining read. He was an excellent writer, much better than when he first started several years ago. Professional editing and publishing had a way of making an author a better writer, sometimes kicking and screaming.

When they announced the boarding of our Swissair flight, tears were streaming down my face as I read a very familiar break-up scene which, at the time, I thought had not affected him at all.

When I looked up from the book to figure out my next move, a couple tables from me, I noticed a quirky-looking, fortyish blonde wearing a black leather pants and a two thousand dollar Saint Laurent white satin tie blouse that would have required a report to the fashion police on nearly anyone else, but seemed to work on her. She was finishing off a drink definitely stronger than my wine.

Just as I standing to catch my plane, she caught my eye and sauntered over to my table. She stuck out her hand. "Margo," she hesitated as if she were trying to remember her last name. "Prentice. I guess I have to get used to using my maiden name again. I'm headed to the Alps to forget husband number five. How about you?"

We walked to our gate and as we talked. I wasn't sure how much detail I wanted to get into. She looked like the type who could talk my ear off for the entire eleven-hour flight and I was planning on sleeping most of the way, but I figured the odds of us sitting together were pretty slim since the first-class lounge was virtually empty.

I rolled my eyes. "Nothing as exciting as you're going to do. I'm going to court."

Margo grabbed my shoulders affectionately. "Don't tell me you're divorcing a Swiss prince, and they were making you travel back to his homeland to grant you the divorce? That's what happened to me with husband number three."

While I had absolutely no reason to believe this woman, for some reason, I did. "No, nothing like that. It's a murder trial."

She looked at me with disbelief. "No way! That's how I got rid of husband number one. Just cry a lot and tell them he hit you. That's how I got off." She rolled her eyes as if being accused of murdering her husband was a dreadful inconvenience.

I couldn't tell when this woman was serious, but she looked stone-cold serious, then burst into spontaneous laughter. Then she looked around suspiciously and whispered. "At least I can't say that publicly. It was a terrible accident." She winked.

She studied my face, and I become immediately self-conscious about my scars. We were next to enter the plane, so she stopped talking just long enough for me to take a couple of deep breaths. I was somewhat relieved when she sat across the aisle from me as opposed to in the next seat. The idea of having her in my personal space for eleven hours was enough to raise my anxiety level twenty points.

Just when I thought I was home free, a middle-aged guy started up the aisle. I prayed, crossed myself, and held my breath. Old childhood habits die hard. At this point, I wasn't even sure if there was a God, but I figured I needed all the help I could get. At first, it seemed to have worked; his seat was the window seat next to Margo. I pretended not to notice as he peppered her with questions with a heavy German accent. She smiled politely as she responded, but then gave the international sign of a woman in distress: she pushed up her sunglasses with her middle finger. She then turned toward me, making sure we made eye contact, and mouthed, "Help!"

Having been in that situation more times than I care to remember, I responded immediately loudly enough for 'Herr Sprecher' to hear, "Margo, I know you're superstitious about riding on the right side of a plane. Would you like to join me over on this side?"

She nearly jumped out of her seat and wasted no time climbing over me to claim the window seat. She whispered, "Thank you, thank you, thank you, thank you, thank you."

Margo and I drank wine. We talked. We laughed. We cried. We slept. Then we did it all over again. By the time we landed in Zurich, I felt like I had known her my whole life. We hugged like we were long lost sisters after we found our suitcases in baggage claim, knowing that she was heading south to Lucerne, and I was headed west to Bern and on to Thun. We had become so close during that eleven hours, we had even tried to plan some time together while we were in Switzerland, but the logistics weren't coming together, so we settled on our original plans.

Her train came before mine did, so I watched her board while she waved and yelled back to me, "Long Beach is not that far from Malibu, so you aren't rid of me by a long shot."

167

I blew her a kiss, waved, and headed off to my track, hoping the rest of my journey went as smoothly. Remembering that I would probably run into Patricia while I was here, made me less optimistic.

Chapter 22

I was traveling on SBB, the national Swiss rail line. There seemed to be varying opinions online, whether SBB or DB, the German equivalent, was a better rail system. Travel plans from the airport, through Bern and on to Thun, including my hotel, had been made by Gretchen or her staff, so I just settled in, assuming they knew what they were doing.

I had forgotten how beautiful Switzerland was with its snow-capped mountain views, lush green landscapes, and unmistakable Swiss architecture. I spent most of my time on the one-hour train ride taking in the sights and thinking as little as possible. After my whirlwind flight with Margo, I hadn't had any time to obsess about my meeting with the panel of judges tomorrow, and that was probably for the best.

I closed my eyes briefly, or what I thought would be briefly, but when I opened them, we were pulling into the Thun train station. While I had never been there, the mountains, the Thunersee, or Lake Thun as the American tourists like to call it, and the castles, were unmistakable from pictures I had seen on Trip Advisor. It was like a storybook Alpen Stadt.

What I never expected, though, was the vibrancy of Thun. There were cars and people everywhere, clogging the cobblestone streets and narrow bridges. Granted, it was precisely 5 p.m. when we pulled in, but my feeling was due to more than the traffic and crowds, there was a positive energy I didn't feel in LA. It was hard to put my finger on the feeling, but the people I watched seemed to have a purpose. So often in cities in the U.S., people seemed to wander aimlessly, and if they displayed any energy, it was fueled more by desperation than anything good.

Despite there only being 44,000 residents in Thun, it had a feel of cities much larger, although it was also very walkable and, from what I had read, safe at all hours.

I was excited to explore the old city, which was where I was staying, and craned my neck to see out the windows as I followed my fellow passengers down the middle aisle and off the train. As I disembarked, Gretchen was standing about ten feet from the door, holding a sign that said, "Miranda Marquette." She looked just like she sounded, mid-thirties, long brunette braids running down her back, a welcoming smile, and a twinkle in her eye.

She dropped the sign and ran to me as soon as I stepped off the train. I assumed she was a hugger due to the speed with which she approached me with her arms flung open. After our embrace, she held my shoulders at arm's length and nearly burst with excitement. "Miranda! Thank God for the internet so I could see what you looked like before you arrived. From what I could glean on you, you've had a couple of exciting years."

I laughed. "You probably don't know the half of it, but I'm a survivor. I got that from my Grandpapa." I nodded briefly toward heaven as I usually do when I speak of him.

She grabbed my suitcase, leading the way, leaving me with just my carry-on. She glanced back to make sure I was keeping up. "The Hotel Freienhof is just around the rotary and across the bridge." Gretchen didn't do anything slowly. She walked fast and talked fast. I almost had to break into a jog to keep up when she finally noticed me fading further and further back. "I'm so sorry! I just want to get you settled in as quickly as I can," she yelled back in my direction.

I was only slightly out of breath. "I'm fine. How far did you say it was?"

She came to a stop as we approached a rotary called the Maulbeerkreisel. Traffic was constant, coming and going from the three streets that intersected the traffic circle. Just when it looked like we'd never get a chance to cross, she crossed in a Frogger-like move, nearly getting run over as she reached a safe lily pad. It took me another five minutes to cross while she encouraged me to go for it, and I did, nearly getting run over myself.

By the time we walked across the bridge and to the hotel, which was only a couple of blocks, I felt like I had run a marathon. The eleven-hour flight, and nine-hour time change probably had something to do with it. I had spent the night in my clothes, intermittently sleeping, talking, and drinking with Margo, but it felt like I had been wearing them for a couple of days, at least.

As we approached the grand front entrance to the hotel, she asked hopefully, "Would you like to get dinner with me somewhere? There are tons of restaurants and bars within walking distance."

As much fun as Gretchen seemed to be, I wanted nothing more than to check into the hotel, get cleaned up, and have some *me* time. I hoped I didn't hurt her feelings when I responded. "I think I'm going to take a shower and relax a little. It's been a long day."

Thankfully, she didn't take offense. "I figured, but I didn't want to desert you in a strange place." She gave me directions to the courthouse and started down the walkway toward the street. "I'll meet you on the steps out front on Scheibenstrasse at ten tomorrow morning," she yelled back to me without turning around.

I wasn't sure if I should be offended that she didn't hug me good-bye, but that may have had something to do with the fact that I needed a shower. Badly.

As I approached the entrance of the building that appeared to have been built in the seventeenth or eighteenth century, I never expected an ultra-modern lobby with a curved gray marble front desk, a comfortable-looking seating area with black leather couches and chairs, ceramic tile floors and recessed lighting. I felt like I had been transported to one of the newer hotels in LA or San Francisco.

Heidi, the twenty-something woman at the front desk, spoke with a moderate German accent and served me as if I was the only other person on earth. I wished that some of the hotels I had stayed at recently in the US would come here for training. Heidi insisted that a bellman carry my bags upstairs and recommended that I not provide a tip unless his service was excellent. She explained, "This is the only way we can guarantee outstanding service every time."

For the pleasure of not having to drag my bags another hundred feet to my room, I tipped him fifty dollars. He questioned whether I realized that this was a fifty and not a ten or twenty, and I assured him it was well worth it to me. He seemed elated as he exited the room, which made me feel like it had been worthwhile despite the front desk clerk's warning.

Seasoned travelers warn against unpacking your bags when staying in a hotel room. I usually concurred, but considering I was likely to be here a week or more, the idea of living out of a suitcase was not at all appealing. I would do it for a night or two like I had in San Francisco, but I never felt quite settled, though, if I didn't hang up my blouses, dresses, and skirts or put my jammies and underwear in a dresser drawer. I had learned the telltale signs of bedbugs years ago: thin red lines on the walls or elsewhere, bugs or bug parts in or near the bed, and worst of all, unexpected movement on the sheets when you pull the covers back. I hadn't seen one in years, but I still remember the first time, and it makes my skill crawl.

After carefully examining the room, I unpacked and laid down on the bed. It was clear from how exhausted I felt, that if I stayed where I was, I would be asleep in a matter of minutes. It would be hard to beat jetlag if I fell asleep for the night at 6 p.m. I'd probably wake up alert and ready to go at 3 a.m., which wouldn't be good at all.

I searched Google Maps for someplace nearby to grab a bite to eat. The two-level outdoor bar and restaurant off the hotel lobby looked great, but I wanted to save that for another day, maybe with Gretchen or Patricia, depending on whether or not she liked me this week.

I took a right after exiting the hotel through the main entrance. I assumed the street, Freienhofgasse, which crossed over to the other side of the Aare River, was named after the hotel, but it may have been vice versa. I took an immediate left on Obere Haubtgasse and found the perfect spot for a drink and a bite to eat at the El Camino Cafe Bar. It almost felt like I was at the Santa Monica pier with the large Ferris wheel within fifty feet of the entrance.

More a bar than a cafe, the polished mahogany bar sported five Western European beers on draught and Guinness, which was socially acceptable anywhere. The barstools were full of locals, mostly men, and mostly around my age. After I was quickly seated at a small table on the wall across from the bar, I ordered a Hopfenperle, the only beer in the place brewed in Switzerland, according to my waiter, Dieter. After my first swig, I regretted not ordering my typical Cabernet. The beer was overly carbonated, and the taste was bland and boring.

I must have groaned out loud at my first taste because, Dieter, probably working his way through college on tips, nearly ran back to the table to make sure he hadn't offended my pallet in some way.

I smiled at his attentive service. "Oh no, it's fine, I'm sure. I'm just not used to these stronger European beers. Can I just have some red wine? Cabernet if you have it?"

He swept my beer glass off the table and returned with an excellent glass of Bordeaux Cabernet, which was far more satisfying than the lager, even if the French, in my opinion, could never match a California Cab. Surprisingly, California wine generally had more alcohol than the Bordeaux and a deeper flavor.

I looked up from my wine to see a handsome Italian thirty-something standing in front of my table. "May I join you?" He hesitated, apparently waiting for me to give him my name.

I extended my hand to signal that he was welcome to sit down. "Miranda."

He took my fingers in his and kissed my hand. "Such a beautiful name for such a beautiful woman." He sat gracefully across from me. "I am Françesco."

Despite the corny line that I was sure he used on every available woman that walked into the place, I was flattered. I could feel my face grow warm, and I knew I was blushing. Rather than drawing attention to my reaction, he continued. "I could not stop looking at you from the bar."

I protested, "But the barstools all face the other way."

He pointed toward the bar. "You forget the mirror, my love."

He was right, of course. The mirror behind the bar allowed the patrons sitting at the bar to get a view of anyone at a table.

He had obviously done this before, but I was enjoying every second or his adoration. "Whatever has brought such a beautiful creature to our humble town, and how can we convince you to stay?" He held both of my hands in his.

I couldn't help but smile at the feeling that I had been transformed onto a 40's movie set, and I was Lana Turner wearing only a trench coat and high heels. "It's mostly business with a little bit of pleasure, then more business."

He smiled with delight. "Even the smallest amount of pleasure will be enough."

As fun as it was leading this guy on, I realized that all good things had to come to an end, and I didn't want this to take a turn I couldn't retreat from. I looked him straight in the eye. "Françesco, you have no idea how flattered I am, but I'm here to

174

give my statement to the court and to attend a trial, so I don't think I would be much fun."

He stared at me with disbelief. "The murder trial? That's all anyone has been talking about for weeks. Are you here for the prosecution or the defense?"

I was taken aback by where the conversation was headed even though I had brought it up. I figured the townspeople wouldn't even know or care about it. The murder took place a few towns away, but Thun was the official court in the Canton of Bern, which is why it was happening here. Because I hadn't encountered the press when I disembarked the train, I figured this trial wasn't even news in these parts. "I'd rather not go into that kind of detail right now if you don't mind."

He stared at me blankly as if he were at a loss for words. Finally, he said, "Well, if you change your mind, you know where to find me." He stood up and walked back to his stool at the bar and sat down.

I wasn't sure whether to laugh or cry when another young man from the bar approached me. By the time I had been there two hours and nursed three glasses of wine, five men had sat across from me at my table. Each had been charming in their own way, and at a different time or place in my life, I might have been convinced to spend a lost weekend with any one of them. But I had business to attend to, and I needed to be sharp for my inquisition.

As I stood to walk out, each of them bade me adieu, all expressing regret that we couldn't get to know one another better. Several of them offered to walk me back to my hotel, but I declined. How could I decide which one? I couldn't remember the last time five men competed for my attention, and I liked it. It made being single feel right. Within minutes, I was back at the hotel and in my room, still on an emotional high after being wooed and adored for a couple of hours. I drifted to a peaceful and deep sleep.

Chapter 23

I woke refreshed and impressed with myself that I had beaten jet lag successfully. Even though I was in Switzerland, not Austria, songs from "The Sound of Music" kept popping into my head as I flitted around the room, toweling off after my shower, looking in the closet and drawers for the right, conservative outfit for the judges, while trying to remember the words to Edelweiss.

I finally settled on a mid-length gray wool skirt and a black turtleneck sweater with an S pattern crocheted across the front, mid-calf boots, and a Gucci bag to tie it all together.

I had seen Ristorante el Porte, an Italian restaurant across the street, advertising breakfast on their chalkboard easel, which was sitting on the sidewalk when I returned last night. Having no idea what Italians ate for breakfast, I was intrigued.

When I entered, I was confused. The restaurant was empty. No customers, no host or hostess, no waiter or waitresses. I figured they weren't open yet and turned to walk out. Seconds before I reached the door, I heard voices coming from the back. They were faint as if they were coming from a basement or outside the back door, but increased in volume and intensity as I stood and listened

Suddenly, two men dressed in white, broke through the kitchen door and into the restaurant. One was probably forty, the other twenty, if that.

The younger yelled in the face of the elder, "*Smetto!*" threw down his apron and ran past me out the door. I didn't need to know Italian to figure out he had just quit.

I hadn't noticed how disarmingly attractive the remaining cook was, until he smiled and winked at me. "These young people today. It's not how it was when we were young. They don't want to work, just get paid."

I smiled as he swept me into a table in a corner toward the back and sat across from me. I was immediately overtaken by the scent of sweat, cologne, and musk. The sensation was not altogether unpleasant. I managed to get a couple of words out of my flushed and hot face. "Caffe Americano?"

He practically ran to the kitchen. "It'll be right out. Cream or sugar?" he yelled, turning back to me.

"Both!" I giggled like a schoolgirl just before he disappeared behind the swinging stainless steel door. "You need to get a grip," I whispered to myself. I could have had any one of those guys last night and resisted nearly to the death. Now, I was falling for the first incredibly attractive man I ran into the next morning.

I closed my eyes and took a couple of deep breaths. When I opened then, Antonio, according to his name tag, was carefully setting my coffee on the table while he handed me a menu and placed some silverware and a paper placemat in front of me. I held my breath, knowing that if I breathed him in again, I'd be a goner.

He watched me curiously. "Are you all right, *signorina*?"

I opened my menu, attempting to get my usual level of control back, ignoring his question. "I'll have a *Sfogliatella*," which I was pretty sure was a cream-filled pastry.

He scribbled something on a pad and said, "Very good," and retreated to the kitchen.

I figured a pastry wouldn't take too long, assuming they either had already made them earlier, before they opened, or purchased them from a local baker. Other than the cook who recently quit, he seemed to be the only person in the place.

It took him a couple of minutes to bring my pastry, so I had time to prepare for my date with three judges. I had no idea what to expect. I knew that Larry had lied to the police in San Francisco, so I had to assume he would do the same here. I

177

needed to practice my credible deniability before I panicked in front of them.

Luckily, as I waited, the place started filling up, and a couple of waitresses joined Antonio, who retreated to the kitchen to fill in for the guy who quit.

Brigitte, my new waitress, was anything but Italian but was efficient and pleasant. I thanked my lucky stars that Antonio had passed off my table because I had no idea what might have happened next, but I think it would have involved exchanging phone numbers. That was the last thing I needed right now.

I had a couple more cups of their version of café Americano while I waited for my appointment, watching and listening to the local businesspeople and tourists speaking in German, Italian, French, and other dialects I didn't recognize. It was like nowhere I had ever been, and I savored the feeling of being immersed in so many cultures.

At 9:30, I paid my check and started my walk to the courthouse, confident and light-hearted. It was only supposed to be a ten-minute walk, but I didn't want to be late.

Heading up Balliz, I made a mental note to stop at some of the local shops tomorrow. So far, I had nothing planned, and I thought I'd do some sightseeing. That was rare for me to take some time just for myself.

True to my phone navigation, I arrived twenty minutes early, so I headed across the street to a park-like area overlooking the river, adjacent to a row of town homes. I watched a young couple strolling along the river, throwing stones in the water, teasing each other, then hovering closely, kissing then running away, then repeating the ritual. It made me long for someone, anyone, to be that close to. I figured the feeling would pass.

I strolled back toward the courthouse with ten minutes to spare and found Gretchen, true to her word, sitting on the front step of the building, which looked more like an office building than a courthouse.

Gretchen came to life as I approached, enthusiastically talking with her hands as she showed me the courthouse building. "The first thing you will notice is that we have no security, unlike the U.S., where a public building is like a prison."

I didn't comment except for an, "Uh-huh." But it took me back to a simpler time when people trusted one another. Since 9-11, it seemed like we thought the worst of everyone. The more we increased security; the more crazies figured out a way to get around it. It appeared that massacres like Columbine and Virginia Tech would just become more and more prevalent until people started trying to love one another again, like in the sixties.

Gretchen didn't seem to notice my contemplation of life and death, which was probably for the best. She led us to the elevator and pointed to the right as we stepped out. "The judges' conference room is down the hall and on the left, last door." She did her best to stay perky and positive, but I couldn't escape a feeling of impending doom.

I felt cold and small, entering the large conference room with multiple conference tables connected and at least twenty leather chairs lining each side of the table. I took my time picking the best chair on the opposite side of the table, imagining that if I never sat down, the proceedings would never begin.

As if the universe had something to prove, the judges opened the conference room door and filed in as soon as I sat down.

Because she would be acting as the interpreter, Gretchen sat on the opposite side of the table with the judges and introduced them one by one. "Miranda, this is judge Daimler. He will be leading the proceedings. He is the standing judge in the Thun Court and has sought out the other two judges from Bern."

Justice Daimler nodded and spoke in German through Gretchen. He was probably in his early sixties, around six foot two with short graying hair. I couldn't understand most of the words, but his demeanor was very stern.

179

"Our courts are very different from yours. Most of the evidence gathering and witness interviewing will take place before the trial officially begins. All the evidence will have been evaluated and analyzed by experts in their field with written reports provided to this panel of judges. I see our goal as adding the human touch to the process. Interviewing you or other witnesses will allow us to test our hypotheses regarding the innocence or guilt of the defendant so that when the trial commences, probably on Monday of next week, it will be concise and efficient, not a spectacle as is often the case in your country."

When he said "your country," which I could decipher from the one semester German I had taken in high school, it was clear that he was not a big fan of the United States, which was not uncommon throughout Europe.

I nodded my understanding of Gretchen's translation, and he continued.

"We will ask questions that might, in your country, come from either the prosecution or the defense. As long as you provide us the truth, we will all get along fine."

He motioned with his hand to the other judges who were his junior, age-wise. I wondered, for simplicity sake if that would mean they would defer to Judge Daimler.

My hopes were almost immediately dashed when Judge Friedenhof, short in stature, dark-haired and dark-eyed, spoke. "I feel it is my job to poke holes in the case. I intend to listen very carefully to your responses for inconsistencies. I have been trained as an expert witness in forensics, and I handle all lie detector tests in the Canton of Bern."

I could only hope the third judge, who appeared to be barely my age, was not even worse than the other two.

He started softly and slowly. "My name is Emil Spitzer. I have been a judge in Bern for five years and specialize in criminal cases. Please relax. I know this process can be stressful, and I want you to know that we just want to find out what the truth is."

The other two judges glared at Emil as he attempted to bring a more human touch to the process. He smiled at me in defiance of the other two, which made me smile in spite of myself.

There was a short break while the judges gave Gretchen various instructions, but because they were speaking in German, I had no idea what they were talking about. I asked Gretchen if I could use the restroom and if they had any water. I knew my mouth would get dry if I were going to spend hours answering questions, especially if they were difficult questions, although I was hoping for the best. Within ten minutes, we were all in place and ready to go. I smiled when I saw that Gretchen had left a cold bottle of water at my place. She winked.

Judge Daimler had a full page of questions in front of him. The other two did not, so I figured they would just be reacting to answers I provided or asking follow-up questions. He started with a bang.

"Miss Marquette, did you kill Tara Androsio?"

I had seen enough Law and Order reruns to know that he was trying to trip me up by making me incriminate myself early in the process. I responded, "No." Mark would have instructed me only to answer the question asked and not embellish. It was good to know an attorney.

He was quick to follow-up. "Can you tell me, to the best of your recollection, the events that led to Miss Androsio's death?"

I realized that I should have rehearsed my answers, but it was too late to think about that now.

"I had put together an all-girl extreme sports team, and we had come to Lauterbrunnen to BASE jump. We each had various experiences with skydiving or BASE jumping in the past and believed we were ready to take on High Ultimate, which was one of the more challenging exit points but was the easiest to get to from the cable car from the Village of Lauterbrunnen to

Murren. We each carried our own equipment from the hotel to the cable car that morning, although we had all touched each other's parachutes at one point or another over the last several months of practicing and skydiving."

I wanted to address any possible DNA questions upfront since they had requested a sample before I arrived.

He motioned for me to continue.

I started to feel more at ease now that I had broken the ice. "Tara and Larry, uh, the defendant, had gotten to know one another over the previous couple of days, and he helped her with her equipment. Because we were proud of our self-sufficiency, the other three of us made several good-natured comments about how Tara couldn't handle doing it by herself. I felt terrible later that those were among the final words we had shared." I smiled a sad smile, remembering how we used to tease one another, and wiped a tear from my eye.

I took a minute to grab a tissue while they waited for me to continue.

It was hard to read the panel. Daimler was very stoic, Friedenhof averted his eyes when I focused on him, and Spitzer smiled and nodded with my every word. I continued, focusing mostly on Spitzer because I felt like he was listening.

"The four of us were most worried about jumping out far enough to clear to protruding cliff. It was the first fifty feet and the fact that you needed to propel yourself out far enough that made this a perilous jump. Several people had died attempting it in the last couple of years, but I never expected any of my teammates to die because of an equipment issue. We checked and double-checked our equipment before each jump."

I tried to make eye contact with each of them before I delivered my most crucial line. "I believe Tara's equipment was tampered with before she jumped. And the defendant was the only one in a position to do that before her jump."

The judges didn't react to my statement at all. I wasn't sure if that was because I was stating the obvious or because they didn't want to give anything away. Finally, after scribbling some notes, Judge Daimler spoke.

"I'd like to shift gears a little bit. But first, do either of you on the panel have any other questions?" he addressed the other two judges. Both of them shook their heads.

Daimler flipped to another page of questions and started asking them immediately. "The defendant indicated to us that you and he have a long-standing relationship. Would you speak about that, please?"

I was so thankful the detective in San Francisco had clued me in on Larry's statement to them on this issue. I felt confident I could address it effectively, even though I was having heart palpitations, realizing that I might be considered an accessory or even a co-conspirator at this point.

"When we were here in Switzerland, I had no idea that the defendant was someone I had met in my past. I was informed by the San Francisco police that he indicated he had grown up in a neighboring town and had attended the same school I did. I have no recollection of ever meeting him in the past, and we certainly do not have a long-standing relationship as he apparently told you."

Friedenhof raised his hand, indicating he had a question. "So, you are testifying that you did not conspire with the defendant to kill Ms. Androsio?"

I struggled to make sure my voice was not shaking. "Tara was my friend. I was devastated by her death. I did not conspire with him or anyone else to kill her. That is outrageous, and frankly, insulting."

Judge Spitzer jumped in. "We are sorry to have to ask these questions, and my colleagues promised me that we would keep them to a minimum, and I believe we have concluded this line of questioning."

The other two judges nodded, but not particularly convincingly.

The panel spent the next half hour or so confirming other facts that seemed irrelevant to the case but might have been related to witness credibility. Then they thanked me, stood suddenly, and walked out of the conference room. They left so quickly, and without warning, it was hard at first to comprehend that they were done.

Gretchen stood and stretched as if she had just woken up from a nap. "Well, that went well, I thought." She smiled.

I stared at her in disbelief. "Were you at the same proceeding I was? I thought it was really hard."

She brushed me off with her hand. "Hard? No way. You should have been at some of the other ones. Those were mostly just the standard questions. It's when they ask tons of follow-up questions that you know you are in trouble. You got off easy."

I considered the process and thought back on the questioning. "What about the part where Larry and I went to school together? I'm sure they didn't ask anyone else about that."

She smiled. "Oh, that was more the defendant's credibility that yours. Friedenhof is just a little full of himself. He's not a big fan of Americans or women."

I whispered, "Are you sure you should be telling me this stuff? Couldn't it get you in trouble?"

She laughed. "I suppose, but you're not on trial here. It's my job to keep you relaxed and happy, so your visit to Thun is as enjoyable as possible." She whispered, "Honestly, it's so you stay until the trial on Monday."

I breathed a sigh of relief. "I'm not going anywhere. Now that I'm here, I wouldn't miss the trial, although it sounds like it might be a little anticlimactic."

"It probably will be, but the town folk are always an interesting wild card. Just in case there are points of evidence that need clarification or questions from the locals that they can't answer, they really would like you to stay around, although other than finding you in contempt of court, there isn't much they could do if you do skip town. There's not a country in the world who would extradite you for contempt of court." She gathered up the pad of paper in front of her and motioned me to follow her.

I suddenly felt lighthearted. "Hey, want to go out for a drink or something when you get off?"

She checked her watch. "I'd love to, but I have to pick up my kids from school this afternoon for doctor appointments, then make dinner and all that." She turned to look me straight in the eye. "I'm sorry, Miranda, I'd really enjoy that. I really would. Maybe we can do something tomorrow."

Chapter 24

I was disappointed but figured I'd find something to do. It was early afternoon, so I decided to find someplace to get a bite to eat. I promised myself to avoid that Italian restaurant I had gone to this morning. Gretchen walked me downstairs and hugged me as we approached the front door. We waved our goodbyes, promising to try to connect over the weekend.

The interrogation ended so quickly, I was still coming to terms with the fact that it was over. I felt like yelling, "I'm free!" and throwing my hat up in the air. Unfortunately, I wasn't wearing one and didn't want people to think I was crazy, even though I often felt that I might be. I nearly skipped down Scheiberstrasse as I left the Regionalgericht Oberland, their fancy name for the courthouse. Within a couple of blocks, I stood in front of Kino Rex, a theatre at the intersection of Route 6 near the bridge over to the northern part of the island where my hotel was located.

I scanned the films running today and nearly opted for Star Wars dubbed in German, but I thought that might be too much work. I was more in the mood for shopping anyway. Lunch would have to wait as I approached the stores on Balliz. My stomach churned as I passed McDonald's. It seemed like such a travesty to ruin the landscape with such a thing. I also avoided the New Yorker and Esprit stores and opted for Schaufelberger, a local department store.

I browsed for probably an hour, feeling like I hadn't shopped in years. My passion for Amazon was taking a toll on my in-person shopping, and I missed it. I tried on a couple of dresses, but they didn't fit to my liking.

I remembered seeing a women's clothing store, Anouk, a couple of blocks to the south, so I sauntered in. From the clothes featured on the manakins in the window and throughout the store, I knew this was my style. After trying on a couple of pairs of pants, I opted for a black leather mini-skirt and an off-white collared blouse. I was tempted to get a bag to coordinate with the outfit but reminded myself I had limited space in my suitcases.

It was nearly dinner time when I finally reached the hotel, happily, with my shopping bags in tow. The bar and restaurant overlooking the river were filling up with hotel patrons and locals. The aroma of traditional Swiss cuisine intermingled with steaks and seafood got my growling stomach's attention.

I was just about to enter the elevator when I spotted Patricia at the front desk with her bags. She appeared to be having an issue, and I couldn't bear to see her in distress despite our recent differences. She was nearly in tears as I approached her. "What do you mean you don't have a reservation, and the hotel is full? You've got to be kidding me."

The desk clerk was flustered. "Perhaps we can get you a room in our sister hotel, Krone, which is an easy cab ride from here."

Patricia, who hadn't noticed me yet, raised her voice. "I don't want to stay at the Krone. I have an appointment first thing in the morning, and this hotel was chosen because it is nearby!" Her eyes filled with tears.

Brigitte, the twenty-something clerk, appeared to be running out of options. "Do you want me to call the hotel manager?"

I saw my opportunity. "That won't be necessary. She can stay with me."

I must have startled Patricia, who had no idea I was there. "Oh my gosh, Miranda, you nearly scared me to death," she said curtly.

I surmised that she was still upset, and it was hard to read her reaction to my offer, especially when I thought about how angry she had been with me when we last met in Texas. Risking complete rejection, I reached out to hug her. Much to my relief, she dropped her bags and pulled me close to her. Tears streamed down her cheeks.

I slowly pulled away from Patricia and glanced at Brigitte, who still had the phone in her hand to call the manager. I motioned to her that we were okay, and I grabbed Patricia's bags, and she followed me toward the elevators.

She was quiet until we got to my room, then she sat on the bed and patted it so I'd sit next to her. She took a deep breath and began talking. "Miranda, I am so sorry for everything I said to you at Annika's funeral. I was so lost and alone, and I blamed you for everything. I've also been terribly moody since I got pregnant. But, the last few weeks have been an essential time for reflection and soul searching, and thankfully," she whispered, "I found a good therapist."

I chuckled. "You don't have to whisper with me around, I've been in therapy since I left the police force."

Her jaw dropped, "Really, don't you mess with me. I always thought you had it all together."

I thought for a second. "I think that's my fault. I wanted you to believe that. When we first met on that trip we took as a team, your looks completely threatened me." I could feel sweat dripping down my back as I confessed. "I swore I'd never tell you this, but I was utterly jealous of you. I tried to get the other girls to like me better than you."

I thought she would be angry with me, so I was taken aback by her reaction. She burst into laughter. "That's exactly what I was trying to do to you. You made me feel so inadequate. You had built a multi-million-dollar business, and the only thing I had ever accomplished was placing second in the Miss Colorado Pageant. I'm still living with my wealthy parents because I don't have the confidence to get out there and try something. I'm terrified of failing."

We hugged for the longest time, and finally, I broke the silence as I pulled away to look her in the eye. "I am so hungry I can hardly stand it, and I'm sure you'd love to freshen up."

She nodded, grabbing a tissue from the bedside stand, wiping her eyes and blowing her nose.

I stood up. "I'm going downstairs to the hotel restaurant before I starve to death. Will you meet me down there? I feel like we have so much more to talk about."

She threw her suitcase on the bed and opened it. "Yes," she responded breathlessly, "I would love that."

The combination of being done with the panel of judges and my eye-opening reunion with Patricia had me feeling ecstatic by the time I reached the outdoor restaurant overlooking the Aare River. The charming maître d showed me to a two-person table right on the water. As he seated me, I wondered why the men I had met since arriving here made me feel like I was the only woman on earth, when most American men didn't give me the time of day. By the time I finished my first glass of Cabernet, I debated why I would ever want to leave Europe. By my second glass, I considered moving permanently into this hotel.

I was considering ordering a third glass when the voice of reason, Patricia, joined me. She took one look at me, my empty wine glass and the table with no dishes, and asked the very attentive waiter, Hans, for menus.

The fact that she was six months pregnant was a blessing, because had she also started drinking when she joined me, I would have been under the table in no time. She hadn't eaten since she got off the plane and was starving also, so food was a priority.

Because the menu was in German, Hans was accommodating, steering us toward delicious and fresh salads, with cornmeal ragout and spaetzle on the side, as opposed to the bar food I had been craving.

Patricia and I talked about our experiences flying to Switzerland, seeking comfort in small talk while we worked our way back to more delicate topics. It was inevitable our conversation would eventually land on our trip to San Francisco. I hadn't seen things through her eyes and felt remorse and regret about how I had handled matters.

"I was so angry with you, Miranda. I had finally found someone who I was pretty sure no one would try to steal from me, and, in a way, you took him."

I put my hand on hers, resting on the table. "I am so sorry about that. I realize that I can get a little obsessed with things. My heart was in the right place, but I realize now there were better ways to handle that whole situation. Can you forgive me?"

Patricia smiled. "I've already forgiven you, but I can't say I was able to get there without an excellent counselor."

I was so relieved to talk about therapy with someone other than my brother. "Like I said earlier, I've been in therapy for years, since I had my accident."

Her look of confusion told me we had never even discussed one of the most significant experiences of my life. I closed my eyes, briefly reliving the tragedy. "You knew I was an undercover cop and left the force after an ambush and a severe gunshot wound, right?"

With her finger on her chin, she said, "I think I would remember that." She laughed. "We really haven't been very good friends, have we?"

I nodded. "That's going to change. Right now."

Tears filled Patricia's eyes. "You have no idea what that means to me, Miranda."

I touched her arm on the table, letting her know I felt the same way. "Well, I was on an undercover bust, and my back-up never showed up, resulting in me being shot in the face."

She cringed. "How horrible. But you look—"

I cut her off. "That's another long story, but I had multiple surgeries over two years. I started blogging about it which I found very therapeutic. That was how I circuitously ended up in the cosmetic surgery referral business." I hesitated a second before I added, "I'm still working on the anxiety this whole thing caused, but I'm a little better every day." I rarely shared my affliction with anxiety attacks even with close friends.

Patricia sat quietly eating, but I could tell she had something on her mind. She wrung her hands in front of her and looked distressed. "Most people don't know this about me, but since you shared your trauma with me, I feel like you deserve the truth. My parents aren't my birth parents. My birth mother was a heroin addict, and I never really knew her or my father. I was placed in foster care when I was two. I was adopted by the kindest, most loving parents anyone could ever hope for. They didn't tell me this until I was in my teens, and I completely revolted, feeling like I had no idea who I was. I started running with the wrong crowd, staying out all night, drinking, and taking drugs. I'm honestly, lucky to be alive. I went through rehab and eventually got back to nearly where I had been, excelling in school and playing sports, but I always felt like I had shifting sands under my feet."

I nodded.

She blushed. "I'm sorry, Miranda. Am I talking too much?"

I was happy she was talking because I knew I would get choked up if I shared any more of my most personal experiences. "God, no. I'm so honored you have chosen to share your life with me."

She adjusted her seat. "My parents were always there for me through my ups and downs. They couldn't have children, and they treated me like a queen. I often wondered since I found out I was adopted, if they chose me because I was the spitting image of my mom. She also has very light skin and black hair. It's almost spooky. It was partially the reason we started competing

191

in mother/daughter pageants. She was a fashion model who had been on the runway since she was a pre-teen, and it came very naturally to her. But I was like a fish out of water. I was painfully shy and hated being in front of people."

She twirled her black hair nervously as she spoke, her red lips pursed while she thought of what to say next. "I think it was this lookalike modeling that made me so resentful when they told me I was adopted. I felt like the joke was on me. I looked the part, but I never really belonged."

I knew she would appreciate my story, so I didn't hold back. "Last year, when I was visiting my mother, she sprung something similar on me. It turned out that she had been married before, and my biological father was the man I thought was my uncle, my father's brother."

She almost fell out of her chair. "No! Way!"

I smiled. "Way."

Exhausted from her flight and my court appearance, we retreated to the room after dinner. I thought it might be awkward staying in the same room with just one bed, but Sabine and I had done it so many times while visiting our grandpapa, it felt like just another sleepover.

Chapter 25

We were up, showered and dressed by eight, and similar to my court date yesterday, Patricia didn't need to be there until ten. I put on the outfit I bought yesterday, and I was secretly thrilled when Patricia whistled. She wore a sleek gray suit that accentuated her alabaster skin. She looked stunning. We strolled up the Balliz, attracting admiring smiles and stares from an assortment of men on the street. We decided on the Alte Oele for breakfast, which doubled as a cafe during the day and a bar and theatre with live music, in the evening.

They had a few tables outside, which we opted for. While it was a little chilly outside, the leftover smell of stale beer and cigarettes made the inside tables not an option.

As seemed to be the norm here in Thun, breakfast was not celebrated like lunch or dinner. It was more of an afterthought. Pastries or some other baked goods were usually the order of the day, similar to Italy. But the café Americano was always hot and fresh, making breakfast as least tolerable.

Already on her second cup, Patricia fidgeted in her seat, appearing to get anxious over her meeting with the panel of judges. "So, what do you think they will ask me?"

I thought back on their questioning, which was pretty routine for the most part. "I think the judges will try to tie your current relationship with Larry to Tara's death. Because of how we always helped one another with equipment, all of our DNA is probably on Tara's parachute, so DNA evidence alone may not prove to be conclusive."

It just struck me that I hadn't told Patricia about Larry's contention that he and I knew each other from childhood. I had avoided the topic last night because we were bonding, and I didn't think that conversation would go well. I plunged in, hoping for the best. "So, Patricia, has Larry ever mentioned to you that we might have gone to school together?"

I got her attention immediately. "What?"

"Has Larry—"

She interrupted, "You don't have to repeat it. I mean, what are you talking about? He never mentioned knowing you."

Her jealous bone was kicking in, and there wasn't a thing I could do about it. I tried to sound calm and soothing. "The police in San Francisco told them I had gone to school with him and had embarrassed him in front of his classmates when he asked me out, and I said 'no.'"

Her face was beet red, and she was drumming the table with her nails. "Why would he have not told me this? Why didn't you tell me this until now? Do you two still have feelings for one another? I'm being played for a fool again. Right, Miranda?"

I was so stunned by her sudden anger; I was speechless.

She pounded the table. "Right?" She stood up. "I've never seen you at a loss for words, so maybe you need to make up a believable story!" She hurried away, up the street. She turned to yell to me, "Good-bye, Miranda. Don't expect to see me later." She was gone around the corner.

I looked around to see no less than ten people staring at me. I took a sip of coffee, contemplating my next move, and said, "The show's over folks." I whispered to myself, "The show's over."

Shortly, I paid the check. Behind the Alte Ole was the Untere Schleuse, the covered walking bridge across the River Aare. The bridge was one of the most photographed spots in Thun with its flower boxes in full bloom. Bungee surfing was a popular activity just upriver from the Schleuse. I had never heard of the sport until arriving here, and I very much wanted to try it, but I wasn't dressed for it. Tourists lined the bridge, clapping when a surfer stayed up and groaning when they fell. It took my mind off of Patricia if only for a few minutes.

194

I proceeded across the bridge, passing the massive Ferris wheel I had seen my first night at the El Camino. I was almost tempted to go back into the bar but thought better of it when I glanced through the door and saw at least two of the guys I had met the other night. Clearly, they were full-time trolls, besides it was only ten in the morning.

I thought of Patricia and hoped that she had calmed down before she reached the court. I guess I knew the conversation about Larry wouldn't go well, but I could never have predicted just how angry she would get. I felt like we were back to square zero, and I second-guessed bringing it up at all. Perhaps the judges wouldn't have mentioned it.

I decided it would ruin my day of sightseeing in Thun if I worried the whole time about Patricia. She certainly was angry with me in Texas and had recovered by the time she got here. Maybe she would bounce back by the end of the day. Or, better yet, if the judges did get into that line of questioning, perhaps she would appreciate the head's up. I was going to hope for that to keep my anxiety in tow.

Old City was a charming and delightful part of Thun. The shops were one-of-a-kind and eclectic. I spent hours browsing at Sister Boy Clothing, specializing in 1950s to 1970s Rock and Roll wear, Dekowerkstat, which carried all sorts of home accents, and the Secret Nature Herb Shop, which sold many things that I thought were still illegal.

I nearly bought a poodle skirt at Sister Boy, but then I wondered if I would ever wear it when I returned to civilization. The good news was that my Patricia-induced funk had cleared, and I was ready to move on. I had read on Trip Adviser that there were multiple castles in Thun, so I set out to find them.

I was lucky that I checked my phone before leaving the neighborhood because the famous Thun castle was a two-minute walk from Secret Nature. Had I been paying closer attention, I would have known that the spired 12th-century building on top of the hill overlooking this part of town was Thun Castle. I spent a couple of hours in the spire admiring the views, taking pictures, and touring the museum, which included tons of artifacts from the 1300s, a jousting ring, and, allegedly, ghosts.

From there, I walked across the island, past the train station, and toward the lake. I had been so consumed with Old City; I hadn't ventured to any of the outlying areas of Thun. As I approached the lake, I was overwhelmed by the beauty of the mountains and the surrounding countryside in contrast to the deep blue lake.

I spent an hour in Schadau Park, which was right on the lake, and then took a ferry to Spiez Castle, which housed some fascinating people over the years, including Franz Ludwig von Erlach who lived from 1575 to 1651 and spawned thirty-five children with two wives. The historians had done a great job recreating the lifestyles of the times in various rooms and halls.

I was surprised when I looked at my watch to find that it was after five as my ferry headed back into the port of Thun. The views from the boat were breathtaking, and I was so glad I had taken the time for myself to sightsee. I might never get back to this part of the world.

I hadn't spent much time thinking about my last encounter with Patricia but immediately got a pit in my stomach as I walked back to the hotel. She was not the type of person I wanted angry with me. It was too stressful to be on the receiving end of her ire. I was surprised to see Patricia and Gretchen sitting together on one of the couches in the modernized lobby. They were talking and laughing, so I decided to join them despite my concerns. Because Patricia wore her heart on her sleeve, I, at least, always knew where she was coming from.

As I approached the two of them, Patricia caught my eye. "Miranda, come join us!" She waved me over. I felt like the world had been lifted from my shoulders.

I started to speak, but she cut me off.

196

She stood up and came to me, grabbing my hands. "I have to apologize to you once again, Miranda. Thank God you told me that Larry knew you from the past, and I wasn't hearing it for the first time in court. I would have been mortified and confused, and the judges might have wondered what was up, possibly casting doubt on the rest of my responses. Because of what you confided in me, I did pretty well, I think."

Gretchen looked like she was going to burst. "Pretty well? You both did great! I know those judges, and had they had any doubts about either of you, the questioning would have taken a lot longer and been much more pointed. Believe me. I've been involved in every interrogation." She whispered, "And if I didn't know any better, I would say that Spitzer had a bit of a crush on you, Miranda."

I waved her off. "You're kidding, right? There's no way any of those judges had any opinion of me other than as a witness."

Patricia supported Gretchen. "That young one was relentless when it came to questions about Larry and my relationship. So, if Gretchen says he was easy on you, take her word for it."

I didn't know what to say or want the spotlight on me. I was just thrilled that Patricia had gotten over her earlier jealous rage and that everyone was happy. "Are you guys hungry? I'm starving."

We agreed to go to Restaurant Krone attached to the Krone Hotel, not far from the shops I had visited earlier in the day. The inviting aroma of the grill, cooking up some good old-fashioned burgers had made me promise myself to return there before I left Old City.

Patricia reddened when she realized how close it was to our hotel when she had refused to stay there. "I guess I could have walked here in the time it took me to argue about it."

I gave her a quick hug. "I'm glad it worked out the way it did, now that we are sisters for life."

Tears streamed down her face, and I knew just what she was feeling. It amazed me how we had gotten off on the wrong foot, and it was only a quirk of fate that had forced us together so that we could reconcile our differences.

"I always wanted a sister," she whispered loud enough so only I could hear.

Gretchen, Patricia, and I spent three hours talking, laughing, and sharing embarrassing stories about the wrong men we had chosen in our lives. I was surprised and pleased that I wasn't the only one who had made monumental mistakes when it came to men.

Of course, I was the only one who had chosen a man more than twice my age right out of high school and ran halfway across the country with him, but I had to admit their choices hadn't been much better. I could understand why Patricia was living with her parents and why Gretchen had retreated back to Switzerland after sowing her wild oats.

Heading back toward our hotel, Patricia and I vowed to stay in touch with Gretchen, at least on Facebook, which seemed to be the communication tool of the future. I wasn't a huge fan but didn't feel I could completely ignore it either. And if that were a way to stay in touch with Gretchen, it would be easier than traveling eleven hours to see one another. Although, I relished the idea of coming back to Switzerland after this was all behind us.

She yelled to us as she headed the opposite way, "I'll be coming back to the states one of these days too. Besides, I'll see you both on Monday."

Patricia and I walked in silence. It seemed like neither one of us wanted to think about Monday yet since we were feeling carefree. I decided to change the subject. "Do you still want to head up to Lauterbrunnen tomorrow?"

She looked straight ahead as we walked. "I think we need to, Miranda. And I think Tara and Annika need us to."

I nodded. "I think you're right. For whatever reason, they both died doing what they loved to do. I don't know that there's a better way to go."

Even with the tragedy we had faced together, everything felt right, like life did have a meaning, and that we were close to figuring out what it was. We walked silently again to our room. Right now, there were no words we needed to say.

Chapter 26

We woke early and skipped breakfast, except for coffee in the hotel lobby. The trip to Lauterbrunnen was about an hour and required us to switch trains in Interlaken. We had passed through Interlaken on our first trip since it was further east and directly south of Zurich. Once we were on the Lauterbrunnen train, my stomach started doing backflips, and I wished I had eaten something.

Patricia didn't say anything, but I could see she was suffering too.

Just a couple blocks from the train station was the Air Time Cafe, which we had gone to just before our fateful BASE jump. It was an eclectic combination of baked goods, gourmet gluten-free, and a sense of humor. No one in Lauterbrunnen, especially the business-owners, seemed to take themselves too seriously. I surmised it had something to do with the fact that so many of them defied death every day, participating in dangerous sports, such as BASE jumping, regularly. It reminded me of the survival techniques cops, or first responders often used.

Keeping a sense of humor was necessary to battle stress because you didn't know if you'd be around to enjoy the next day. But having experienced death at the hands of the mountains that surrounded us, nothing seemed funny to me right now.

As we sat at a small table near a large window, overlooking the perilous peaks, Patricia studied my face.

"What?" I responded with nervous laughter.

She searched my eyes even though I tried to avoid hers. "What happened to the happy-go-lucky Miranda who would normally be trying to talk me off the ledge?"

She was right. I was feeling more anxiety than I expected being here in Lauterbrunnen and was trying to use some of my relaxation techniques, like deep breathing and picturing myself in a safer place. My biggest issue was that I was consumed with guilt. If it weren't for me, and my dream of fame and fortune, two of my teammates and friends would be alive today.

"It's all my fault," I finally was able to express.

She took a sip from her coffee cup. "No, I think the fact that the coffee is three hours old is their fault."

I smiled weakly. "No, if I hadn't put the team together, Tara and Annika would still be alive. I've done my best to avoid having that thought but coming up here brings it all back. I can still see Tara plummeting to the ground as I floated safely with my parachute. Why did my parachute open, and hers didn't?"

Patricia grabbed my hand. "Miranda, you can't blame yourself. We were all here of our own free will. We had a great time together. Your dream of the first all-girl extreme team was a good one. Things just happened. Whether Tara's death was an accident or something worse, I guess we'll find out next week. The police are working on Annika's accident too, and I'm sure we will hear something soon. You can't take on everything yourself. Besides, remember what we talked about yesterday? You have me now too. Sisters. Right?"

I smiled through tears that streamed down my cheeks. "Sisters."

We didn't talk much as we rode the cable car from Lauterbrunnen to Murren. High Ultimate, our entry point, was only steps from the platform. As we exited the cable car, two jumpers made their way onto the metal grate platform extending from the ledge like a pirate ship's plank then plunged 2,360 feet to the valley below. We watched in awe, barely believing that we had done the same just a few months ago.

We climbed solemnly up the hill to the edge of the cliff. Patricia quietly said a prayer, and we sat looking down into the valley for quite a while. As we sat, a sense of peace and contentment settled over me. I couldn't put it into words, but I could tell by the look on her face, that Patricia could feel it too.

201

Finally, we stood together, hugged, and climbed down the hill to catch the next cable car to Lauterbrunnen so we could head back to Thun.

The train rides went by in a blur. Patricia and I had grown so close in such a short time, it surprised me that we had barely even been acquainted when we arrived here.

We spent the rest of the weekend sightseeing, shopping and avoiding the topic of the trial which started on Monday. I had been a little worried that sleeping in one bed might be awkward, but we talked and talked into the night like Sabine, and I had done years ago.

She also slept more peacefully than anyone I had ever seen. Once she went to sleep, she slept for at least eight straight hours and never moved or stirred at all. There were times when I listened carefully to hear her breathing to be sure she was still alive.

She had opened up to me about how she felt, being pregnant with the baby's father on trial. She had seemed so much in love in San Francisco; I was surprised when she confessed about not being sure if she wanted to raise her child with a man.

She turned on her side to face me on Sunday night with her head resting on her hand and her elbow resting on the bed. "I'd like to be able to make my own mistakes and have my own victories. Larry acted excited when I first told him I was pregnant but seemed to have a lot of doubts after that. There is no room for doubt. It's 'do or die' time." She turned on her back to face the ceiling with her hands behind her head on the pillow.

I did the same and was reminded of my brother and me as we lay in the grass underneath the stars the summer before our parents separated. Before that summer, I thought everything would go on as childhood had forever. Granted, it wasn't perfect, but it was predictable and secure. My life after that was anything but.

Even though we chose not to talk about the inevitable trial, before we knew it, it was Monday morning, and we were in court. While the courtroom was similar to ours in appearance, several things were laid out very differently. The panel of judges sat at a small conference table near where the typical witness stand would be. The defense table was on the left side from our viewpoint, and a witness table was on the right, where a prosecution table would typically be.

The judges were already seated at the table when we walked in and sat in the second row of the gallery. Gretchen was sitting at the end of their table facing front. She smiled demurely, but I figured that waving to Patricia and me would not have been politically correct.

I wondered how Patricia would react to seeing Larry in court. She glanced briefly at the defense table and slowly rubbed her stomach. I imagined she was coming to terms with raising their baby alone, but she didn't comment.

We sat quietly while a few other stragglers sat behind us in the gallery. I pegged them as natives by their dress and disdainful looks at the two of us.

Judge Friedenhof stood to address the courtroom, which I thought was a nice touch. He spoke in German, and Gretchen translated. The court wasn't exactly standing room only, but there were probably thirty people in the gallery, which I was sure surpassed their usual trial.

"Ladies and gentlemen, we are in the final phase of the second-degree murder trial of Mr. L, the defendant."

I found it odd that they never used the defendant's name, but that was customary in the Swiss court system.

He continued with a confident and business-like presence. "As many of you know, much of the trial: the gathering of evidence, the interviewing of witnesses, and other pertinent parties, and the initial deliberation by the panel of judges has already taken place. Today, after my opening statement, we will have a brief recess and then we will be summarizing the findings in the case including evidence, interviews, statements and overall impressions of the court. This will take most of the day.

"If we have time, we will then open up the court to questions from the gallery or any other interested parties excluding, of course, the press who will remain outside. If we don't have time for questions today, we will be taking questions tomorrow."

He spent another half hour summarizing the evidence they had reviewed, describing the witnesses who had been interviewed, and from my perspective, providing no information that might be the least bit helpful to the defense. While an attorney sat at the defense table with Larry, he never once asked a question or even spoke. We certainly were not in Kansas as Gretchen so aptly noted.

As promised, there was a brief recess around 10:30. Patricia and I went outside for some fresh air. There wasn't much to say, but Patricia seemed to be in a place where she could accept whatever the outcome of the trial was.

The trial resumed at eleven. Judge Daimler summarized the meetings with all witnesses, and there was nothing particularly interesting introduced during that segment, although there was a buzz in the gallery when the judge mentioned that Larry and I had gone to school together.

Judge Spitzer then proceeded with the forensic evidence. I figured this was where their case would either be made or not. He seemed to enjoy the presentation aspect of his job. He spoke very dramatically with every piece of information he shared.

"The victim's parachute was the center of attention of the DNA testing. Our initial finding was that there was DNA of several of the victim's teammates and crew. However, when we focused only on the area where zip ties had been applied, preventing the ripcord from functioning correctly, we only found DNA consistent with the defendant's."

Several members of the gallery gasped. I didn't recognize them and didn't know if they were relatives of Larry's or just interested onlookers.

After Judge Spitzer was finished, Judge Friedenhof re-assumed control of the trial. He scanned the gallery, probably anticipating the types of questions they would receive. He folded his hands in front of him. "We will now open up the trial to questions."

A man down the row from us, probably in his fifties and dressed in typical Swiss farming clothes, including a white shirt with a black vest, brown woolen trousers, and brown boots, raised his hand.

The judge pointed at him. "Yes, Herr Muller."

Based on the judge's familiarity with him, I figured that this was not Mr. Muller's first rodeo.

He stood and gathered his thoughts. "Judge Friedenhof, I do not even understand why you are conducting a murder trial. These people, jumping off cliffs, clearly have a death wish. More of them die every year, but still, they keep jumping. And as if that isn't bad enough, the 25 Francs the Swiss BASE Association charges them for a permit to die, to reimburse us for damage to our crops and our land, it is not nearly enough to cover the cost."

At first, I thought Judge Spitzer was going to take this one, but he surprised me when he opened his hand, gesturing to me and said, "Fraulein Marquette, would you like to address this question?"

While it was posed as a question, I knew I didn't have any other options. I smiled and stood up, facing the farmer. "Herr Muller, while it may seem like we have a death wish, that couldn't be further from the truth. We represent a growing portion of the world population, not satisfied with traditional sports or entertainment. Yes, we are risk-takers, but we also pride ourselves on preparing safely before any of our activities.

"We are as concerned as you are that a small percentage of BASE jumpers are not qualified or trained sufficiently to take on these mountains. However, as a percentage of jumpers, there are fewer and fewer casualties every year." I wasn't sure if anyone was going to address the 25 Franc fee, so I continued. "We agree that the 25 Franc permit fee should be raised to compensate residents from damage to crops and property and we certainly support that."

Patricia whispered, "Brilliant." She, much to my surprise, raised her hand.

The judge recognized her, giving her the floor.

She spoke directly to the judges. "I respect the fact that you have your own court system and customs. However, the way that you conduct a trial has me baffled. I guess it's possible the defense was allowed to make their case at some point behind the scenes, but will we be provided with any information regarding that defense, how it was conducted, and what the outcome was?"

Judge Daimler responded. "We, the panel of judges, have interviewed the defendant with his attorney present, as well as various other witnesses who did not have an ax to grind with the defendant. We believe that this process, including the physical and other evidence, much of which had been presented in this courtroom serve as a credible basis for the determination of the outcome of this trial. Does this answer your question?"

Patricia nodded but remained standing. "I just want to state that the defendant is the father of my child and a good man. I can't fathom that he was involved in causing Tara's death, and I stand by him to the end." She sat down with a stoic look on her face but with no tears.

There were a few more questions asked, but nothing pertinent to the case at hand. The local residents seemed to use the opportunity to air other local grievances, which didn't seem like the best use of time, but the judges were generally patient and kind in their responses.

Once that information had been presented, the judges left as a group to deliberate in Judge Friedenhof's chambers. We stayed seated as we didn't expect their discussion to take long. I figured it was pretty much a formality since there was no new evidence introduced during the trial that they hadn't already reviewed.

They were only gone for fifteen minutes, which was even shorter than I had expected. They filed in, and the two junior judges sat while Friedenhof remained standing. There was a hush in the gallery in anticipation of the verdict.

"I would like to thank the citizens of Thun and Lauterbrunnen and the witnesses who provided invaluable information," he gestured to Patricia and me, "especially those of you who came from the United States."

We both nodded and smiled.

He continued quickly as if he had a two o'clock tee time. "We have deliberated and have decided on the verdict in this trial. We find the defendant guilty of second-degree murder." He hesitated briefly as if awaiting a reaction. There was none. "We request a sentencing order from the prosecution within a week, seven days from today. You are dismissed."

I stared straight ahead at the panel of judges. I was afraid to look at Patricia, not knowing what state she might be in. Before I had time to catch my breath, she stood up and said matter-of-factly, "I guess that's it."

Wondering if she was just in shock, I didn't question it. I asked, "Ready to get out of here?"

She bolted in front of me toward the door. "You bet I am. This place to so stuffy, I could barely breathe." I followed her until we got outside, then she stopped short. She continued, talking faster than she normally did. "Do you think we can still catch a plane back today? I am so ready to get back to life; I can't stand it."

I couldn't help but stare at her, wondering who this Patricia was. "Are you sure you don't want to take some time, get a good night's sleep, and go tomorrow? You seem, well, I don't know what you seem, but I'm a little worried about you."

She turned to look me straight in the eye. "I'm fine, Miranda. I had to be prepared for any outcome, and I meant what I said yesterday. I really don't know if I want any man mucking around in my life right now. I want to concentrate on being the best mother to my child and the best friend I can be to you. And I hope you'll take me up on being my friend after we leave here and go back to real life."

I was excited that she seemed to be in a better place than I had ever seen her and was accepting the inevitability of Larry's conviction. We walked back to the hotel and talked about life after Switzerland. "Hey," I stopped just short of Balliz in serious danger of getting run over. "I know you don't want to live with your parents forever. Why don't you come and live with Heather and me? There's plenty of room. We could all take care of the baby together."

She was quiet most of the way back to the hotel. When we got inside the lobby, she motioned me to sit with her on one of the couches. She faced me and took my hands in hers. "That is such a kind and selfless offer, Miranda. And there is a big part of me that would absolutely love to take you up on it." I could tell there was a but coming sooner than later. "But my parents have been waiting so long to be grandparents and I hate to deprive them of that, especially during the first few precious months. But after that, who knows? Denver isn't that far from LA, and they've been talking about moving somewhere warmer anyway. I know I'm rambling here, but what I'm trying to say is, I will seriously consider it once I have the baby and get settled into a routine."

I hugged her. "I'm so glad, Patricia. I really hope you do. That would be so much fun. You could be the sister I never had. Well, I actually do have a sister, but you could be like the sister I never see." I felt a pang of guilt, knowing that I was equally responsible for not seeing Sabine as often as I should. "Now, let's get upstairs and pack and see about booking a flight."

Before we knew it, we were touching down in Denver. We hugged in the airport before she headed off to baggage claims, and me, to my next gate. We swore to stay in close touch. I was thrilled when she asked me to come out for her delivery. Her mother was very squeamish and wasn't sure she could handle staying in the room while she delivered. I promised I'd be there, and I meant it.

Chapter 27

Having flown Lufthansa from Zurich, I had to switch to American Airlines in Denver. Just over two hours later, I was taxiing into LAX. An hour and a half later, nearly 9 o'clock on Monday, I was home. It was only five hours later on the clock than when I left Zurich due to the time change. But I could feel every minute of the fourteen-hour flight. I bent forward and back at the waist, trying to get a kink out of my middle back as I watched the airport limo drive away.

No inside lights were visible from the driveway. I scratched my head, wondering if Heather was out or if she had just gone to bed early. Her car was here, but that didn't always mean anything these days. I sometimes worried that she was reverting to her drug-induced days, but I never asked. We hadn't been as close since Annika died, and I wondered if she was fighting depression. I know I was, but the therapy was helping.

As I put my key in the lock, I exhaled deeply, relieved to be home at last. I switched on the downstairs lights, which lit up the kitchen and the living room. The open living space meant the kitchen, living room, and dining room were all just one big area, defined by furniture arrangement. Heather's laptop screen was still active on the countertop, so I assumed she had recently gone to bed.

I hoped to catch up with her tomorrow to see how she was doing. She never complained and never asked for help, so I always got the impression that she was happy, but maybe she had just gotten good at putting on a smiling face. I knew what that was like. I did it for years.

I dragged my suitcase, my carryon, and the wardrobe bag up the stairs to my room. I bought the wardrobe while I was in Thun so I could get my new clothes home. It felt good to buy some new duds. I had been in a fashion rut for a while now, wearing jeans or jean shorts and t-shirts most of the time.

Sitting on my bed, I suddenly felt exhausted. There was no point in unpacking now when I could do it tomorrow. I opened my second dresser drawer and pulled out my Strawberry Shortcake Jammies. I didn't care for them when an ex gave them as a joke gift, but now I loved them. I got the last laugh because they've lasted way longer than he did.

When I was en route from LAX, I told myself I would shower when I got home, after wearing the same clothes in a train, a tram, two planes, and a limo, all of which had probably transported God knows how many germy people before me. But even that fact only motivated me to wash my hands and face and brush my teeth.

I was asleep by the time my head hit the pillow and slept dreamlessly. I was half asleep when I heard a loud pounding sound. I wondered if they were doing construction next door, but it sounded closer than that. I listened to see if I'd hear it again.

The next time I heard it, it seemed closer. I rubbed my eyes and got out of bed. Suddenly, I realized someone was knocking on my front door. I grabbed my shorty silk robe and vaulted down the stairs. I figured that Heather went running and locked herself out. It wouldn't be the first time.

I flung the door open, laughing, expecting a sweaty and out-of-breath Heather, only to be greeted by two armed cops in uniform. The junior officer was barely out of the academy and almost made me laugh again with fear written all over his face. I was anything but a threat and didn't think I looked scary in my Strawberry Shortcake jammies and a shorty robe. The second was around my age and immediately demonstrated that he was in charge. He held a piece of paper. They both had their weapons holstered.

Not having any reason to believe they were here for anything other than some early morning fundraising for the Police

Benevolent Association, I decided I should mind my manners at least until I found out the real reason for their visit.

I smiled, securing my robe to hide my jammies. "What can I do for you today, officers?"

The elder smiled back. "I am Officer Johnson, and this is Officer Cantone. May we step inside, Ma'am?"

This situation was already moving too quickly for me, but I forced myself to respond pleasantly again. I extended my hand. "I'm Miranda Marquette. Pleased to meet you, gentlemen." I realized I had been working so hard to sound pleasant that I might have crossed the line into sarcasm. "I see you have a piece of paper with you, Officer Johnson. Is that a warrant by any chance?"

They stepped forward in unison, entering my personal space. I instinctively took a step backward. "Yes, we have a warrant. May we step inside?"

The smile on my face faded. I wondered if this had anything to do with the information the federal government had requested about the business. I figured it couldn't be because these weren't feds. They were local cops. I had to see it before they took control of the premises. "I hate to ask, but can I see the warrant? I have no idea why you're here. I just know that I haven't done anything wrong."

Then he dropped the bomb. "Is Heather McIntosh inside the premises? We have a warrant for her arrest."

My mind was running wild with possibilities. Was Heather involved in drugs again? Or was it something worse? I never imagined they were here for Heather. I figured it was me, and based on my last couple of years, it was a reasonable assumption. I realized I was talking to myself in my head and not responding to the officers.

Finally, I responded. "Why? Why would you want to arrest Heather?"

The officer debated whether or not to provide that information, and before he responded, I heard a voice behind me. "Hey, Miranda, welcome home! Do we have company?"

I mumbled under my breath, "You might say that." I had pulled the door nearly closed as I spoke with the officers on the front stoop.

When Heather got to the door, she opened it wide and gasped, "My God, Miranda, are you in trouble again?"

The officers immediately jumped into action, turning their attention to Heather, who had just gotten out of bed and was dressed in "Kiss My . . ." shorts. I prayed they would let her change before taking her in.

The senior officer stepped toward the front door, approaching Heather and bypassing me and my best attempt to block his way. "Heather McIntosh, you are under arrest for the murder to Annika Bloom." He continued speaking as he, in one motion, pulled her hands behind her back and applied handcuffs. "You have the right to remain silent. Anything you say can and will be used against you in a court of law. You have the right to an attorney. If you cannot afford one, one will be appointed for you. Do you understand these rights as I have provided them to you?"

Heather wasn't paying attention to the officer virtually dragging her to their squad car and was trying to communicate with me with facial expressions and eye movements. I had no idea what she was trying to say, but I responded, "I'll follow you to the station, and we'll figure this out."

My police experience taught me that the officers wanted to get Heather out of her home as soon as possible. The sooner you had the perp in custody and out of their comfort zone, the less likely it was that things would turn bad. In my own experience, I had seen it all, friends coming over to visit while an arrest was taking place, a suspect reaching for a weapon in a nearby drawer, even children biting the arresting officer.

On the other hand, I felt terrible that they hadn't at least let her change from her sleeping clothes. Then again, she wasn't likely to be in her own clothes for long either way.

While they were loading her in the squad car, I stepped into a pair of jeans that needed to be washed and a Hollywood T-shirt I bought when I first moved to L.A. My mind was going a mile a minute. But one thing I was sure of was there was no way Heather killed Annika. Number one, they barely knew each other. Number two, they had become quick friends, and they seemed to hit it off great. I was even a little jealous of their friendship. Number three, Heather was my most trustworthy friend. I trusted her with my life.

As I rushed to catch up with them, I realized I hadn't even asked them if she would be arraigned here or be immediately transported to San Francisco. My experience was that police didn't do anything particularly quickly when it came to prisoners, so they might let her languish in Malibu in a holding cell for a couple of days before she was transported.

As soon as I hopped in the car, I hooked up my phone to the Bluetooth and dialed Mark Peterson, my sister's boyfriend, my ex-attorney, and my friend from school. He answered on the second ring. "Mark Peterson."

I took a deep breath and crossed my fingers just for luck. "Mark, it's Miranda."

He sounded more relaxed than I had heard him in a while. Of course, he was defending me for murder the last time we spoke, so that might have explained it. "Miranda! To what do I owe this pleasure?"

I wasn't much for small talk, especially in an emergency. "I've got a huge problem."

He gave me his full attention, which was never guaranteed with Mark. "Okay, I'm listening."

I knew I was talking fast, but I had to get it out before I arrived at the police station. "Heather, my roommate, and most

214

trusted friend and employee has been arrested for the murder of my teammate."

He interrupted. "I thought that trial just took place in Switzerland."

I didn't have time for long explanations and was getting impatient. "Mark, get with the program. That was my other teammate, Tara, who was killed BASE jumping. This is Annika, who was killed in San Francisco during a street luge race."

"Sorry, Miranda, I know you've had your share of tragedy lately. I should have remembered two of your friends died." He was sincere in his apology.

I was hoping he was so sorry he would do the impossible for me. "Mark, you're licensed to practice in California, right?"

He hesitated, "Well, yes, but—"

I interrupted, "Before you blow me off, hear me out. Heather is my best friend, and I need a great attorney now. I don't have time to break in a new one. Besides, you and I are practically family. I am in the car following the police to the station, and they have Heather in custody. I won't know when the arraignment is, probably in a day or two. I imagine it'll be in San Francisco, so we might have a little time to coordinate this."

He sighed. "I don't know why I even try. Between you and Sabine, I already know I'll be doing this."

I squealed. "Thank you so much, Mark. I love you, um, like a future brother-in- law."

He sounded defeated. "How do I know I'll end up regretting this?"

I retorted, "Oh, I don't know, Mark. I think you'd end up regretting not doing it much more. Anyway, when do you think you can get out here? I would hate to have some stranger have to represent her even on an interim basis. I'm sure she's scared to death. How could they possibly think it was her? God, just when they finally convicted Larry of killing Tara, I figured that would seal the deal on this case. I'm sure he killed Annika too.

215

God knows what deranged motive he had for either killing, but there is definitely something not right with that guy."

There was silence on the other end. Mark probably figured my rant would go on for another couple of minutes so he could multi-task.

Finally, he said, "Hey, Miranda, I'd better get going. I'm gonna have to juggle several court appearances to make this happen. Believe it or not, I do represent other people."

I was happy we were back to being sparring partners. That was the relationship that suited us best. "Okay, Markie, you do that. When can I expect you out here?"

He was slow to respond. "How about Thursday?"

I honestly had no idea how quickly things moved here or even if they would do the arraignment here and then transport her to San Francisco. I smiled and shifted into sweet voice mode, trying to get on his good side. "I really think you can do tomorrow, don't you?"

I could tell he was losing patience. "Okay, Miranda. Tomorrow. I'll be in touch with the police and the court so I can figure out whether I should fly into L.A. or San Francisco. But you owe me."

I mustered a half-sarcastic laugh. "Actually, I think you owed me from our last case, don't you?"

He chuckled. "That's debatable since neither of us solved the case."

I decided it wasn't a good time to argue the point. "I'll see you tomorrow either way. Thanks. Bye."

I heard a faint, "Bye," as I hung up the phone.

Chapter 28

Since I wasn't her attorney, just her closest friend, there wasn't much I was able to do at the police station while they processed Heather. I felt horrible for her having gone through a similar humiliation not long ago.

I would have done anything to prevent her from having to spend the night alone in a holding cell. I hoped she was alone anyway since spending it with some criminal would be even worse.

I went home feeling frustrated, guilty, and alone. I made the Desk Sergeant promise to call me with her disposition as soon as he knew what was going on with Heather.

I spent the night tossing and turning, anticipating a meeting with Mark tomorrow. He was likely not to be very happy about spending time in California, where he didn't know anyone but me.

True to their word, the Malibu police called me at 7 a.m. to let me know that Heather would be extradited to San Francisco by mid-morning. They would probably arrive there by around four-thirty.

Mark texted me that he was heading to the airport for a noon flight that should arrive in San Francisco around three, taking in account the time change. I took his text to mean he didn't want to talk to me right now, which was fine with me. He'd be over it by the time we met up later today. I decided it would be good form to meet him at the airport, so I locked up the house, grabbing a carry on with a couple day's changes of clothes and my laptop. With Heather out of commission, I also had to run the business. I had gotten so used to Heather handling the day to day issues; it was going to be a challenge without her, but I'd have to manage.

Mark was gracious when I texted him that I would pick him up at the airport and take him to the hotel. I felt like it was the least I could do after railroading him into flying out here on a moment's notice, especially since I was staying at the same hotel. I booked him a one-bedroom suite with a parlor at the Hilton San Francisco Union Square, which was a seven-block walk from the U.S. Northern District Court on Golden Gate Avenue.

The hotel was a modern high-rise with an outdoor pool, a trendy restaurant, and a cocktail bar with city views. I booked a queen room for myself, hoping only to spend one night, but prepared for more. You never knew how long these court things were going to last.

He looked haggard when I spotted him trying to track down his suitcase in the baggage claim area. I tapped him on the shoulder, and he jumped a mile, which cracked me up. He didn't always appreciate my sense of humor, but he laughed in spite of himself. "I didn't see you there, Miranda. You're lucky I didn't take you down with my lightning-fast reflexes."

I punched him on the arm. "Don't get too full of yourself, Mr. America. I can call Sabine in a second to get you back under control."

He smiled confidently. "Oh, Sabine already knows I'm a superhero."

I narrowed my eyes. "Oh, she does, does she?" I knew he was putty in her hands, scared to death of her, or some combination thereof.

In a few minutes, he found his bag, and we were heading for my convertible. It was unlike me to leave the top down, but I figured the people sharing the short-term parking lot at the airport had other things to worry about than stealing my CDs or carving their initials in my leather seats.

Once we got in the car, I asked him for an update on Heather.

Looking up at the parking garage ceiling above us, he started listing the minimal information he had, then started pummeling me with questions. "The arraignment is tomorrow morning. Luckily, in California, the bail hearing is usually included in the same proceeding. So, with any luck, Heather will be free tomorrow. So, what do you know about this? Did you suspect Heather at all? I know she's your friend, but I thought you might have a feeling either way."

He didn't take much time to aggravate me. "Mark, you've got to be kidding me. She's my best friend in the world and practically a partner in the business. Besides, she barely knew Annika. There is no motive."

He clearly had decided to get the difficult questions out of the way first. He continued to look up, but now at the sky since we were on our route to San Francisco from the airport. "Now, don't take my head off, but could there have been a mistake, since it seems like probably a sled was tampered with, that she was targeting either you or Patricia?"

I looked over at him, which was not the smartest driving move considering traffic on the 280 can go from eighty to twenty in a matter of seconds. "Okay, Mark, I trust Heather with my life. I would place you higher on a list of possible suspects than Heather. I've been wracking my brain as to what evidence led to an arrest. I guess you'll find out soon enough, but I'm baffled."

He settled into his typical lawyerly investigation. "From what you said on the phone, she had helped out quite a bit with the sleds. I imagine she showed up positive on a DNA test."

I rolled my eyes. "Okay, Captain Obvious, even I figured that out, but where's the motive? Besides, all of our DNA was on those sleds, along with employees officiating the race."

He grimaced after I smacked him on the arm. "Ouch, hey, I'm not the enemy here."

I shook my head and laughed with a touch of sarcasm. "You're getting soft back there in the Big Easy. I've gotta talk to Sabine. She's clearly not keeping you on your toes the way she should be."

He mock-groaned. "I don't think you need to worry about that." He watched the traffic line up in front of us. "So, what's your gut. Who's your suspect?"

I slammed on the break as traffic came to complete stop with no explanation. "Until I spent last week in Switzerland, I was sure it was Larry, the guy who just was convicted of killing Tara. It all fit together for me. He was a psycho with a bizarre life-long vendetta toward me and was killing my teammates one at a time to get back at me for ruining his life. But something doesn't feel right. It's almost too obvious. I nearly went to see him in jail after he was convicted to see if he might give me a clue, but there simply wasn't time. I hope I don't end up regretting that decision."

Mark spoke in his typically soothing tone, "Is there anyone else, other than him, your teammates, and you, who were in Switzerland and here? What if Larry was falsely convicted and somebody else killed both of them?"

I grimaced. "Believe me, Mark, that question has had me lying awake at night more times than I can count. The only person I can think of is Rocky Blanchard. He was the second cameraman on the Switzerland trip and was also filming here."

He looked at me thoughtfully. "Well, there's somewhere to start anyway. You're going to help me with this, right? I've got no staff out here."

I chewed on my thumbnail. I needed to break that habit. "Of course, I'll help. It would be beneficial if you could get Heather out on bail, or I'm going to have to run the company by myself, which would leave me less time to assist." I smiled and batted my eyelashes and spoke in my best 'Southern Belle' accent. I still love to flirt with Mark even though he's hopelessly in love with Sabine.

He laughed. "You can bat your eyelashes all you want, but I'll get her out on bail either way."

I hit his arm again, "Aw, you're no fun."

Other than the one unexplainable backup, traffic was unusually light, so we were at the Hilton within a half hour. Mark had a bunch of calls to make about work he was still tending to at his practice in New Orleans.

I mindlessly watched Law and Order reruns for several hours then went to bed early.

We met in the lobby in the morning and debated walking to court but opted to drive. My exercising kick would have to wait another week.

We parked a couple of blocks from the Northern District Federal Court on Golden Gate Avenue. We stopped at Philz Coffee across the street for some high test before we entered the court building. As many Starbucks as there were in San Francisco, I couldn't believe there wasn't one within walking distance of the court.

While Mark and I discussed the case, I still found it hard to believe that Heather had been arrested for the murder. Either I was missing something, or the police and DA's office were off on this one.

While we sipped on Philz super-hot coffee, Mark said as if he read my mind, "I'll be interested in seeing what the evidence is in the case the prosecution is bringing forward. San Francisco isn't some Podunk town where the sheriff and his posse can just get away with arresting any suspect under the sun because they have a hunch."

I chewed on my thumbnail again. "I can't even think of anyone to interrogate with Larry in prison, except maybe Rocky, the other cameraman. I have a gut feeling that he's involved in this."

Mark stared out the window at the court building. "How serious a competition was this street luge race? Could it have been one of the competitors? Did anyone stand to lose big money or reputation by being beaten in this race?"

I thought for a minute. "I can't believe I didn't think of that. I was so convinced that Larry did this, I never considered any other possibilities. I'm still not confident that he didn't do it, but, on the other hand, the law enforcement community doesn't seem to agree with me even after I delivered him to them on a silver platter."

Mark pressed on. "So, any other racers who come to mind?"

I wracked my brain. "Well, there was a bit of bad blood between Annika and Felix Loch, the German bobsled racer. But I can't imagine him sabotaging her sled. I'll check it out, though, to see if there's more to him than meets the eye."

Mark checked his watch. "We better get over there to the hearing."

We dodged cars, busses, and trucks to get across the street to the court building. Mark and I split up so that he could have a moment with Heather before the hearing began.

I had a pit in my stomach, sitting in the gallery, waiting for Heather to appear. Within a few seconds, she walked in, led by an armed guard. She was handcuffed and looked even smaller and more vulnerable than usual, in an oversized orange jumpsuit. I had never seen her looking so meek and defeated. I wish I could say I couldn't imagine what it felt like, but considering it was less than a year since I was in the same situation, the memory was all too fresh.

I couldn't hear what she and Mark, who followed them to the table, were talking about. I imagine he was giving her a description of what was to take place and what her role was.

If her hearing was anything like mine, she would plead innocent, and Mark would take care of the rest.

The judge was a stern gentleman by the name of Andrew Turner. He spoke to the prosecution and defense regarding the procedure relating to bail and the approximate timing of the preliminary hearing, which was scheduled three weeks out. He never cracked a smile or made an off-the-cuff comment. I realized how lucky I was to have the judge I had in New Orleans. She kept things under control in her court but also maintained a relaxed air, which left you wondering what she was going to say next.

The arraignment was over very quickly. True to form, the prosecution argued for not allowing Heather out on bail, and Mark presented a case that she should be released on her own recognizance. They settled on $500,000, and it was over.

Mark and I sat in the coffee shop, waiting for Heather to be released. There was no reason for us to stick around town. I assumed that Mark would stay with Heather and me at least until the Preliminary Hearing, but I'd confirm that with him later. After the hearing, it would probably depend on how much pre-trial preparation was necessary and when the trial was scheduled, assuming it had to go to trial.

Mark didn't know Heather well, and he spent much of the six-hour ride to Malibu finding out about her background. While she happily soaked up the attention of an attractive male, I was aware that he was doing his job, trying to access her character and any possible flaws that the prosecution could take advantage of.

We all went to bed when we got home, exhausted from the early court date and six-hour drive. I went downstairs to get some water around eleven and found Mark sitting at the kitchen counter working on his laptop. I sat down next to him. "Couldn't sleep?"

He rubbed his eyes. "I'm in this pattern where I fall asleep for a couple of hours and then wake up, tossing and turning for hours afterward. I decided to make it productive since I couldn't sleep." He hit send on a lengthy work-related email, from what I could tell.

I downed most of my water in one gulp. "So, what do you think of Heather?" I asked, trying to sound casual.

He hesitated as if he were in court, not wanting to spill too much information. "She seems nice." He opened up another email.

I turned to glare at him.

He worked for a minute or two until my eyes nearly burned a hole in the side of his face. "What?" He responded as if we were an old married couple with a predictable communication pattern.

I lit into him. "That's all you've got after spending nearly six hours talking with Heather in the car? She seems nice? I wasn't paying complete attention to the conversation, but it seems like you two hit it off pretty well. I, frankly, was a little jealous for Sabine. I can't imagine the conversation would have been the same if she had been in the car."

He smiled weakly. "Okay, you're probably right, which is why I don't take my girlfriend to work. Part of being a competent attorney is building trust with your client. Sometimes when a client is a woman, part of achieving that trust can border on flirting." He hesitated and then looked me in the eye as if he just remembered who he was talking to. "For God's sake, Miranda, you were a cop for years, don't tell me I'm telling you anything you don't already know."

I bit my lip, knowing he was right. "Just be careful, Mark. Heather can be very persuasive. And, yes, she's my best friend, and she's adorable, but she has a dark side. She pulled herself out of a pretty bad situation down in Venice Beach, and sometimes I wonder if she's getting sucked back into it. Lately she's been gone for days at a time without explanation, and I have no idea where she was."

Deep wrinkles rutted his forehead. "Have you asked her about it? Maybe there's a logical explanation."

I went to the fridge for more water from the door dispenser. "I haven't seen Heather much. Last week, I went back to San Francisco to answer questions about this case that the police had before they turned Larry over to the Swiss government. For a minute, I thought they were going to arrest me."

I looked up from his computer. "Really? Why?"

I didn't want to get into an extended conversation about it, since it all turned out okay. "Well, he claimed that he knew me from home and that we conspired to kill Tara."

He scratched his head. "What was his name again?"

I didn't get my wish on the extended conversation. "Larry Lechter."

He thought for a minute. "Sounds familiar, and not in a good way. I may have defended his brother in an arson case."

I thought for a minute. "I'm not sure if he has a brother, but anything's possible." I decided it was up to me to change the subject. "Before I went back to San Francisco to talk to the police, I was in Texas for Annika's funeral, and then I went home for a couple of days."

He nodded, "I heard you were back. Sorry I missed you."

I laughed. "That was fine. At least I had Sabine all to myself. Then I went to Switzerland for Larry's trial, and the morning after I got home, Heather was arrested. It's been crazy."

He nodded, half paying attention and half-reading his work email.

I continued anyway. "I'm just a little worried. She had a tough childhood, and I'd hate to see her getting back on heroin. She's been clean for a few years, but I know she didn't take Annika's death very well, and now to be accused of her murder has to be driving her crazy."

Mark scratched his head and shut his laptop. "That was one thing that took me by surprise in the car. She seemed so cheerful and unaffected by the whole thing. Even in court during the arraignment, she was joking around with me. Most of my clients are either scared to death or angry like you were." He winked.

I turned some shade of red. "Yeah, I guess I wasn't too nice to you at that time, but I had to take it out on someone."

He nodded, "I've got pretty thick skin. I'm used to it. But that was the weird thing about Heather and probably why I talked to her for so long in the car. I kept waiting for her to breakdown or have an emotional moment, but it didn't happen. I'm trying to decide if she should testify on her own behalf. She'd either be the best or worst witness I have ever had. I'm just not sure which one right now."

Having lived with Heather, I knew what he meant. "She is probably the most positive person I know. She's reliable. She's funny. She's kind to animals. She's like a Girl Scout in so many ways. But occasionally, she shows her other side. Sometimes, it's just a look, or a word or a sentence, and then she shifts back to the Heather we think we know."

He studied my face until I started to get self-conscious about my nearly non-existent scars. "Well, tell me this, Miranda. Do you think she's capable of murder?"

I nearly responded with a resounding "No!" but I waited to let the question sink in. "I don't think so, Mark. I'm ninety-nine percent sure. But I don't think anyone knows what Heather's one percent is capable of."

He nodded. "I get what you mean, and both you, as Heather's best friend, and I, as her attorney, need to crack that one percent, or we won't be doing the best job we can in defending her."

We both sat in silence for a few minutes, pondering how that could be accomplished. I knew Heather pretty well and didn't have a clue. I tossed my hands up. "I don't know Mark, and I don't know that anyone ever will. Do you plan to stay until the preliminary hearing, or are you going to go back to New Orleans while I work on things here?"

Mark stood up from the stool at my breakfast bar and stretched, leaning on the counter across from me. "I plan on spending at least a couple more days here, getting to know Heather. Three weeks is a long time if you aren't doing anything or a very short time if you have a lot to do. I, at least, need to determine if I'm going to have Heather testify on her own behalf. That could easily sway the jury. It would be hard for the prosecution to make a case that she's some kind of psycho killer. Obviously, the most intensive period will be after the hearing and before the trial, especially if I get buried in discovery requests. With Andrea back in New Orleans, I'd have to field most of those requests myself unless you want to help."

That didn't sound the least bit appealing. "I'd be happy to do interviews, investigation, and anything that requires action, but paperwork is not my thing."

He started toward the stairs. "Let's play it by ear. In the meantime, I'm going to try to get some sleep."

I was happy to be using three of the six bedrooms upstairs. I had never had them all filled at the same time, which was indicative of the number of friends I had or family that visited regularly.

I followed him up after switching off the lights. Tomorrow I would formulate a plan to assist with Heather's defense. I hoped, in exchange, Heather would continue to take care of the business, which would keep her mind off her impending murder trial.

Chapter 29

I tossed and turned for most of the remainder of the night, finally getting out of bed at 6:30. I dreamt of frustration with setting up interviews with prospective suspects like Felix Loch and Rocky Blanchard.

I was immediately rewarded for opening my underwear drawer with Rocky's business card lying in the corner of the drawer. The one he had given me when I ran into him during the luge races at Halfmoon Bay Beach. My mood suddenly improved. Getting in touch with Felix Loch was another thing altogether since I had no contact information on him and didn't even know if he was still in the country. But one thing at a time.

After taking a quick shower and throwing on a pair of jean shorts and a tank top, I bounded down the stairs, attempting to convince myself that I wasn't dressing to get Mark's attention. Sometimes I was so transparent, but my therapist said it was better if I admitted my motives to myself rather than denying them.

I was the first one up, and I was soaking up being home after so much traveling lately. I took a cup of coffee out on the deck and listened to waves crashing on the beach. I took a moment to scan the mail sitting on the counter. A U.S. Government Official Business return address caught my attention. Since it was sorted with the other envelopes, I assumed it came while I was in Switzerland. It was stamped in red, "Third Attempt. Please contact us immediately, or the license to operate your business will be suspended or revoked."

Sweat started dripping down my back. I braced myself against the deck railing and took several deep breaths and closed my eyes.

My initial anxiety reaction subsided in a few minutes, so I moved to the kitchen counter to read whatever was inside the manilla envelope. I was shocked that Heather hadn't mentioned this, but on the other hand, we hadn't spoken since I got back.

I waded through three pages of legalese, and none of it looked good. They continued to have questions about the legality of my contract and wanted a face to face meeting. I balanced on a stool as my anxiety level increased again. My ears were ringing, and my skin was hot. Sweat ran down my face, and I couldn't focus on anything. I started to feel my way toward the couch for safety and lost consciousness.

~*~

Sometime later, I opened my eyes. The left side of my face stung, rug burn, I figured. From this angle, all I could see were furniture legs, baseboards, hardwood floors, rugs, and dirt. Heather was not as meticulous a cleaner as I am.

After a few minutes, I was able to pull myself onto the couch. I was happy no-one was up yet. I hated for people to know that I was debilitated by anxiety attacks. I had thought they might be getting better. I managed to make it through my whole trip to Switzerland with only some minor pangs of panic, and even Heather's arrest hadn't taken me down.

When I thought about it, I wasn't all that surprised that this issue with the government had had that impact on me. I had been ignoring them for months, hoping they would just go away. I knew that there was only so much Heather could do, and she had tried to protect me as much as possible, but that wasn't her job.

I sat on the couch for a few minutes, getting my sea legs back. I knew I had to deal with this and decided to call my business attorney, Tonya Bloomsburg. She was one of the best in LA, and I was lucky to get on her roster when I first moved to town, before she gained the notoriety she has today. She had developed the most recent version of my provider contract. When I thought about it, I should have forwarded the

229

government inquiries to her earlier, but I had been in denial. At a thousand dollars an hour, it took a lot for me to get motivated to use her.

I went to my filing cabinet and dug out her file. On her stationery was a fax number. I jotted off a note for her to call me after she reviewed the document and faxed it to her. Once I checked that off my list, I started to feel better, if only for now.

After my second cup of coffee, nearly an hour after I made it, Mark sauntered down the stairs. I figured I must have been out of commission for at least fifteen minutes. I breathed a sigh of relief that Mark hadn't found me on the floor.

I nearly forgot about my rug burn until Mark asked, "What happened to your face? You haven't been picking fights in bars again, have you?" He snickered.

I could feel my face getting red. "One barroom brawl in high school and I will never live it down." I tried to minimize it, although at the time I was fighting for my life. I quickly made up a lie. "I guess it's been too long since I've been home, I ran into the closet door on the way to the bathroom last night."

He looked at me quizzically, but let it drop. "So, what's your plan for the day? I'm going to contact the court and let them know to send any discovery requests here. Then I plan on spending some more time with Heather, assessing her credibility. I'm leaning toward having her take the stand if possible, but I don't want her to blow it for herself either. I've seen several defendants lose their own case by confusing or alienating the jury. I've eventually been able to get them off on appeal, but it was a long, slow process."

I bit my lip. "I know what you mean. On Law and Order, the defendants can be their own worst enemy even if they are innocent. The Swiss court system may have gotten it right. They carry out most of the process during pre-trial proceedings and have no juries. In serious cases, like murder trials, they rely on panels of judges to make the final decision. I was impressed with how efficient the process was."

Mark grumbled. "That's all I'd need, multiple judges to deal with. Don't get me started on the attributes of the jury trial. That is what this country's judicial system was based on. To take that apart would be like dismantling the constitution."

I was surprised he was so closed-minded on the topic, but I guess when you live and breathe it every day, it could be a sensitive topic. I decided it wasn't worth debating. "Okay. I see what you mean." I figured changing the subject was the best idea. "I plan on calling Rocky Blanchard and, hopefully, set up a time to get together. We could have a conversation on the phone, but it's so hard to read people, especially when they are lying, on the phone."

He had a yellow pad in front of him that I hadn't noticed, jotting down notes at the counter as he sipped coffee. "Did you figure out how to get in touch with any of the other racers?" He chewed on the end of his pencil—a man after my own heart.

I thought for a minute. "I know. I can call Bernie Weinstein, my publicist. He worked with the race organizers on marketing our team. Maybe he has some contacts I can use."

Typical of Mark, still jotting down notes, he was only half paying attention. "Sounds like a good start."

Knowing we were all tired last night, I decided to repeat the warning to Mark. "I know I said it last night, but just be careful with Heather. She's about as 'touchy-feely' as a person can get, and I'm sure that can get very confusing for a man. Your life is your life, but I've got a vested interest here. You're going to marry my sister, so I won't cast a blind eye if I think something is going on."

That finally got his attention, and he looked directly at me. "Miranda, I said it last night. I need to have Heather's full trust, or I will not get anywhere with this defense. I have very healthy boundaries, and I am very much in love with Sabine. I already spoke to her last night, and this morning and talked about Heather and our conversation and, yes, even about your concerns. So, don't worry. I'm a big boy."

I felt a little better and slightly foolish in my jean shorts. "Okay. I'm just looking out for you two."

We hugged briefly and platonically. Mark held me at arm's length, looked me in the eye, and said, "Thanks for caring."

I still felt uneasy about the government situation but figured there was nothing I could do until Tonya got back to me, so I spent the morning answering work emails. Heather slinked out of her bedroom close to noon. I've never seen anyone who can sleep as deeply and as long as she does. She claims that she's making up for lost sleep in her childhood. I figure she must live a guilt-free life.

"Good morning, sleepyhead," I hugged her and gave her a mug of coffee.

She sat between Mark and me at the counter, inhaling the nectar of the gods. She whispered hoarsely, "Good morning."

I gave Mark the evil eye as he appeared to admire her in her shorty nightgown.

I whispered in Heather's left ear. "Maybe you should get dressed. There is a man in the house."

She giggled. "You're such a prude, Miranda. Besides, it's just Mark. He's practically family."

I thought to myself, "Yes, practically family to me, but not to you," but I scooted her upstairs to her whining protests and said instead, "'Practically' is the key word here. 'Man' is the other one. If he's going to be here for a while, we need to make some adjustments."

She glared at me like she was a spoiled teen, and I was her mother, then stuck her tongue out playfully and disappeared up the stairs and into her room.

232

I had no idea what Rocky's work schedule was, but I figured it was late enough to call anyone at this point. I grabbed his business card and punched in his number.

He answered after two rings. "Rocky Blanchard."

I could hear the nervousness in my voice and was sure he could too. "Hi. I'm not sure you remember me, but this is Miranda Marquette. You were at our photoshoot in Switzerland, and I ran into you on the bus at the street luge races."

Rocky didn't hesitate. "Oh yeah, absolutely. What can I do for you? Do you need a cameraman? I heard that Larry guy was convicted of murdering your friend. Serves him right as far as I'm concerned."

I was surprised how quickly word had spread, but the internet had sped mass communication up considerably.

I didn't want to spook him, but I figured being direct was the best way to go. "I'd like to get together to talk about the day my teammate Annika died in San Francisco during the street luge race."

He hesitated. "Oh, I don't know anything about that. I was just doing my job. I pretty much keep to myself. I'm sorry to hear about her death, though."

I wasn't surprised. Most people didn't want to get involved in anything that had nothing to do with them. Then again, maybe he knew something or even did something and didn't want to get caught. I wasn't quite ready to give up. "I understand. I used to be a cop, and I know how it is getting asked questions about something you know nothing about." I decided to try a different angle. "Let me ask you this. Are you single?"

He laughed. "Well, there's an interesting question."

Evidently, one he chose not to answer. I stayed with it, though. "Where are you located? Maybe we can combine business with pleasure and go out for a drink."

I could hear laughter in the background and wondered where he was. "Sorry about that. I'm with a couple of buddies who think they're smart. I'm in Long Beach. How about you?"

I thought I might be making progress. "Malibu. Want to meet at 26 Beach Cafe on Washington Boulevard near Lincoln in Venice? It's probably about halfway for both of us."

In the background, his buddies seemed to be giving him a hard time. "Okay, you got me. I don't have a random woman call me from out of the blue every day. Maybe it'll be fun."

I was relieved, but a little nervous. I really didn't want to meet on false pretenses, or to get Rocky's hopes up about anything personal. I decided to worry about that later. "How does two work for you?" I really wanted to get this out of the way.

It was getting increasingly louder at his end. He yelled over the din. "I'll see you then."

While I was on the phone, Heather came downstairs in a cotton print sundress and flipflops. That was a vast improvement over her previous outfit, but I still thought she was dressing to impress Mark. I had no excuse since I had pretty much done the same thing.

I had been on the couch, talking to Rocky, and they were huddled together at the kitchen counter. "I'm heading out to meet Rocky. Wish me luck!"

Heather clicked her tongue. "You're going out like that? Just what kind of interrogation is this going to be?"

I knew she was right, which was why I just said, "I'll see you two later," and went out the door.

I jumped in the convertible feeling out of control. I squealed the tires on the way out of the neighborhood as I headed down the canyon to the PCH. I sat at the intersection before I took a left down the coast to L.A. I took a couple of deep breaths are started talking to myself.

"Okay, Miranda, that wasn't too bright. You want the neighbors, most of whom already hate you, calling the cops?" Luckily, there was no-one behind me. It gave me and myself some time to talk.

"Remember, your therapist talked about how you always feel like the odd man out. 'Third wheel syndrome' I think she called it. That's what's going on with you, Mark and Heather. When they laugh, you feel like you are the butt of the joke. Whenever they whisper, you think they are talking about you. This is all in your head. You felt the same way about Annika and Patricia in San Francisco, and now Patricia is one of your best friends. Get out of your head, Miranda. It's not a good place to be." I took ten deep breaths with my eyes closed.

I was jolted back to reality when a car pulled up behind me and hit his horn. I took a left on the PCH.

Traffic was heavy, as usual, and it took the two hours I had allotted to make it to Venice Beach. I hoped to take a few minutes to languish on the beach after our lunch. Venice Beach was always an entertaining place to people-watch. Whether it was a street magician wowing the crowd or a singer just short of their first break, it was never dull.

After the frustration of sitting in a line of traffic for a half-hour on Washington to go the last mile, I finally arrived. I found a table on the muralled wall featuring multi-colored poodles, who led the brunch babes. I smiled. Sometimes I actually missed L.A., but it was rare.

My waiter, Thomas, was friendly, helpful and really good looking. My face flushed red nearly every time he spoke to me. I thought I had gotten over that in Switzerland, but definitely not. His meticulous look and flair for style told me he was probably gay, but I didn't care. Within a matter of seconds, he had delivered my glass of Josh Cabernet, an up-and-coming Napa winery run by an East Coast family. Who knew Connecticut even had wineries? It was surprisingly smooth.

I scanned the place to make sure Rocky hadn't beaten me there and already taken up with some other bachelorette. While perusing the half-full restaurant, I saw a guy that I thought might be him walk in the door. I wasn't sure I'd recognize him if I saw him and I was right. I wasn't sure. Further inspection confirmed that he was looking for someone. When he found me, our eyes met, and he practically ran over to the table. I stood and stuck out my hand. He shook mine and looked me up and down. I was a little embarrassed by my outfit, but he didn't seem to mind.

"Sorry, I'm late. Traffic," he said as we were sitting down.

I nodded. It was a reality in L.A. It could take fifteen minutes to go twenty miles or three hours. Most of the time, you never found out why, an accident, construction, a UFO. It was just what it was, the price of living in La La Land.

I wanted to keep things light at the beginning, so he didn't feel like it was the interrogation that it was. I motioned to the quickly filling restaurant and asked, "Have you ever been here?"

He opened the twelve-page menu, perusing it while we talked. "Yeah. When I first moved out here from Ohio, I didn't live far from here, Marina Del Ray."

I snorted and almost inhaled my wine. "How could you afford those swanky digs?"

He chuckled. "I had a childhood friend who struck it rich in Vegas and spent everything on a boat moored there. I moved in with him for a while. It wasn't long before he gambled it all away and we were both on the street. That's how I started my career as a cameraman."

He leaned back in his chair with his hands behind his head. "I play a little music on the side. Of course, back then, I thought I was going to come out here and strike it rich. I was busking on Venice Beach, and they were filming a documentary about the homeless situation in L.A. The cameraman was stuck in traffic with no hope of making it by the time they needed to wrap it up, so this young producer came up to me and asked if I'd like to earn a thousand dollars."

He smiled at the memory. "I hadn't come close to seeing that kind of money since I'd been out here, and I jumped at the chance. They trained me in the basics in about fifteen minutes, and I was ready to roll. I was, apparently, a natural because they used me for the rest of the film, which took six months to shoot."

I nodded and took another sip of Cabernet. "So, what got you into filming sports? I imagine that's very different from film?"

He closed his menu. I figured he knew what he wanted. "You'd be surprised. It's not all that different. There are different demands when you are filming live, and you have one chance to get it right, but the concepts are the same. I'm a freelancer, so I'll do just about anything."

We talked and ate and laughed. It felt good just to let down for a few minutes.

He surprised me when he brought up the case. "So, you said something about investigating the murder of your teammate at the street luge race in San Francisco? I thought they arrested some broad. And I figure she did it. Probably a fight over a man."

My initial reaction was to jump down his throat, but I sat silently for a minute or two. Then I said, "She's my best friend, so I'm betting she didn't do it."

I felt something in the air change almost immediately. His body posture closed. He stopped making eye contact, and he started sweating, red-faced. I thought he was going to burst, but he finally spoke. "So, you come down here thinking, 'well, let me try to think of someone to hang this murder on. I don't want my best friend to go to jail. So, I'll go visit Rocky and see if I can get him to confess.'"

I had to admit that he wasn't far off, but I couldn't admit it to him.

I spoke in a Mark-like calming voice. It always seemed to work for him. "It's not like that at all, Rocky. I just knew you were at the race where Annika was killed, so I thought you might have seen or heard something."

He wasn't buying it. "So, you think you can come down here in short-shorts and a crop-top, and I'm going to just be putty in your hands." His tone was more and more abrasive and sarcastic, and his face was more contorted with every word. He stood up to go.

I stood too, trying to reason with him. "Rocky, listen—"

He screamed at me. "Sit!"

The restaurant got deadly silent as he walked out to whispers and points.

Ever obedient when I think my life is being threatened, I sat.

Thomas returned with a glass of cabernet. He whispered, "Don't worry about it, honey. He's not your type. You could do so much better."

I nearly laughed at the irony of the situation and was almost tempted to explain, but I said, "You're probably right, Thomas."

He retreated to the kitchen while I sipped on my wine and planned my next move.

Chapter 30

I took my time getting home. Mark and Heather would probably just give one another knowing winks if I told them what happened, blaming my results on the wrong outfit.

My plan to go to Venice Beach had been pre-empted by my sour mood. I wasn't in a place where I could be amused by some comedian or a mime displaced from Paris. I hate mimes.

I decided that my best course of action was to go to Santa Monica Pier. Years ago, when I first arrived here, when I didn't know what else to do, I would buy an unlimited wrist band for $29.95 and ride the Ferris Wheel all day. It was a place I could think. The last time I did that, I rode so long without a break, I was forcibly removed by a ride operator with no teeth and gin on his breath.

Generally, my mental state was much better today than it was then. But between my panic attack this morning and my 'interrogation gone bad,' I wasn't feeling so great. I hadn't seen my therapist in a couple of weeks due to travel. That was a mistake. I needed to call her and get one of her ASAP appointments.

When I got to the Pier, I bought two tickets for ten dollars, which seemed like a real rip off compared to the unlimited wrist band, but I tried to keep my obsession under control.

Before getting on the ride, since the line was longer than I preferred, I walked to the end of the pier and looked out to sea. I did the next best thing to talking to my best friend. I spoke to myself. "What was up with Rocky? We were having a pretty good time until I mentioned that Heather was my best friend. Then he went crazy. Was that anger, guilt, paranoia, or fear? Or was it something else entirely?"

I watched the waves break out to sea like there was a distant storm brewing. I started to brighten. "Now, wait a minute. If Rocky and I had had a nice chat and he hadn't reacted at all, what would that have proven? I know a lot more by the fact that he reacted as he did. He just moved way up on the suspect list." If I was going to play detective, I needed to get my thick skin back. I took my two rides on the Ferris Wheel and headed home with a new sense of optimism and purpose.

When I got back to the house, it was empty. Perhaps Mark and Heather had gone on a field trip so that he could observe her in her native environment. I badly needed an attitude change about those two. I'd work on that later.

I was at a loss at how to get in touch with Felix Loch. It also struck me that there were other luge racers that I never met who could have had it out for Annika. Or maybe it wasn't a murder at all. Perhaps it was an attempt to take Annika out of the competition with a minor crash, and it went terribly wrong.

Finally, after thinking until my brain hurt, I decided to call Bernie Weinstein, my publicist. He had a relationship with the organizers of the race, and maybe he could get contact information. We hadn't spoken since he saved me from vicious reporters in Texas, so I was due to follow-up with him anyway. Bernie could run hot and cold, so I often avoided calling him, not knowing which Bernie I would get.

He answered on the first ring. "Bernie Weinstein."

I didn't hesitate, trying to throw off a positive vibe. "Bernie, it's Miranda. How are you today?"

He didn't sound good. "Miranda, I was just about to call you. The Bravo people called me this morning and canceled tomorrow's meeting. They said they aren't investing in any new reality shows right now."

I glanced at the date on my phone. I couldn't believe it was the sixteenth. I had completely forgotten about the meeting scheduled tomorrow. But I was suddenly hit with a tremendous relief. Maybe reality TV wasn't for me. Patricia was right. Having people in my business twenty-four hours a day would drive me crazy. I thought about telling Bernie, but I figured it was better if the network canceled the show as opposed to me. So, I kept it upbeat. "Well, I guess it wasn't meant to be."

He said nothing and since I couldn't tell what he was thinking, I decided to move on. "Hey, I have a favor to ask of you."

I was relieved he seemed to be in his fatherly persona today as opposed to his manic businessman mode. "Sure, Miranda. Whatever you need."

I breathed a sigh of relief. "Can you either give me the number of the people who ran the Street Luge race in San Francisco or contact them for me? I'm looking for names and contact information for participants and employees. I know it's a long shot, but I had to ask. Heather has been arrested for Annika's murder."

He gasped. "Your Heather? I heard that someone had been arrested, but I didn't put two and two together. I don't know what the prosecutor is thinking. She'd be the last person I would suspect."

I was so glad I didn't listen to my apprehensions and called Bernie. "Thanks, Bernie. I'm glad you feel that way. Sometimes I feel like I'm the only one."

He started talking faster and shifted gears. "I will see what I can do on your request. I'm assuming you need it right away."

"Yes, I do." I was just about to sign off when I remembered one detail. "Hey Bernie, even if you can't get the whole list, if you could get Felix Loch's contact information, that would give me a place to start. I'm looking for suspects and Annika, and he didn't seem to hit it off."

He responded quickly. "I'll see what I can do. I'll send you an email with whatever I get as soon as possible."

I was just about to get off but said, "Hey, Bernie, thanks for everything. I'm sorry the reality show didn't work out."

He replied, "Water under the bridge, Miranda. I'm sure we will work together in the future."

I smiled. "I hope we do." We both hung up.

I spent the next couple of hours answering work emails. I was starting to get used to being the only one working the business. With everything that was going on with Heather, I didn't feel it was necessary to require her to work while she was fighting for her life. I decided, too, that it wouldn't be a bad idea to start taking back control of the essential things like the bank deposits and paying the bills. As an internet-based business, we didn't have too many expenses, but we spent quite a bit on marketing to doctors to keep our network viable.

I was almost tempted to call my attorney about the government issue, but I figured no news was good news. My therapist would tell me that I was exhibiting avoidance behavior, and she would be right. I reminded myself that I was a work in progress.

By mid-afternoon, Bernie had emailed me all the information I requested and more. There was also a cross-reference of each racer by sled number from the competition. A few, including mine, had been crossed out with a different number written in. I had no idea why. With no sign of Mark and Heather, I started perusing the list to find people I could identify and their phone numbers.

I made a pot of coffee, and I made it about halfway through the list. Besides Felix and a couple of employees, I didn't recognize anyone's name. I rubbed the back of my neck as I sat back down on the stool at the granite countertop. The combination of staying in one position too long and the stress and frustration of making little progress sent shooting pains down my neck.

242

My therapist would have suggested I quit for the day and do some yoga and deep breathing exercises. While that would have been an excellent suggestion for a native Californian, yoga was not my thing. You'd be laughed out of town for doing yoga in New Orleans. They had their own means of relaxation, but the only exercise involved was hoisting a drink off the table and putting it back down when the glass was empty.

When I got to Felix Loch's name on the list, I was excited that there was a phone number identified as his cell. I had no idea if he had gone back to Germany after the races or if he was spending some extended time in the states. I remembered some of the racers talking about traveling to Lake Placid, New York, to their summer bobsled training facility. Perhaps he had gone there. With only a four-hour time difference, it would still be a decent hour there. I told myself that I could always leave a voicemail if he was in Germany and fast asleep.

I held my breath and punched the numbers into my iPhone. He answered on the first ring. Judging from the noise in the background, he hadn't been sleeping. "Hello?" His German accent identified him right away.

I hadn't expected him to answer, and I hadn't rehearsed my opening to the conversation. "Hello, Felix. This is Miranda Marquette. Perhaps you remember me from the street luge races in California."

He interrupted. "Miranda! How nice to hear from you! I don't remember giving me your number. Perhaps you are a clairvoyant of some kind." He laughed, and the people around him seemed to be laughing with him. I wasn't sure, but I thought he might be slurring his words a little.

I laughed, hoping to stay on his good side. I was still a little gun-shy after my experience earlier with Rocky. "Not clairvoyant, just resourceful. Did I catch you at a bad time?"

243

He chuckled, "Only if you consider throwing back some beers with some old friends a bad time. What can I do for you? Are you nearby? I'd love to see you."

That was definitely the beer talking since I was at least ten years his senior, and he had expressed absolutely no interest in getting to know me when we were competing the Northern California. I decided to tell the truth, and maybe he would divulge me where he was. "I'm home in Malibu."

There was a muffled sound as if he was covering the receiver, then a new round of laughter, I imagined, at my expense. "That's a shame. We are in New York City on our way to the Lake Placid training center. We haven't entirely made it there yet." He hesitated as if he was either thinking of something to say or miming the line to his buddies before he said it. "So, to what do I owe the pleasure of your call?"

Due to the circumstances, I was tempted to hang up, but I never knew if I'd get the chance to speak with him again, so I forged ahead. I tried to sound in control even though I felt defensive. "I'm sure you remember about the death of my friend and teammate Annika Bloom, right?"

His voice sneered, "How could I forget?" Then he realized who he was talking to. "That was so sad." He lied. It was no surprise because he and Annika lost no love over one another.

I felt like I was wasting my time. "I know that people talk, especially after a tragedy like this one, one that canceled the finals to an important race. Did you hear any grumbling either before or after that race about Annika from any of the other racers?"

His voice hardened. "I already spoke to the police about this. I don't know anything. Did you call me to try to get me in trouble?" He was rising from a simmer to a boil. "Yes, the whole world knows that I didn't like her. To be honest, I'm not all that fond of you or that Patricia on your team, either. You all made a mockery of the race with your faces slathered all over town. It was embarrassing, or at least it should have been for you. I told my manager this is the last time I get roped into a publicity stunt. I am a world-class athlete, and the rest of you in those races weren't strong enough to pick up your own sleds. Street Luge is not a sport and never will be one, and I'm happy about that."

I interrupted. "It's well known that you weren't thrilled about racing against women, especially when they were better than you were."

I expected a quick retort, but all I got was dead air. Felix had hung up. "Great interrogation technique, Miranda."

I moved from the kitchen to the couch in the Great Room. I felt like I was floundering. Both suspects I contacted could very well be guilty, but I had no idea how to make that case. I could only assume that Heather was arrested based on DNA evidence alone. Well, of course, her DNA was all over the sleds. She had transported them from here to Northern California and had helped with several maintenance-related issues along the way.

I am a huge fan of DNA evidence because I believe that many fewer people are wrongly convicted. On the other hand, I felt like it was being used as a substitute for good police work. There had to be a happy medium, and this wasn't it. I guess that there were multiple DNA samples on Annika's sled, but Heather was the only suspect being considered by the police. It was unlikely the prosecution had gotten DNA samples from all racing personnel and racers, so it was likely that a killer was running around loose unless something changed quickly.

I scanned the list of racers and their sled numbers. Something didn't seem correct, but I couldn't put my finger on it.

Chapter 31

Soon Mark and Heather returned home. Heather was not as happy-go-lucky as she had been earlier. I wondered if the reality of her possible murder trial had kicked in. I remembered being in the same situation and the mood swings I encountered.

Time went by quickly, and the three of us developed a rhythm. We rarely hung out as three, because that never seemed to work. So, if it was Heather and me, Mark and me or Mark and Heather, everything was fine. Otherwise, someone always felt slighted.

I eventually contacted nearly everyone on the list of racers and employees provided to me by Bernie but didn't turn up anything useful.

In a couple of weeks, the preliminary hearing came and went. Heather was going to trial. Two months, to the day, from her arrest, Heather's trial began.

It felt like Deja Vu being in a courtroom at a murder trial, but I didn't have that sense of optimism that surrounded Mark and me before my exoneration. Heather, Mark, and I had gotten to a point where we didn't discuss the trial much. I updated Mark daily on my progress in interviewing potential witnesses, but it only got more depressing as time went on. I wracked my brain for another strategy to prove Heather's innocence but never found one. I felt more and more guilty as the trial approached and less and less effective as an investigator.

The first two days of the trial consisted of DNA evidence, all pointing to Heather. The brakes on the sled that had killed Annika had been tampered with, and the only DNA consistently found on that sled belonged to Heather.

The focus of DNA testing was on sled number 214. As racers, we were identified with scanned bar codes that matched the sled number we were assigned to. Each rider was provided with the sled that matched their wrist band electronically before the race began. We were provided with the number by race staff, in case there was a mix-up or an issue with the scanning device, but we never needed it.

Months after the race, I had no clue what my sled number had been. I thought I had put it in my phone comments section just in case I forgot it, I'd have to check later since I hadn't brought my phone to court because they were forbidden. Once the prosecution had completed their presentation of data, Mark called several witnesses, including Rocky, and Felix, who was allowed to testify by video conference. While they both came off as defensive and impatient, even I had a hard time believing either one was the smoking gun I was hoping for.

Both sides to case their made their final plea to the jury, the prosecution first. "Ladies and gentlemen of the jury. During this trial, we have sought to prove that the defendant, Heather McIntosh," the DA gestured towards the defense table, "is guilty of murdering Annika Bloom. We have presented a very technical display of evidence because that was what was required here. The DNA evidence is clear; Ms. McIntosh was the only person proven to have touched the braking area, which was tampered with causing Ms. Bloom's death. The defense would have us believe that the evidence is faulty and that his client had no motive. We may never know what Ms. McIntosh's motive was, and that may go with her to the grave. However, based on clear evidence, we can say without a shadow of a doubt that she is guilty."

Mark looked haggard. I knew he was reaching but would do his best. He walked up to the jury box and spoke directly to them. Most of them watched him intently. "DNA. That's all we seem to hear about these days in court. The prosecution would have you believe that the three tenets of a murder: intent, motive and opportunity, are no longer valid.

"But, ladies and gentlemen, we are missing two of the critical items: intent and motive. Sure, Heather had the opportunity and means. She had unlimited access to the sleds. Her DNA was all over all the team's sleds as the prosecution so very kindly demonstrated. But did she have intent or motive, the other two out of three? I have to say an undeniable, 'No.' She had only recently met Annika, and the evidence showed that they got along very well.

"So, with no motive, why would Heather intend to kill her? She wouldn't. Let's be reasonable. Picture yourself sitting here at the defense table. All you did was help your friend with some sleds, and now you are facing a first-degree murder charge. This trial is a farce, a waste of your time and a waste of government money. Please vote with your conscience. Please find this beautiful, kind, and trustworthy woman, innocent."

I had to admit, I would have had second thoughts if I were on the jury, and hopefully, they would too.

The judge instructed the jury to begin deliberations, and this phase of the trial was over. I stepped outside to get some air.

For the time being, Mark stayed with Heather at the defense table. Clearly, he was expecting a fast verdict. I wished I had brought my phone because I had nothing to do except to sit outside or go back into the courtroom. Much to my surprise, when I returned, the jury was filing back in. I wondered if they had questions for the court or if they had actually reached a verdict in less than fifteen minutes.

Mark was whispering something to Heather, but I had no idea what it was. I knew from the past that a quick verdict usually meant innocent but not always. The timing usually meant there were a few strong personalities on the jury who shared the same opinion.

When everyone was seated at their respective tables, and the judge instructed the jury to provide him with their verdict, the foreman passed a piece of paper to the judge, who read it and handed it back.

The foreman was a fiftyish gentleman who wore a suit to court every day. He looked proud to have been given this responsibility. In a loud voice that could be heard clearly throughout the room, he announced, "Judge, we find the defendant, Heather McIntosh, innocent on all counts."

The courtroom erupted with a combination of cheers, claps, and various other exclamations. I hadn't realized that Heather was that popular with the gallery. She and Mark hugged, and the prosecution looked concerned and dejected.

Mark and Heather had ridden up together in Heather's car, and I had taken my motorcycle. They wanted to discuss the case on the way up, and I was pretty much talked out about it.

I walked down to the front of the courtroom and hugged them both. "Congratulations," I said to them, and while I was happy, I felt an emotional letdown. I was glad to have six hours on the motorcycle to process whatever I was going through. Had I expected Heather to be convicted? Did I want her to be found guilty? What was wrong with me? She was my best friend. What kind of friend was I?

"Earth to Miranda," I heard Heather say in a distant voice. I had been far away.

I jumped, having been interrupted from the serene world in my head. "Sorry, I was figuring out my route home."

Heather whined, "Home? I don't want to go home. I want to celebrate! Mark's coming. Are you with me?"

Of course, they were in the same vehicle, so he didn't have a choice. Partying was the last thing I wanted to do. I never even drank an ounce of alcohol while I on the motorcycle. It was too risky, especially with these crazy California roads and drivers. But I remembered the excitement and relief I felt when my trial was over, so I didn't want to be a downer. I forced some enthusiasm out. "Of course, I'll go. I wouldn't miss it for the world."

We walked over to White Chapel, a San Francisco landmark on Polk Street. When we arrived, half the gallery was already there, and they cheered when Heather walked in. She curtsied and nearly fell on her face but recovered at the last second. This was Heather with no alcohol. I hoped Mark would follow my lead on the wagon.

I didn't intend to stay too long, but I hadn't come up with a credible excuse to leave yet.

Mark sat down next to me with an iced tea. "That's not a Long Island Iced Tea, is it?" I teased.

He took a sip through the straw. "Nope, we have a six-hour drive ahead of us. I just figured Heather might want to blow off some steam before we got back in the car.

Heather was off talking to a few of her well-wishers, but I spoke in a low voice. "So, Mark, did you think it was going to be that easy? Let's face it; we didn't put together much of a defense."

He chuckled, "Speak for yourself, Miranda. I was amazing."

I knew Mark well enough to know he was bluffing. "Yeah, right."

He thought for a minute. "Well, when I have a case like this, I never really know what the outcome is going to be. They didn't have much of a case except for the DNA evidence, and since Heather was, in fact, innocent, it made sense that she wasn't convicted."

I wasn't convinced. "Yeah, I know that defense. That was the one I tried when I was arrested. It wasn't very comforting. Don't you wonder, now, who actually did it and why the prosecution didn't figure it out?" I thought for a second. "Maybe that's why I'm feeling uneasy. There's still a killer out there. Annika's family deserves the truth about her death."

Mark took another sip of iced tea. "I agree, but the reality is, this case will probably never be solved. There will be pressure on the department to close the case and spend more time and money on cases they can actually win. I can't even imagine the amount they spent on DNA testing alone."

I was suddenly flashing back to Larry's trial in Switzerland. I hadn't thought about it until now, but these cases were nearly identical. "Hey Mark, remember my trip to Switzerland for the case against Tara's killer? I'll bet the only reason they were able to get a conviction is because they don't have jury trials over there."

He laughed. "Good thing this one wasn't tried there."

I didn't see anything funny. "Think, though, about how many cases are reversed every year now that DNA evidence is available, victims who have been falsely imprisoned for decades. Maybe the Swiss aren't so far off."

He stood up. "You're a killjoy, Miranda. I was feeling pretty good about today, but now it sounds like I was lucky I had an ignorant jury."

I thought about trying to stop him from walking away, but he was right. Besides, I needed to hit the road sooner than later. Maybe a six-hour bike ride could help me solve this case once and for all.

I got up and plodded toward Heather, who was yucking it up with a bunch of people I had never met. She motioned me over when she spotted me. "Hey, Miranda, I want to introduce you to some people." She was already slurring her words. She had little tolerance for alcohol due to her petite size and the fact that she rarely drank. "People, this is Miranda, my bestest friend. Miranda, these are people."

I smiled politely. I wasn't sure if she didn't know all their names, couldn't remember their names or if she even knew them at all. "Nice meeting you all," I spoke to Heather in a lower

251

voice. "I'm going to hit the road. You know I don't like to ride in the dark."

She frowned like the spoiled child she sometimes was. "Oh, Miranda, don't be a party pooper."

I hugged her. "I'll see you back at the ranch." I knew she'd get over it before I reached the exit door.

The weather was typical California, seventy-two and sunny. No wonder so many people wanted to live here. Sometimes I wondered if the weather was worth the crime, the traffic and the threat of earthquakes, but the feeling usually passed quickly when I thought about the humidity in New Orleans, the blinding heat of the Southwest, or the snow of the North.

I took the Pacific Coast Highway for the views and the smell of the saltwater. On one stop, I remembered to check the notes on my phone for my sled number from the race. I couldn't remember which one it was supposed have been. I'd have to look at the list when I got back to the house.

I got home just after ten. I was relieved that Mark and Heather hadn't beat me since they would have taken the interstate. I planned on staying up and tying up some loose ends, but when I got up to my bedroom, it looked so inviting, I laid down intending to take a short nap. When I woke up, it was 7 a.m.

Chapter 32

I dreamed all night about numbers, mix-ups, ambiguities, and confusion. I awoke in a fog. I dug out the list that Bernie had provided for me and searched out my name. The roster was a copy of a computer print-out with several manual cross-outs and written in numbers. By my name was a printed number 214. It was crossed out in red, and 213 was written in. I sought out Annika's name, and there was the opposite notation. The number printed by her name was 213, but 214 was written in.

After some coffee, I called Bernie for clarification. He sounded very business-like. "Bernie Weinstein."

I was still waking up but tried to sound like I had my act together. "Hey, Bernie, thanks for much for the racing roster. I did have one question, though."

He sounded like he was multi-tasking. "Okay, shoot."

I scanned the report for others with a similar situation to Annika's and mine. There were several others. "On the report you provided, there were several sled numbers that had been crossed out and replaced. Do you remember why that was?"

He thought for a minute. "That list was preliminary. I can't remember why, but on the first day of racing, some of the sleds didn't match the wrist band of the racer, so they printed a final list later that day. I just made the notation and kept the original."

I thought back to the first day of racing. "Oh yeah, I remember. We had a delay in the first heat because several racers' wrist bands didn't match their sleds. Mine and Annika's got mixed up at some point. I had forgotten that."

There was silence on the other end of the line. I wasn't sure if it because he was listening and had nothing to add or if he was busy and not really paying attention. My answer came in a few seconds. "Hey, Miranda, I hate to cut you off, but I've gotta run. Is there anything else I can do for you?"

"No, Bernie. Thanks."

"You bet," he said, and he was gone.

I originally had a copy of the same list at the time we were racing, but either lost it or threw it away. We were all provided with one on the first day at registration. I probably gave mine to Heather.

Mark plodded downstairs with his suitcase in tow. I couldn't blame him for wanting to get home. I noticed he was moving slower than usual. "Hey, big-time attorney, I hope you didn't stay out too late last night."

He chuckled, "It wasn't that late, but when you add the six-hour drive, it was a long day. Happily, I was able to get an eleven o'clock flight back to the Crescent City, and from what I've heard, you can't arrive too early at LAX, no matter when your plane is scheduled to take off."

I corrected him. "Well, your biggest issue could be the traffic between here and the airport. The airport is such a mess, they almost require people to skip in front of the security line if their plane is boarding. It doesn't encourage the local residents to heed the typical 'Get there at least two hours before your flight' warnings."

He swigged a half cup of coffee, gave me a quick hug, and headed toward the door. "Take care of yourself, and don't forget to visit your mother. She isn't going to be around forever."

I felt a pang of guilt, knowing that I never visited enough, and I had promised her when she was diagnosed with breast cancer that I would come around more often. "I will definitely be back soon. I've just been over my head with murder and trials lately."

He yelled back as he went out the door, "Well, I promised Sabine I'd remind you, so consider yourself reminded."

He jumped in an airport limo that I hadn't even noticed had arrived, and he was gone.

I wrapped my hands around my coffee mug. I couldn't explain why a chill had suddenly come over me, but I needed to turn the temperature on the air conditioning up.

I looked up from my coffee to see Heather heading down the stairs, fully dressed, which was unusual for this time of day. She also had a suitcase dragging behind. She looked horrible like she had just lost her best friend.

I ignored it, thinking she had a late night and had decided to take a vacation now that her trial was over. I was sick of the gloom and doom that had spread over the house as it approached and was glad to have it behind us. "Hey, sleepy-head, where are you headed?"

Heather sat down next to me and started talking in a somber and nearly unintelligible voice. "I'm leaving, Miranda."

I chuckled, "I got that idea when I saw the suitcase."

She shook her head. "No, Miranda, I'm leaving for good."

I nearly did a double take because I was not looking at the Heather I knew. "What? Why?"

Her hands shook, and tears ran down her cheeks. She struggled to talk but clearly wanted to get whatever it was out. "I did it, Miranda. I killed Annika."

At first, I thought she was joking, but nothing in her body language supported that supposition. I just stared at her.

She hesitated, searching for words. "It gets worse."

I spoke in a soft voice, anticipating her response. "How could it get worse?"

She had stopped crying. She looked me straight in the eye. "I meant to kill you."

I sat there staring at her, trying to get a handle on what I was feeling. I couldn't say I was shocked or even surprised. Something in me had known all along, I couldn't face it, but now I would be forced to. "Why, Heather. You're my best friend."

She put her hand up. "No, Miranda. I'm no one's friend. I've never had anything that I could call my own. I've been mooching off people's kindness for as long as I can remember. Venice Beach wasn't the first place. It was just an easy place to stay anonymous."

I felt the color draining from my face.

She talked louder as she spoke. "You were an easy mark, Miranda. You paid virtually no attention to your business. For a while there, I thought you might even make me your partner. But then when you said you'd give everything to me if you died, it seemed too good to be true. But then the Feds started snooping around. And I don't know if they've got anything on you or not, but I wasn't willing to take that risk. I had to get rid of you before they got any closer, liquidate, and leave town."

I was having a hard time keeping up. "So why Annika?"

She started pacing. "It was a mistake, a crazy mistake. Everything was set. I had all the information I needed, the list of riders, and sled numbers. 214 was the sled you were riding. But I had to time everything perfectly because only the San Francisco course was dangerous enough to do the deed. Injuring you would only have made my problems worse. I was likely the one who would have to care for you, and if I killed you, then, I'd be the first and most obvious suspect."

I was starting to worry. The only other times in my life when suspects had confessed to a crime in this much detail, they had no intention of letting me live to tell the tale.

She barely seemed to know I was there, mired in her story. "I guess I was the only one who didn't get the memo that you and Annika's sled numbers had been reversed. I was confidently watching your race, waiting for the fateful moment when you collided with destiny, and it never happened. I did everything I could do to get to Annika's sled before her race when I figured it out, but it was too late."

She didn't seem remorseful at all, just angry that she hadn't pulled it off, even though she had been acquitted. Ironically, had she murdered me, the police and prosecution might have figured

256

out her motive and been able to get a conviction. But, because she had no reason to kill Annika, they had a much weaker case.

As if she suddenly realized where she was and who she was talking to, she picked up her bag and headed toward the door. I breathed a sigh of relief, which she detected immediately. "God, Miranda, you didn't think I was going to go to all the trouble of killing you now, did you? I got my half a million dollars from the company bank account, so even if you go to the police, I will be long gone. But, go for it if you need to."

I spoke just above a whisper. "I think you know I would never do that. I'm sure that living with what you've done will be enough punishment."

She stopped in her tracks, her face bright red. "Don't even give me that 'holier than thou' garbage, Miranda. You're no better than I am. You just got lucky. Well, I have a feeling your luck is about to change." She picked up her bag and walked out the door just as a taxi arrived.

I grabbed another cup of coffee and made my way onto the deck. My knees were weak, my respiration was fast, and my heart rate was elevated. I concentrated on slowing my breathing for five or ten minutes. I stared out at the ocean for a long time until I started to feel like I wasn't going to pass out.

I had to laugh to myself and said out loud, "I can't believe she only took half a million. What was she thinking?"

I spent the rest of the day making sure Heather had caused no other damage to the company other than theft of assets. I prevented further damage by changing passwords and sign-on names. I reviewed customer service emails, telephone messages, and bank accounts. I called my contacts at my highest volume physician groups and got nothing but compliments about Heather and her efficiency.

Early in the evening, a DHL envelope arrived from the Kantanle Verwaltung Reginalgefangnis, Allmendstrasse 34,

3600 Thun, Switzerland. I stood at my front door and opened it. It contained a letter addressed to me.

"Dear Miranda,

I hope all is well with you. I am writing to you as part of a sentence reduction program at the prison in Thun, Switzerland. Similar to a twelve-step Alcoholics Anonymous program, all steps must be completed to start toward rehabilitation into society. If I finish it successfully, I may be qualified for release in as soon as five years. The relevant steps as far as my relationship with you goes are five, eight, and nine, and I plan to address those in this letter.

The fifth step is 'Admitting to God, to ourselves and another human being, the exact nature of our wrongs.' The eighth step is to 'Make a list of all persons we have harmed and become willing to make amends to them all.' The ninth step is to 'Make direct amends to people wherever possible, except when to do so would injure them or others.'

So here goes. I purposely caused the death of your friend and teammate, Tara. I did this because of a deep-seated hatred of you because I believed that you ruined my life. When I was at the tender age of thirteen, you thoroughly destroyed my self-esteem by rejecting me and labeling me a leper. The name Larry Leper stuck with me from that fateful day forward, and I have never been able to shake it, no matter how much schooling and professional success I achieved, I never felt good enough. I believed the label.

However, through counseling, I am learning that it was my own self-loathing that has been at the root of my issues, not the rude comment of a twelve-year-old girl. I wish I had received the help that I needed before

Tara, who I had grown quite fond of, died a needless and careless death.

Miranda, I am genuinely sorry for the pain that I have caused you. I have been consumed with anger for so long; I was blinded by it. I will strive every day to address my issues in more appropriate ways or even to extricate the demons from my being. Counseling and a newfound belief in God have made me believe it is possible.

Sincerely,
Larry Lechter"

I stood for a long time, reading and re-reading the letter. Having been filled in by the detective in San Francisco, none of it came as a shock, but there was something about seeing it in writing from the man who murdered my friend. It was far too real and unnerving.

I had heard that sentences in Switzerland were generally light, but five years for murder was unfathomable.

I needed to call Patricia to see if she had received one. Besides, I needed to see how her pregnancy was coming. She wasn't far from her delivery date, and I hadn't stayed in touch as I had promised. That sounded very familiar to my mother's breast cancer and how I had promised to see her more, or at least call more, but I hadn't done it.

I sat at the kitchen counter in a funk. Two people had confessed murdering separate friends of mine today, both of which I was, at least indirectly, responsible for. One thing was for sure. Had I not put together the extreme team, both of them would be alive today.

On the other hand, with someone like Larry Lechter running around consumed with anger for me, he could have just as easily killed me or someone else I knew with or without an extreme team. I just made it easier for him.

And judging from Heather's obsession with material wealth, had she not attempted to murder me in San Francisco, she probably would have killed me here when the time was right.

But for some reason, I had been spared. I had more work to do.

If you enjoyed this book, please rate it on Amazon or even really make the author happy, and write a review either on Amazon or Goodreads. This will let other readers know what a satisfying read this was for you.

Enjoy JT Kunkel's first story in the Miranda Marquette series:

Blood on the Bayou

Available on line at Amazon and Kindle.

Made in the USA
Coppell, TX
07 December 2020

43532891R00148